The Art of Falling

in

Love with You

By

A. A. Jaeon

Alliance Kingdom Studios

Cover Design by A. A. Jaeon & Tanjibo

Book Cover Illustration by Fran Hao Shuang

Cover Formatting & Illustrations by Tanjibo

Proofreading by Jennifer Herrington

Visit the author's website at www.aajaeon.com.

First Edition: May 2023

"This is your life. Don't let others discourage or judge you for your choices. Your happiness is what matters most."

–A. A. Jaeon

Chapter 1

Don't open the door to strangers. Something every parent tells their kid at a young age.

Or should tell.

And it's one of the few things I am thankful my parents taught me. But presently, what does a full-grown, twenty-one-year-old adult like me do?

Exactly that.

Either my teenage rebellion stage finally catches up to me or how I only had five hours of sleep yesterday makes my brain forgo one of my most important life lessons.

"Hi. I have a package for Lydia Zhang," says the tall man I need to angle my head up to look at.

In most cases, this would seem like a very normal situation and nothing worth alarm bells sounding. But the fact that he is wearing the opposite of a delivery carrier uniform with his light blue shirt jacket over a white T-shirt, khakis, and Timberland boots keeps me on my toes. Last time I checked, this neighborhood was pretty safe and had a low crime rate.

Maybe because I recently stumbled upon a video where two delivery carriers charged into a person's house to attack and ransack their place after pretending to deliver a package to them, I can't seem to let my guard down. Yet at the same time, I might be overthinking, since if he was going to rob me, he probably would have at least dressed the part.

The man clears his throat and speaks again after realizing his greeting was not enough to garner a response from me. "Oh, um...I think someone sent me the wrong package so I came here to drop it off." With a sheepish smile, he extends the package closer for me to read the address label.

Lydia Zhang

LiArte Studio

30 Lornia St.

San Willmore, California

The little light bulb icon lights up in my brain. This must be the two gallons of lavender Pine-Sol I ordered online. Everything he said processes in my brain, but instead of responding like a normal human being, I stare at him dumbfounded. I realize that this stranger specifically walked over to personally deliver the package when he could have just kept the goods himself, something I would have totally not done.

Or he could have informed the FedEx carrier, who would then dump my package out in the street for anyone to take with no prior phone call or notice like they usually do despite my numerous complaints. I feel embarrassed and guilty for ever thinking he was going to rob me. My body's earlier fight or flight response starts to relax back to normalcy and I open the door wider, no longer planning to slam it in his face.

"Thank you," I say with my most sincere smile as I transmit apologies for thinking the worst of him with my non-existent telepathy abilities.

In another life, I would directly apologize to him for my earlier unfair assumptions, but as a petite five-foot-three Asian-American female, there's no such thing as too safe for people like me in this world.

"Is there somewhere you would like me to put it?" he asks before I can outstretch my hands.

Pointing my finger at the empty patch of space on the new, beautifully wood-patterned vinyl floor, I say, "If it's not too much trouble, can you put the box on the floor right there?"

"Sure thing."

The guy sets the package down and I thank him again, but pause when I realize I don't know what his name is. "Sorry, I didn't catch your name."

"Connor."

"I'm Lydia, but you can call me Lia. Thank you so much for carrying that heavy box all the way here. I really appreciate it."

His raven black hair covering his forehead sways ever so slightly as he tilts his head vaguely in the direction of my neighboring building and answers, "I'm right next door over at the SW Youth Center, so it's no problem at all."

"Oh, are you taking a class there or something?"

"No, I teach a cooking class there. The previous teacher for the class is traveling overseas and they needed someone to temporarily take over his position."

"I guess that makes us neighbors from now on," I reply and my own sheepish smile forms on my lips.

"I saw the signs outside about art classes being held here." He does a quick turn to the outside of my studio where the flyers are posted before facing me again. "I've been teaching at the youth center for six months now and it still surprises me that they offer a bunch of extracurricular classes. Cooking, linguistics, home economics—" Connor lists them one by one on his fingers. "Basically everything you can think of except art. It's nice to see art classes being offered somewhere close by, especially right next door."

"Some people would rather invest time and money in something else. I mean, I get it. I think art is not something you can really teach, you know? Just like how you can tell what type of person someone is through their driving or by the way they organize their rooms, your artwork really shows a lot about you." My mouth practically moves on its own and I can't stop myself from rambling. "Art is more like a creative outlet than a skill you need in life, and it's not guaranteed to make you money. That's why I want my art classes to be a place where people feel safe and just have fun expressing themselves. I always lacked that as a kid which is what inspired me to teach art classes in my studio too, kinda like a two-in-one thing."

My brain finally works at normal speed again and I mentally clamp the brakes on my mouth to stop me from embarrassing myself even more. My new neighbor and I were having a casual conversation like normal people so why the heck did I turn it into Lydia Zhang's monologue? I usually watch what I say and avoid oversharing in front of people. My lack of sleep is definitely putting me off my game today.

(Note to self: When having less than six hours of sleep, try to limit your interactions with strangers to the bare minimum. You will thank yourself later for it.)

After shoving my hands in the pockets of my Levi jeans, I'm about to navigate the conversation in a different direction but Connor stops me.

"Wow. You're amazing, Lia." He speaks with so much genuine sincerity that my eyes glide back to his face. Instantly, I'm caught off guard by the way he is looking at me with his brown eyes. I've seen numerous brown eyes before—mine included—but it's the way his See's Candies dark chocolate brown eyes are looking at me full of admiration that makes me feel a tad on edge.

As if knowing I need a few more seconds to fully register his words, he gestures to the whole space around us. "All of this. You know what you want and work hard to make it into reality. Your passion for art is very apparent and I think many people will find comfort and solace in that."

In my junior year of high school, I felt unsure of many things but the one thing I was certain of was what I wanted to do with my life. I wanted to be an artist so I could draw and paint all day. But knowing how far-fetched and not financially stable that idea was, I scrapped it in the back of my mind as a foolish dream.

Choosing to go down this career path cost me things I can't get back, maybe even never get back, but it is something I don't regret and love doing more than anything. Hearing this stranger compliment my efforts send a strange feeling of warmth and fullness in my heart I didn't expect to feel.

"I can't wait to see how this place will look after you finish unloading everything. Speaking of which, I don't want to intrude any longer so I'm going to get going," Connor says as he opens the door, letting the blazing sun brighten my space.

"No, not at all. You saved FedEx and I from having another long chat. Is there anything I can do to repay the favor?"

Connor lets out a hearty laugh. "It was nice meeting you, Lia. If we run into each other again, just don't act like a stranger. That's more than enough for me."

"For sure. Thank you," I say hoping those two words can convey all of my gratitude for the kindness he showed me.

Connor salutes me as he walks out of the studio. I smile before shutting the front door and taking a moment to lean my back against it. My current random urge to jump up and down reminds me of the same feeling my old—or still—dorky self got after befriending someone new. Snapping out of my giddiness, I glance down at my digital watch that reads 9 a.m. and gasp.

Why does time pass by so fast? I need to finish cleaning and unloading all these boxes before noon! After calming my nerves with three deep breaths, I put my headphones on and play my playlist of K-pop dance-pop bangers. Nothing more motivating than listening to BEAST's "Beautiful Night", SISTAR's "Shake it", or B1A4's "What's Happening?" to get things done.

After I finish cleaning and setting everything up, I take a small break and sit down on the freshly mopped floor to admire my handiwork. The whole space is now rid of any dust and smells like lavender—bless you, Connor. Five wooden easels are lined up in a line near the wall to display a few of my paintings. In the center of the room are ten wooden tables and chairs in a circle.

On the sides of the room are cabinets full of paint, canvases, paintbrushes, and other art supplies. My little own workstation is off to the right where my Wacom Cintiq tablet and stylus sit. Reading web-comics or webtoons has been a hobby of mine ever since high school and the rise of popularity in them led me to try digital art and I fell in love with it ever since. My art studio is set exactly the way I envisioned and it all still feels unreal.

Right when I think life cannot possibly get any better, I remember it can.

The light gray plaid shirt jacket and black tank top with jeans I have on is comfortable but not exactly what I want to wear for a lunch date. After freshening up and changing into a white floral-patterned knee-length summer dress paired with beige wedges, I remove the pencil from my messy bun letting my jet-black hair fall to my shoulders before tying it back up into a high ponytail. Looking at myself in the bathroom mirror, I do the finishing touches of adjusting my bangs.

Ever since I could remember, my hair always parted on either the left or right side. Wanting something new and refreshing, Isa suggested trying the famous Korean see-through bangs. In the beginning, I was unsure of it since as a little girl, I had bangs and hated them.

Hated them, as in despised them.

I refused to have any photos taken of me with the bangs clearly visible. I refused to leave the house without wearing clips to part them to the side and an extra set of clips in case they broke. And despite my mother's reassurances that I looked adorable, my bangs were one of the many things where we didn't see eye to eye.

But fast forward many years later, when it comes to basically anything relating to fashion or trends, my BFF is the first person I go to. Isa helps me cut and trim my bangs whenever they start poking my eyeballs. See-through bangs surprisingly make my face look not half bad in photos. It's insane how covering my forehead with a few strands of hair can frame and give my face more character.

Finally satisfied with my appearance, I slide my pink cross-body purse over my shoulder and head to the sidewalk where we agreed to meet. I let out a sigh of relief that I'm not late and even have four minutes to catch my breath.

"Lia?" a voice calls out.

On my left, I see my new friend standing a few feet away from me. "Oh, hey, Connor. I didn't expect to run into you so soon. Not that it's a bad thing." An awkward laugh escapes from my mouth but he thankfully didn't think it was weird.

I hope.

"My class finished so I'm heading out to grab lunch," my neighbor says, pointing his thumb behind him.

"I didn't know you can't eat during a cooking class?"

"Well, technically you can eat all you want, but something I learned after teaching is it's best to wait a few weeks before eating anything made from the class. We received many new students recently so it will be a few weeks before I try anything," he answers with a wink.

I laugh and ask, "Are you messing with me?"

He gives me a boyish grin before collecting himself and responding, "Yeah, I'm kidding. All the students are great and quick learners. There's just this new café I wanted to try. How about you? Where are you headed to?"

"Same as you, I'm grabbing lunch."

"In that case, would you like to—"

Someone, not my neighbor's voice, calls my name from a different direction. I would recognize that voice anywhere. It's the dreamy voice I have fallen in love with more and more over the past three years.

Reed jogs up beside me and slings his arm around my shoulder.

"Sorry I'm late. Got stuck in traffic," he says slightly out of breath.

"No worries, I didn't wait long." I smile and perk up, even happier than a second ago now that he's here. Unable to resist, I nuzzle closer to him wanting to engulf myself in his warmth.

"Who's this?" Reed asks as he graces me with his lovely smile. He glances down at me and then to Connor.

"Reed, this is Connor. Connor, this is Reed. Connor and I met this morning when he returned a package that belonged to me," I answer using my hands to assist with my introduction.

"Nice to meet you, Connor. Thank you for helping out my girlfriend." Reed offers his hand for my friend to shake.

With a polite smile, he takes Reed's hand and shakes it. "Of course, just doing what anyone would do."

I'm not sure if my lack of sleep is messing with my vision, but I think Connor's jaw tightens. It was so fast that after I blink, his usual bright smile is back and I'm not sure if I saw correctly.

"Sorry, Connor, what were you saying earlier?" I ask remembering that he never got to finish his sentence.

"It's nothing. It was nice meeting you, Reed. Have a good lunch, I'll catch you guys later." Connor waves before turning to walk in the opposite direction with his hands in his front pockets.

"Shall we head to lunch, Lia?" Reed asks drawing my attention back to his gorgeous smile that still makes me all fuzzy inside.

Lacing our fingers together waffle style and smiling from ear to ear, I say, "Yeah, let's go."

Chapter 2

"What are you smiling about, Lia?" Reed asks as he pokes my right cheek with his index finger.

I giggle and smile even more at my boyfriend. "I'm thinking about the first time we met or to be more exact, when we had our first real conversation."

"Oh, I remember. I had the biggest crush on you back then," he says looking up at the sky like he's fondly remembering what happened.

"No, no, no. *I* was the one who crushed on you," I correct him.

Since our hands are still intertwined, my halt in our romantic stroll causes Reed to pause too. He caresses my cheek affectionately with his free hand sending butterflies to my stomach. I don't need a mirror to know my face turned a shade redder than a second ago.

"When we first met three years ago, I was still mainly in charge of finding manuscripts that would be a great fit for our publishing house. Despite all my efforts, my boss told me I needed to work harder and how he was not happy with my selection," Reed tells me with a bitter smile.

Ever since I had known Reed, it was as clear as day that he takes his job seriously as an editor. He has goals and ambitions he wants to achieve and every setback hits him twice as hard. Reed works really hard and it hurts him to see his best is not good enough. That feeling is universal but maybe since I know Reed on a more intimate level, it's like Reed's pain is my pain. My hand instinctively tugs his hand gently to reassure him that I'm here.

My boyfriend smiles at me before continuing, "After a particularly bad Thursday morning at work, I went to grab lunch. I stumbled upon a café I never tried before and the girl who took my order had the most beautiful smile and was literally a burst of walking sunlight. She was patient with me when I asked about the menu and did not rush me on deciding what to order and even wished me a good day at the end."

I mentally screenshot Reed's adorable nervous smile as he directs his eyes downward to the concrete ground beneath us in an almost bashful manner.

"This may seem a little far-fetched and underwhelming, but I was really miserable that day and seeing her made everything better. I found myself going to that café every week and sneaking glimpses of that girl whenever I thought she wasn't looking. I kept falling more in love with her kindness and how she only took out her sketchbook to draw when there was no other work to do. Every time I saw her, she somehow became even more beautiful than before."

My reddened face is now one hundred percent crimson. I know I am the girl Reed is referring to, but hearing what made him attracted to me, from the man himself, makes my heart beat like crazy. Not wanting Reed to see how much I'm blushing right now, I lean my head on his chest.

"I didn't know that. I thought I liked you first," I whisper softly as I try my best not to get lost in his cedar wood scent mixed with Downy fabric softener.

Reed wraps his nicely toned arms around me and kisses my head. "I may have liked you first, but you asked me out before I could ask you."

Even after all this time, I still remember that day vividly. Our manager told Isa and I to close up shop. We were both in the employee locker room getting ready to clean up.

"Lia, now's your chance!" my best friend practically squeals as she nudges my arm.

"What do you mean?"

"You know what I'm talking about. The boy you secretly have a crush on."

I look at Isa and feign ignorance but fail miserably when my voice comes out two octaves higher than normal. "No, I don't have a crush on him."

Isa gives me a knowing look like I'm not fooling her. "Come on, Lia. You can't hide it from me. I see you ogling the cute nerd boy over at table five every Thursday during lunch hours. Go talk to him before he leaves."

"First of all, I do not ogle him. And second of all, you know that's impossible, Isa. I can't just walk up to him and be like 'Hi there. Oh, by the way, I know this may be a few months late but I thought it was really nice of you to give your umbrella to that elderly grandma. Ever since I saw you running across the street with your all too cute brown messenger bag over your head, I started to have a crush on you. Do you want to go out with me?'" I cover my face with my hands before peeking at my best friend and letting out a sigh. "I don't really know anything about him and he doesn't even know me. We have literally no interactions besides 'Hi, what would you like today? Is that all? Have a great day.' He'll be weirded out by me and might think I'm a stalker."

Isa crosses her arms and playfully rolls her eyes. "No, he won't think you're a stalker. He'll think you're a cute stalker and fall in love with you anyways."

Instead of giving into my impulse to gently smack my best friend on her arm, which I'm sure she is expecting me to, I anxiously pace back and forth along the small walkway.

"In my nineteen years of living, I have NEVER dated anyone before, much less asked anyone out. I mean sure I watched a bunch of dramas and movies, but this is real life. I can't do it. Plus, what if he does say 'yes', what's going to happen? We go on our first date and I make a fool of myself and then he breaks up with me? I can't. I can't. I can't. Dating is better left in fiction for me."

"Yes, you can! You are not going to make a fool of yourself. And if you do and he doesn't accept and love you for you, he's not the one. I just don't want you to lose your chance with this guy. Even if you don't ask him out, you can at least introduce yourself. I think a cute guy like him should know that there is a cute girl ten feet away who has been admiring him for a while now. I believe in you, Lia!" my best friend says encouragingly.

Isa always knows what to say to quell my doubts. Even if I don't ask him out, if one day he stops coming here, I think part of me will regret not having a real conversation with him. Straightening my shoulders and nodding in agreement, I declare, "You know what? I'm going to do it. I'm going to go talk to him."

"That's the spirit! I'll finish cleaning and lock up with Manager Kim."

I give her a big hug and whisper into her ear, "Thank you, Isa. You're the best."

She winks and grins at me, "Go get him, girl!"

I nod and exit the locker room with clammy hands and my heart thumping so loud I think anyone within a five feet radius could hear it. When I reach the target, words unfortunately already tumble out of my mouth before I plan out what exactly to say.

"H-hi there," I say lamenting that my nerves made me stutter.

"Oh, sorry. I'm about to leave. I just need to finish packing my stuff," he says placing his laptop in that same lovely messenger bag–I can't help but gush at.

"No, that's not it. I mean yes, it's closing time, but that's not why I'm here."

Reed looks at me curiously but his mouth quirks up in what I think is amusement? He's probably wondering why I came here to talk to him. Quick, say something, Lia!

"I'm Lydia, but I go by Lia since I used to have this classmate with the same name as me so I started going by that nickname to avoid confusion." My nervousness betrays me making my introduction sound very awkward even to my ears.

He responds with an easy smile that makes me forget all common sense, "Nice to meet you, Lia. I'm Reed, Reed Wang."

"I know," I blurt dreamily, realizing a second too late I said that aloud.

He raises an eyebrow clearly surprised at my totally not normal revelation. I panic and then attempt to cover my own butt by adding, "One caramel macchiato with no whip cream and two prosciutto salami sandwiches for Reed. You're one of our regulars so that's why I know your name."

Afraid I introduced myself in the worst possible scenario, I feel my courage to ask him out slipping away. If I stay here any longer, I am going to literally die from embarrassment.

"Um, so I just wanted to say that if you ever need anything, you can call me. Not call me, call me. What I mean is I work here Monday to Saturday from 11 a.m. to 2:30 p.m., so yeah...I'll be here if you're interested in me–my work hours. Yes, interested in my work hours. Totally not me. Just my work hours cause I'm here every day. Yeah, ok, bye," I say what I think is officially the cringiest six sentences I have ever uttered in my entire life.

Knowing I definitely ruined any possible chance between me and my crush, I make an escape with the intention of burying myself some place he will never find me. When I am three feet away, Reed calls out my name stopping me in my tracks.

"I don't think two prosciutto salami sandwiches are enough. Do you know of any place to grab some dessert?"

Worried my brain might have conjured his voice as a coping mechanism for my embarrassment, I turn around stiff as stone to look at him and realize that Reed is indeed talking to me. "Um...there's a Baskin-Robbins nearby if you like?"

"Ice cream sounds good. Can you show me where? I'm not really good with directions," he says with a small laugh and pushes his reading glasses up.

Woah, hold up.

Am I reading too much into this or did Reed Wang ask me to show him where the ice cream shop is? Even after what happened and how I was a complete train wreck in front of him? OMG! OMG! O-M-G! To ensure the fireworks going off in my brain stay in my brain, I only manage a small nod in response.

Reed flashes me a wide smile that forms a perfect dimple on his ever so handsome face and says, "I'll be waiting outside then."

Hurrying back to the employee locker room, I trade my uniform for a white *Naruto* T-shirt and light blue jeans. I tighten the shoelaces of my white sneakers and put on a pale pink cardigan extending to my knees. I admit this is not my best look or anywhere near my first outfit choice for the first hangout date with a boy, but I only have the clothes I wore to school earlier.

No matter how much I like Reed, if he does not like graphic tees, that might mean the end of my crush.

I grab my purse from my locker and head out locking eyes with my best friend. She waggles her eyebrows suggestively as she glances from Reed to me. I answer her curiosity by doing a so-so thumbs up. Understanding my message, Isa grins and mouths, "Tell me the details later."

I mouth back, "I will." We cross our fingers and silently fangirl together before waving goodbye. I push open the cafe's front door only to be greeted by Reed, no glasses in sight.

"Sorry for the wait." I do my best to sound as casual as I possibly can while my heart internally does a somersault at his overwhelming visuals.

"Not at all." He gives me such a blinding smile that I am forced to look away before he can notice my mouth drop in awe.

"So, what's your favorite ice cream flavor? Mine is Oreo," I say in an attempt to start a conversation.

"Nice, mine is Mint Chocolate Chip."

"Oh, cool."

I run out of ideas of what to say next so we walk in silence for a little bit. Coincidence or not, I find it sweet that

Reed is walking on my right side where cars drive by. Ever since I learned how a gentleman stands on the side with cars through an anime I watched, I always wanted to have a boyfriend who would do that for me.

"I um..." Reed says breaking the silence. "I wanted to say I like your T-shirt."

Looking down at my shirt and then to Reed, I notice how he is looking at the road straight ahead, but there is a small smile forming on his lips. Finally processing his words, I try to contain my enthusiasm about my crush being even more perfect boyfriend material.

"You know what anime this is?"

Reed stops walking and says in a familiar determined voice, "Believe it!"

Laughter bursts out of me before I could stop it. "You watch *Naruto*?"

"I watched it as a kid whenever it showed on TV but never finished the whole thing." Reed scratches the back of his head like he is slightly embarrassed. "That's the first anime I ever watched and it introduced me to a ton of other anime series."

"Me too." I rack my brain for something else to say, but my excitement makes it hard to speak in fully coherent sentences.

Reed's phone dings startling both of us. Giving me an

apologetic smile, he takes his phone out of his inner jacket pocket, making me once again envious of male clothing and their many pockets we females lack in our clothes. His eyes scan the words on the screen before his face morphs into a grim, almost regretful expression.

"Is something wrong?" I ask gripping my purse strap nervously, all jubilance gone.

"I'm so sorry. Something came up. I hate to do this right after I asked you for help, but I have to go. Can we take a rain check?"

"Of course, I understand. Don't worry about it," I say trying to sound upbeat despite feeling a little dejected about the news.

We are about to walk our separate ways, but Reed spins around to face me and says, "And just for the record, I lied about being bad at directions. I know how to get to 31 Baskin from here. I was going to use you showing me the way as an excuse to ask you out to dinner."

Judging from his grin, he is obviously pleased to be the reason for me speechlessly gaping at him. Never has a boy said he is interested in me, much less with that much K-drama boyfriend swoonworthiness.

In an even more low and charismatic voice, he continues on, "The next time we meet, I'm going to ask you out properly because I'm interested in you, Lydia Zhang. I'm really interested."

Before I could pinch myself to test if I am dreaming, Reed gives me his thousand-watt smile and winks at me, officially K.O.-ing me with his insane charm.

"I'll see you soon, Lia."

My crush walks away leaving me frozen on the sidewalk still processing what in the world just happened.

Remembering that day, I bury my head deeper into my boyfriend's wonderfully sculpted chest.

"Don't remind me, Reed! I was so awkward and embarrassing."

He strokes my hair gently and has the audacity to chuckle. "Not at all, you were so cute. I wasn't sure if you liked me back or even knew I existed so I didn't have the courage to ask you out earlier. But then when you came up to me, I figured it was worth a shot and you thankfully said yes."

We arrive at my studio porch faster than I wanted to. Eating lunch with Reed and walking back together was nice, but time with him never feels enough. I want him to stay longer, but I know he needs to get back to work and me with mine.

He lets out a sigh. "I'm still bitter over my work emergency that day. If it weren't for that, I would have formally asked you out right then and there, but instead, I had to ask you out the following Thursday. It's only a week difference but having you as my girlfriend one week less than I could have is still something I regret."

Making sure no one's around, I tiptoe and kiss Reed's cheek and whisper in his ear, "It was worth the wait."

Reed cups my face with both of his hands and then looks deep into my eyes. Despite knowing him for a long time, the way his chestnut eyes stare back at me with his full attention still manages to make my heart skip so many beats. Whenever I'm this close to him, it's like everything around me fades. Like the spotlight is shining on us and we are the only two people in the world.

Brushing my cheeks with his thumbs, my boyfriend says, "Meeting you was the best thing that ever happened to me. The more time I spend with you, the harder I fall for you. I love you, Lydia Zhang. Thank you for coming into my life."

He closes the distance between us and his lips press against mine. They are soft and gentle at first but then he deepens the kiss. Wanting him to know that I also reciprocate his feelings, I slowly pull away to look at him after a few seconds.

"I love you too, Reed Wang."

He smiles with so much love in his eyes like I made his day with my confession. I wrap my arms around my boyfriend tighter and kiss him again. Standing on my studio porch with the love of my life, there is nothing else I could ever want in the world.

Most people say first loves don't last long or that they always end in heartbreaks, but I can't help but think we are different.

I know we are still young, but a future without Reed in it is unimaginable. The topic of marriage never comes up and I don't want to jump the gun or anything, but we always talked about having each other in our lives forever.

Whatever happens, whatever life throws at us, I know Reed and I will be able to get through it no matter what because we love each other and that's all that matters.

Chapter 3

Morning jogs are the best. Let me rephrase that, morning jogs listening to music are the best. In general, I consider myself mediocre at sports and not really a physically active person.

However, something I started to implement in my daily life were jogs around my neighborhood. Everyone has their own morning ritual and I guess morning jogs became mine. It's a great way for me to clear my head and relax before the long day ahead. The distance and route of the run changes every day, but I always make sure to pass by Sunrise Beach.

Like the name suggests, the beach is called Sunrise Beach because it has the best view of the sun rising. I don't always make it in time to see the sun rising every morning but simply looking at the ocean and feeling the cool breeze against my skin makes me feel so refreshed that the whole day seems like it will be alright even before it has started.

"Wow," I say in awe at the same time as someone next to me.

I find Connor on my left in a black round-neck T-shirt and dark gray shorts with earbuds on.

"I didn't expect to see you here," we say at the same time.

"Me neither," we answer in unison once again.

Connor and I look at each for a few more seconds before laughing. I hang my earbuds loosely around my neck and say, "I'm surprised the youth center doesn't have a gym."

He shrugs. "It does, but I like to run outdoors because the scenery is breathtaking and there is something about being one with nature that gyms can't replicate for me."

"I feel the same way," I reply with my eyes fixed on the stunning ocean view.

Isa used to be my jogging partner, but the timing clashes with her live stream of DoYogaWithMe. Her fans/followers also known as IsaBells, loved her first upload of her doing yoga and requested her to live stream that every morning. As for Reed, he prefers to work out in the gym mainly because it's close to his apartment and how he is not a morning person.

He is more of a night owl which is the polar opposite of me. I like to start and end my day early because I get really cranky without enough sleep. On the other hand, Reed wakes up later and gets off work an hour or two after me. It's sometimes hard to work around our schedules, but we manage. No one I know shares this hobby of mine so knowing my new friend enjoys it too is for some reason really heartwarming.

"I don't want to be intrusive or anything, but is that "Good Luck" from BEAST?" Connor asks interrupting me from my thoughts.

I give a reluctant nod, surprised and skeptical that someone I know, other than Isa, knows 2nd gen K-pop music.

"I love that song and have it on my playlist too."

"You do?" I ask in disbelief.

Instead of answering, Connor holds up his phone revealing that BEAST's "V.I.U." is currently playing for me to look at.

"You listen to BEAST?"

"I love BEAST/Highlight."

"Ditto," I say not even trying to hide my delight.

"Do you—"

Connor's watch alarm goes off pausing our conversation and he turns it off with a small frown.

"Aw man, I need to head back to the youth center."

I look at my watch and sigh, "Yeah, I need to hurry back too."

"I'm going this way." Connor points behind him.

"I'm headed that way too."

My friend and I grin at each other confident we are both thinking the same thing. For the next fifteen minutes, we jog and gush over K-pop. The two of us talk about our favorite K-pop groups like BEAST/Highlight, SISTAR, Miss A, INFINITE, 2PM, and SNSD. How we love 2nd gen K-pop the most when boy and girl groups interacted with each other freely without any gossip about scandals, how they performed special stages together, and how their official music videos were completely lit with their deep plot lines. K-pop nowadays is great too, but there is something about 2nd gen K-pop that really hits home. The sound of that era and the feel it gives is so incredible and nostalgic.

We move on to talk about solo K-pop artists and artists who also promote individually we love like Fairy IU, Hyolyn the Queen, and Jackson the Gentleman Wang. Isa loves K-pop as much as I do so it's nice to always fangirl over K-pop groups we stan together. Reed and I bond over our interest in classical music and oldie songs as he does not share my interest in K-pop. Finding another person who reciprocates my love for the same music envelops me with even more happiness and excitement.

"I had a lot of fun chatting with you. Hope we can do it again sometime," Connor says as we arrive at the front entrance of the youth center.

"Same here. I guess I'll see you around?"

He gives me another one of his boyish smiles and waves back. "See you around, Lia."

Someone knocks at my studio front door and a bell chimes. My art class starts at 10 a.m. on Fridays. I doubt anyone would arrive to class forty-five minutes early. Looking up from my Wacom, I see Isa wearing a sleeveless white button up blouse with a blue knee-length skirt that only highlights more of her natural beauty. She carries a small brown handbag on one shoulder and at the center of both her hands lie a small potted plant.

"Isa, hey. What are you doing here? I thought you were busy this morning getting ready to introduce Jackson to your parents," I say getting up from my chair and walk towards her.

"I am, but how could I miss the official grand opening of my BFF's art studio? And I got you a gift. I know, I know. You're probably like 'Isa, why did you get me a plant when I know you're a plant killer?' But hear me out. I got you an Echeveria succulent. You can put it near the window so it gets enough sun and just water it once a week or every ten days. It's pretty and some people believe it means good luck," she says lifting the succulent for me to see before placing it on one of the windowsills.

I wrap my best friend in a hug but am careful not to wrinkle her blouse too much. "I love it, thank you."

"It was the least I could do. I've been so busy uploading a video every week that I didn't have time to help with all the moving. I'm sorry," she says and I can hear her disappointment in herself.

"Don't be. You already do more than enough for me. You know that."

Isa and I first met during our freshman year in college. Even though the two of us were roommates, we had different majors and rarely talked. It wasn't until both of us worked together as new employees for Little Mermaid's Cafe did we really click. We bonded over our love of listening to K-pop, reading webtoons, and watching Asian dramas. When Isa and I got closer, we also confided in each other about the difficult relationship we had with our parents.

Isa's parents wanted her to be a doctor and marry some rich dude to take care of her and her family, but she wanted to be a social media influencer. Instead of living our lives for others, she came up with the crazy brilliant idea to quit college, rent an apartment together, and work on saving enough money to fund our dreams. We worked a bunch of miscellaneous jobs and used all our savings to make ends meet.

It was tough, to say the least.

Isa and I have known each other for about five years now give or take, but we have been through thick and thin. She may be my only closest friend, but I love her so much and definitely don't want her to feel bad for not helping me do something as minor as unpacking.

"Still, Lia. The boxes to unload and arranging everything. It must have been hard to do all on your own," Isa protests softly.

I shake my head reassuring her. "No, it wasn't bad at all. There's actually a funny story I forgot to share with you. Apparently FedEx delivered the Pine-Sol I ordered to the youth center instead. Thankfully the person who got my package personally returned it here and since then, he and I keep bumping into each other. It's strange cause we also have a few things in common like enjoying morning jogs at Sunrise Beach and listening to the same K-pop artists."

"Ooh. What's his name?" Isa asks raising her eyebrows curiously.

"Connor. He's the teacher for the cooking class next door."

Isa gives me an incredulous look and gasps, "Connor as in Connor Li?"

"Wait, you know him, Isa?"

"Oh my gosh, no way!" My best friend frantically paces around the room with a hand on her forehead like she is trying to wrap her mind around this new information. She abruptly whirls around to face me. "Do you remember how I met Jackson at C&J's Prime Rib Crib for the vlog I did at the request of my dearest Isa-Bells?"

I stare at her with an "are you serious?" look. "How could I not remember? That was only three months ago. You kept me up until 2 a.m. talking about how dreamy the head pastry chef Jackson was and how the desserts he made tasted like heaven. Even in the vlog, everyone can see the chemistry you guys had."

Isa lets out a happy sigh as if reminiscing about the good old days before shaking her head like she is trying to get back on track. "Jackson is also the co-owner of C&J's and the other owner is his childhood best friend who is also the head chef."

My best friend looks at me like she clarified everything and I should understand whatever the heck she is hinting at me.

I shrug. "I'm not getting it, Isa. I know the other co-owner of C&J's is Jackson's best friend, but I've never met him before."

Isa facepalms her forehead and takes a deep breath before saying, "Jackson's best friend is Connor, Lia!"

My jaw drops slightly but I'm still not as taken aback as she is. "Am I missing something? I mean it's a coincidence but I guess it's a smaller world than we thought, but I still don't get what the big deal is?"

"Jackson's full name is Jackson Chen. The Chens and the Li family are freaking rich! That in turn makes Jackson and Connor 'Fuerdai' rich but not like crazy rich like *Crazy Rich Asians* Nick rich, but they own a good number of expensive properties," Isa explains.

This time my jaw fully drops.

My best friend puts her hand underneath my chin to close my open mouth and then continues to say, "To put it more simply, my boyfriend is rich AF and the Connor guy you're referring to is my rich AF boyfriend's BFF who is also rich AF."

"Are you sure we are talking about the same Connor Li?"

"Is the Connor you're referring to around six feet tall, jet-black hair covering his forehead, puppy brown eyes?" Isa asks as she feigns a bored expression and picks at her fingernails. "Tell me honestly, appearance-wise, he's total eye candy and definitely webtoon boyfriend material."

"Ok, I met Jackson's rich best friend without knowing he's Jackson's rich best friend. How the heck did this happen?" I run my hand through my hair finally understanding why my best friend was in total shock at first.

"Jackson mentioned to me before that Connor took a job

at the SWYC, but I didn't know it was right next door to your art studio. Like OMG, what a coincidence or is it fate? The two Cinderellas finally have a happy ending after they both achieve their dreams and end up marrying handsome sweet rich hubbies?" Isa says with her eyes sparkling and hands dramatically clasped together.

"Isa, everything was just a coincidence. Connor and I met by chance and we're just neighbor friends. Nothing more. Plus, I'm dating Reed."

"Yeah, I was just kidding. But seriously, if I didn't know better, us meeting them seems like some kind of movie or book plot line," my best friend whispers like she revealed a top-secret conspiratorial theory or something.

I playfully push Isa and then reply, "I'll admit it is kind of weird, but I guess stuff like this happens."

Her phone rings and Jackson's attractive face paired with an angelic smile appears on the caller ID.

"Lol talk about timing. I gtg. I'll see you later. We'll talk more about this later and congratulations on your art studio. Love you and bye!"

"Love you too and have fun!" I call out to Isa as she rushes out and gives me a finger heart while she accepts the call with her other hand.

It's 9:45 a.m. and another bell chime sounds. To my surprise, Connor is there. He's holding hands with a young girl with two black twin-sized pigtails wearing a bright floral-patterned dress. She looks to be about six years old and almost half the size of him.

He greets me with a smile before turning to the small girl beside him. "Elly, this is your new art teacher, Lia."

The child looks at Connor and then to me with an adorable smile, "Hi, my name is Emily and I like to draw."

I bend a little lower so I am closer in height to her and then say, "It's nice to meet you, Emily. I like to draw too. How about you go find a seat and we will draw soon, ok?"

"Yes, Ms. Lia!" Emily claps her hand and jubilantly skips to find her seat.

Connor smiles in her direction and then looks back at me with a teasing smile. "I didn't expect to run into you so soon. Not that it's a bad thing."

More blood rushes to my cheeks as I realize that he purposely repeated the exact awkward lines I once said to him before. Crossing my arms, I pretend I don't know what he is talking about. "Are you following me or something?"

My friend lets out a chortle that makes me smile, breaking

my facade. "My older sister asked me if I could take Elly to her art class today. She only just got back from her work trip so she is still jet-lagged and my brother-in-law got called to an important last-minute meeting." Raising his hands in the air like he is innocent, Connor continues to make his case, "I swear I did not know Elly's art class was your art class until an hour ago. My bro-in-law will be picking her up afterward so you won't see me later unless I feel like following you again."

I shake my head in disapproval at him, but the growing upward tilt of my mouth gives me away.

"I'm joking of course. I'm not following you and I don't follow you. If I were, I would be less obvious about it. At least I think I would be," Connor says with a goofy smile causing me to laugh.

Recalling my previous conversation with Isa, I compose myself and clear my throat to speak. "Connor, there's something you should know." He adjusts his relaxed demeanor to match my sudden seriousness as I rub my hands together and spill, "My best friend, Isa, is dating Jackson, your best friend."

Connor blinks a few times and then finally responds, "Wait, you're Isabel's best friend?" I nod. He puts one hand on his chin and stares at me like he is really seeing me for the first time. "I remember Jackson telling me Isabel had a best friend who likes art, but I didn't know that was you."

"I knew Jackson owned C&J's with his best friend, but I didn't know that you were him either."

"I hope this does not make things different between us," Connor says as he puts a hand behind his neck. I tilt my head to the side, not comprehending his words. He smiles boyishly and then reiterates, "I hope we can still be neighbor friends or simply friends and not just because our best friends are dating each other but more because we...like to be friends?"

Connor meets my eyes and I can see a hint of embarrassment in them. He is giving such a cinnamon roll vibe that I can't help but use my hand to cover my open mouth smile. "Of course! I only brought it up because I'm sure we will eventually find out how we kinda low-key already know each other. And while I'm at it, I should probably get this off my chest too."

I take a deep breath before saying, "Isa is my best friend so I'm very protective of her. When I heard about her boyfriend's and his family background, I was worried she might have her heart broken. But Jackson is not a no-strings-attached type of guy and he genuinely loves her with all his heart. For the short time I've known you, you seem like a nice guy and someone I would like to be good friends with. But since you and Jackson share the same, well, social background, I hope you don't think it's weird given that we are pretty different."

What is up with my embarrassing monologues that only come out of my mouth in front of Connor? It seems like I was telling him that although I know you're rich and I'm not, I would still like to be your friend. That's exactly what I wanted to say yet it sounds so weird to have everything spelled out like that. I don't know many rich people so I'm not sure if they are as snobby as the way movies portray them to be.

Hanging around Jackson and spending some time-ish with Connor proves they are not or at least not every rich person is, but I'm not ready to risk making friends with someone if they are not going to be a permanent one.

Connor nods like he knows what I'm saying. "I had the luxury of being comfortable due to my privileges growing up, but I don't like to tie my family's wealth to any of my personal business. I meant what I said about not acting like strangers when we see each other. I want to be friends with you, Lia."

"I want to be friends with you too, Connor," I say emphasizing the "you" like he did earlier too.

A big smile spreads across my friend's face and his eyes seem to shine brighter. It just so happens he comes from a wealthy family, but Connor Li is still the same nice and funny guy I know. I would be a total idiot if I did anything to sabotage my new friendship with him. The bell chimes again and more students come in. My friend moves a few steps closer to me, giving the incoming students more room to enter as I direct them to take their seats.

Glancing at his watch, Connor says, "I should probably head back now" and then calls out, "Bye, Elly!"

Emily gets up from her chair and runs to hug her uncle. He crouches down and says, "I'll give you a piggyback ride the next time I visit."

"Really? Daddy says I'm getting too heavy." Emily pouts, officially making that the cutest pout I've ever seen.

Connor laughs and rubs his niece's head gently, "Don't worry, Elly. I promise I'll always give you a piggyback ride even when you grow taller and I'll make sure I can always carry you as long as you let me."

Emily's eyes twinkle like the stars as she lifts her pinky up to her uncle, "Promise?"

"Promise." Connor returns the pinky promise and gives Emily one last hug before she goes back to her seat.

"You are really good to her," I say to Connor in an almost robotic voice and realize a few seconds too late that that's probably not the usual tone people would use after seeing such a touching family moment.

"My family and I are really close. When Elly was born, our family grew bigger and we couldn't be happier," Connor responds cheerfully and thankfully does not seem to think much about my earlier statement.

"That's nice," I croak out, annoyed that my own bitter feelings about my family relationship surfaces at the worst times.

"Yeah, it is," Connor replies with such a loving smile on his face that makes me wonder for the first time in a long while, what it would be like if my family and I were close. "I want to say, 'see you around' but that now sounds way too creepy so I guess I'll stick with 'see you when I see you,' Lia."

I smile and return his wave. "See you when I see you, Connor."

He grins and closes the door behind him. I turn around fully taking in the sight of my art studio filled with ten people eagerly passionate about art.

Looking at what lies ahead of me, any and all negative feelings disappear as fast as they came. I clap my hands together and start my first official art class.

Chapter 4

Perfect for the occasion, but I wore it too many times already. Cute, but not feeling it today. Yup, this is definitely going in the donation pile. I go through my clothes one by one and nothing feels right.

Why is it so hard to decide what to wear?

Reed suggested a dinner date at my studio tonight since he hasn't had the time to see the whole place in all its glory. I'm excited to show him all my hard work but just knowing that we can spend some quality time together already brings me so much joy. Feeling disappointed at my options, I continue to rummage through more clothes but pause when I see my black halterneck romper with a cute ribbon in the middle.

I have a few rompers, but this is my favorite because the sweet memories of that night always come flooding back to me.

Everyone is probably staring at me and thinking "what the heck is that girl doing?"

I wish I could blame them, but I would think the exact same thing if our positions were reversed. In their eyes, they probably see a girl walking back and forth outside Mel's Drive-In's customer waiting area like a lunatic gripping her purse strap so tight it might snap. This is officially my second date with Reed but first ever restaurant dinner date with a boy.

Of course I'm having a mental breakdown!

We chatted a little during our ice cream raincheck date, but that's all. Isa gave me a great pep talk via phone on my drive here earlier, but all the confidence my best friend bestowed upon me seems to have faded away after I opened the car door. For the first time in my life, a guy asked me out on a second date and I might be late because I'm too nervous to go inside.

"Get a grip, Lia. You can do this!" I whisper chant to myself.

After taking three long deep breaths to calm myself, I finally enter the premise. Scanning the area, I spot Reed sitting in the middle of the diner waving a hand up in greeting. Oh

Lords, he looks so cute I want to draw him. At this distance, I can see Reed styled his hair to the right today and has on a brown blazer jacket over a nicely fitted black V-neck.

Wow, just wow.

Wait, am I dressed too casually? I think my jean jacket looks pretty chic with the whole ensemble but should I have worn boots instead of sneakers?

"Hi, Lia." Reed welcomes me with a gracious smile and that once again perfect dimple.

"H-hi." I put my hand up and wave like for some reason I need to verbally and physically say hi. Before I can make a fool of myself even further, I seat myself in the booth on the opposite side of him.

"I'm glad you're here. I was afraid you might not show," Reed remarks with a hint of nervousness in his voice. He responds to my confused expression with a smile like the smiley emoticon with a sweat drop at the right corner as he leans his head towards the outside of the diner and says, "I saw you...outside the diner."

"You saw me outside the diner?" I repeat after him still not understanding.

Following the direction of where Reed pointed at, I realize this booth has the perfect view of the outside waiting area of Mel's Drive-In.

Oh.

Horrified Reed saw my nervous breakdown just moments ago, I put my face in my hands. "You saw that?"

Reed laughs.

Not like a mean laugh but more like a funny intrigued laugh. I'm not sure if that's a good or bad thing so I stay with my head lowered in shame. A warm hand touches my wrist before making its way to my hand. His hand feels warm and is bigger than mine but we somehow fit together just right.

He squeezes my hand and whispers, "I was really looking forward to seeing you tonight so I came here twenty minutes early."

Hearing that Reed was excited to see me, I can't help but squeal on the inside. I return his squeeze and brush the back of his hand. "I was–am excited to see you too."

Reed gives me a charming smile as he says, "I thought this was a diner, but I must be in a museum because you look like a piece of art."

It takes my brain five seconds for Reed's words to sink in. Never in a million years did I imagine someone from the male species delivering a cheesy pick-up line to me. As a hopeless romantic, I can't help but swoon over this. While I fan my face, I bite down on my lip to hide my overly happy smile. "I don't think that's true but thank you for the compliment."

"I'm being honest." Reed grins and kisses my hand like I'm

a princess honoring him with my presence.

Is this flirting? Are we flirting? It's one thing to be on the other side of the screen fangirling over cute couple moments and actually experiencing those romantic scenes yourself. My heart cannot take this much sweetness.

A waitress whose name tag reads "Carly" gives my heart a much-needed break when she bounces over with her brown pigtails and purple highlights to take our order. I order corn beef hash with scrambled eggs and white toast. Reed orders a New York steak with a side of sautéed vegetables. She puts down two glasses of water on the table and tells us she will be back with our orders soon.

"I'm surprised you chose Mel's Drive-In for our second date," Reed teases with a grin.

"I don't really know what other people do on dates, but I like things simple. I always found two people chatting together and eating at a diner pretty romantic. Lame, right?"

Reed places his hand briefly on mine and says, "No, you're just seeming cuter by the second."

I take a sip of water and avoid eye contact as a futile attempt to keep my reddening face at bay. During our ice cream date, Reed and I mainly talked about animes we love watching like *The Rising of the Shield Hero*, *Darker Than Black*, and *Ouran High School Host Club*. It was getting late so we didn't have enough time to talk about anything else.

Trying my best not to sound too awkward, I say in an almost whisper, "I think we can be considered boyfriend and girlfriend since this is our second date. But at the same time, I don't know too much about you so I was wondering if we could talk more about each other?"

He nods with a pleasant smile. "Yeah, I would like that. For starters, I am not an only child. I have an older brother, Alexander, who's older than me by two years. We're not really close cause he's the epitome of the perfect son and my parents see me as 'the other child.' After moving out of my parents' house and getting a bachelor's degree in English from Stanford, I bought an apartment here back in the city. I'm currently working at the editing department in Moon Bay Publishing."

Hearing about Reed's family situation is a bit shocking. I never pictured Reed Wang as a younger brother or the second son. Every Thursday when he comes by the cafe, he usually multi-tasks in between eating his prosciutto sandwich and typing stuff on his laptop. Along with his computer, he has three thick stacks of paper with a bunch of markings that changes every week. How can his parents not be proud of such a studious and hardworking son? But I guess some things are not that simple.

Reed juts his chin forward towards me and says, "Your turn."

I fidget with my hands unable to hide my nervousness. "Um...I'm an only child and my parents are divorced. I am a freshman in the University of San Willmore majoring in Business. I don't like my major but I majored in it because I don't know what else I should do."

My short summary of myself is the polar opposite of dating material, but if I'm dating someone, complete honesty and the truth are best. Hiding or lying about myself will only hurt me in the long run. I'd rather have Reed know my bad points now than in the future when we get closer and it would hurt more to have our relationship not work out.

He looks at me surprised. "I thought you would be majoring in art."

"My parents expect me to get a good job in the future. Being an artist doesn't fit the criteria. I mean I love it but it's not something I can rely on to pay for college or my living expenses." I laugh with a bitter smile. "Oh my God, sorry. I totally killed the mood. Everything's just really..."

"Complicated?" Reed finishes for me.

I look up at him and Reed gives me a sympathetic smile like he gets that my life is more than a little complicated.

"Yeah, it definitely is complicated. Should we move on to something not as complicated?" I ask with a small hopeful smile.

Reed nods and leans closer to the table and says in a low

voice, "Random fun fact: my favorite color is red, but my lucky underwear is green."

I belly laugh at the absurdity of the turn in conversation. Reed has a wild grin on his face like he's daring me to top that. I like that in a guy. Where he can be serious yet funny in a flash.

"My favorite color is green. I don't have a lucky underwear color but ever since high school, I refuse to wear any socks that do not have any type of graphic on them aside from leggings and pantyhose."

"Graphic socks, really?"

"Hey, better than green underwear," I retort.

Reed laughs and says, "During Senior Prom, my friends and I went without dates. We were planning to have a fun time partying in our all-single guys group together, but we ended up bored, idling at the punch table the entire time. You would think there would be at least one good song after three hours, but the DJ disappointed us big time. Prom is not as fun as everyone makes it sound."

"I've never been to prom or any school dances before. I prefer to stay home and draw."

"Good choice. The prom ticket was way overpriced and the experience was nothing memorable. Cheers to skipping prom." Reed lifts his cup of water and I clink my cup with his. He then says, "Hopes and dreams."

I raise an eyebrow not understanding. He smiles at me before clarifying, "Do you have any dreams you hope to accomplish one day? And you can think in and out of the box."

"Oh...in the box would be making my parents proud with a good paying job?" My answer reflects my uncertainty of even that possibility, but I continue on, "Outside of the box would be...being a famous artist who can leisurely travel around the world...and having a nice house I could go back to where I would draw and do other mundane stuff."

"I like your second answer better."

I smile and then ask, "How about you?"

"In the box would be becoming an important figure in my editing department. Out the box would be being a full-time successful writer."

Reed's answer catches me by surprise. "You want to be a writer?"

"I love words. I enjoy reading other people's works and I want to create something of my own. I don't exactly know what I want to write about yet, but I want people to be interested in what I have to say. I want my words to matter to people."

I nod in understanding. "Me too. I'm not sure if others would be interested in my drawings, but I want to use my art to communicate to people."

We share the same shy childish smile of hoping our real dreams will come true. Carly comes back with our meals placing it down in front of us. We begin eating our food and move on to chatting about TV series we like to watch. Coincidentally, we are big CW fans and love watching *Arrow, Kung Fu,* and *Nikita.*

I don't know what boys usually watch because I never had a boyfriend or a boy that is a friend so talking to Reed feels exhilarating. He likes watching the same stuff I like to watch and enjoys the romance, action, and adventure genres as well.

Reed Wang, oh, Reed Wang, how are you so perfect?

"Miss Zhang, I had a fantastic time tonight. I would like to talk more about why seasons one and two of *Arrow* were hands down the best seasons of the entire series and how Maggie Q is such a Queen in *Nikita* another time. Are you by any chance interested in a third date?" Reed asks in a flirtatious husky voice that has me swooning.

I am not the type of person to play hard-to-get because that takes way too much brain power and I can't keep that pretense up for long. Honest and straightforward are my go-to strategies for times like these.

"Very interested, Mr. Wang. I would love to go on a third date with you."

Reed smiles and reaches his hand out for mine. We interlock our hands smiling at each other all giddy sipping our chocolate milkshakes, exactly like those movie couple montages. As cliché as this sounds, it was so romantic and magical.

My phone sings the English version of "The Boys" by Girl's Generation dragging me back into reality. By the song, I already know it's Isa calling and accept the call.

"Hey girl, just checking in to see how you are doing. Did you choose an outfit for your date with Reed yet?" Isa asks in an enthusiastic voice.

I sigh. "No, you called at the perfect time. I don't know what to wear. I was going through my clothes for the past fifteen minutes and nothing seems good enough. I want something casual and comfortable but also cute."

"How about wearing your plain gray T-shirt underneath your dark blue denim blouse shirt jacket? Tuck in the T-shirt and tie the ends of your shirt jacket. Pair that with your black-mini skirt, and since it's cold, don't forget to wear leggings underneath. And for the shoes, either boots or sneakers, up to you."

I'm silent for a good thirty seconds.

"Hello, Lia? You there?"

"I know you give fashion advice for a living and all, but I'm still shooketh." I put my phone on speaker so I can multi-task between chatting and changing into the outfit Isa came up with.

My best friend laughs. "Like you said, L, it's what I do. And I basically shopped more than half of your closet with you and we take turns doing the laundry."

"Still, Isa. You're so good at what you do." I finish putting on my perfect date outfit and put the phone back to my ear. "Oh right, we didn't get to talk much yesterday. Tell me how your brunch date went with your parents and Jackson."

"The good news is my parents like him. The bad news is they love him. Like they LOVE him. Of course, Jackson won them over with his good-boy mannerisms and laugh-out-loud jokes, but the minute my parents learned he comes from a rich fam, they went bonkers. They started asking how many guests they could invite to our wedding. Jackson played it off cool and said it's fine but I feel terrible," my best friend says and I can practically see Isa twisting the ends of her naturally wavy black hair with her fingers, a habit of hers that kicks in when she's stressed out. "I don't want Jackson to think I love him for his money...of course his wealth is a great additional bonus and all, but I love Jackson for Jackson, first and foremost. He says he believes me, but my parents are not helping."

"Don't worry, Isa. Trust him. He knows you love him for him. It doesn't matter if your parents like his family's money, I think Jackson is thrilled just to know your parents approve of him. I see how he looks at you and how happy he is around you. That boy loves you and I don't think he minds your parents or how he needs to constantly share you with so many Isa-Bells."

"You think so?"

"I know so. Jackson won't stop liking you because of your parents' interest in his financial background," I say as I lock the door to our apartment.

My best friend's voice unexpectedly goes quieter and I have to turn up the volume on my phone to hear her clearly.

"A part of me is relieved that my parents like Jackson. Back then, you know how much they used to nag me about who to date and what to do with my life."

Boy, do I know. When I first met Mr. and Mrs. Wong with their friendly smiles and practiced good-natured attentiveness, they seemed like decent people.

But it was all fake.

I was Isa's shoulder to cry on whenever her parents made off-handed remarks about her life choices and constantly bombarded her phone with links to hospital internships, even months after we dropped out of college. Her parents were ruthless and only stopped their misguided good intentions after Isa started sending them a part of her hard-earned salary.

"And them meeting Jackson yesterday, my parents finally look proud of me, Lia. Like I'm not a failure of a daughter." I'm not sure whether it is the bad connection or not, but there is a strain to my best friend's voice. "They are finally supporting me and my job. And they approve of my boyfriend. They're acting like real parents. I know I should still be mad at them for what they did, but I can't help but feel happy that they're proud of me...it's so stupid, I know."

I now hear the tears my best friend is holding back and I wish I could give her a bear hug this instant.

"Oh, Isa. No, it's not stupid at all."

Isa hiccup sobs through the phone. "I still remember my mom giving me an earful for getting a C- on my mid-terms and telling me to do better on finals while sending me a bunch of pictures of guys she wanted me to go on blind dates with. My dad never really pressured me on his own, but he would take Mom's side and supply more reasons as to why she's right."

"Deep down, Mr. and Mrs. Wong love you. I'm sorry it took them so long to show you that in the right way."

"We've grown a lot, haven't we? Two college dropouts making a name for themselves. Who knew?" Isa laughs through a sob.

Tears well up in my eyes but I blink them away. "We have. I'm proud of you, Isa. Even when you did not have two million subscribers on YouTube, three million followers on Instagram, and fifty thousand followers on TikTok raving about your fashion tips, makeup tutorials, and mukbangs, I was still proud of you." Isa sob laughs making me smile. "I'm glad your parents and you sort of made up. It doesn't make what they did and said ok, but at least you guys are on better terms now. I'm happy for you, Isa."

"I can't hug you right now but know I really want to. Thank you for cheering me up. Now go have fun on your date with Reed," Isa says and I can hear her usual smile–the one that blooms flowers–in her voice.

"I will. Thanks, Isa." I remove the phone from my ear and end the call.

When my best friend and I first started living together, our parents already abandoned us and said we were financially on our own if we didn't do what they wanted. The fact that we proved them wrong by being successful in our pursuits never fails to put a smug triumphant grin on my face. And it also reminds me to send more prayers of thanks to the universe.

Isa and I may not be blood related, but I consider us close like family. Even if my parents and I will never see eye-to-eye, knowing her parents are integrating themselves back in her life for a redemption arc is more than enough for me. A text message notification pops up on my phone.

Reed: "Hey Lia, can we delay our date to 6:15? Boss called for a meeting. It's important and can't get out of it. Sorry."

Me: "Yeah, I can get the takeout and meet you at my studio so take your time with the meeting. Pastrami?"

Reed: "Yes, please. Really sorry. Ty! Text you when I'm on my way."

Me: "No worries, see you soon!" Smile and heart emoticon.

Reed loved your message.

I put my phone in the cup holder and start the car engine. By the time I arrive at Substation 54, get the sandwiches, and drive to my studio, it is already 6:13 p.m. I set the takeout sandwich bag down on my cute little wooden bench table fit for four. One evening when I was browsing through Wayfair, I stumbled upon this wooden bench table.

It was an unwise splurge if I wanted to stay within budget, so although I so badly wanted it, I convinced myself to keep shopping for more options. But then a few weeks later, I checked Wayfair again and BAM, it was on sale. If that's not a sign, I don't know what is. I purchased the bench table and couldn't be happier.

I check my phone but Reed never texted me he was on his way. Maybe he forgot and is close by? I check outside the window to see if he is out there but the street is empty.

That's strange.

Reed is always on time and usually gives an advance notice if he is going to be late. I sit down on the bench with my back leaning against the table for support and text Reed.

Me: "Got you roast beef because they ran out of pastrami. Hope that's ok."

I wait a few seconds and then a minute but no three dots pop up to show Reed is texting me back. Not wanting to seem impatient, I stand up and begin to busy myself. "Busy myself" as in walking around like a teacher giving a lecture. There's nothing in my studio that needs tidying up since I tend to keep my workspace clean and organized.

Ever since I was little, an untidy workspace means a stressed-out and unfocused Lia. I always keep everything neat–not like OCD perfect level–but semi-close to it. That's one of the things I like most about myself, but right now I kind of hate myself for it because I don't have anything to distract me from wondering where Reed is.

On my fifth lap around the room, I give up and dial Reed's number. The phone keeps ringing and right when I think he picked up, I hear his sweet voice send me to voicemail, "Hey, this is Reed. Sorry, I can't come to the phone right now. I will call you back as soon as I can."

The automated voice message lady tells me to leave a voice-mail after the beep, but I hang up. I decide to text Reed again.

> Me: "Hey, I called because I wasn't sure if you were driving, but text or call me back when you can."

No liked, loved, read message or anything. Usually I don't like to be on read but at least that would mean Reed saw my text. Now I don't even know if he saw my text or not. The takeout sandwich bag sits there staring at me. Technically, I can start eating first. But I like eating with Reed. Food tastes better when we are eating together. I sigh and then pull up the Webtoon app on my phone. Nothing kills time like reading webtoons.

After catching up to the latest episode of *Eaternal Noctur-*

nal, the most recent webtoon I'm completely obsessing over, it's 7:30 p.m. Woah, so much time has passed and I didn't even know. Part of me was hoping I'd get a text notification or incoming call mid-chapter or something. I call Reed one more time but am sent to voicemail again. Checking my messages, even though I know nothing has changed, I send one last text to Reed.

> Me: "I'm going to call it a night. We can tour my studio some other time. Text me back when you get the chance."

Taking the sandwich bag with me and switching off the lights, I lock the door to my studio. The night sky is dark but the streetlamp lights and the youth center building lights glow bright enough, making me feel safe walking alone to my car. I mope down the steps of the front porch and am about to unlock my car until I see a familiar figure saunter down the street.

"Connor?"

He turns and looks at me in surprise, "Hey, Lia."

I walk closer to him and ask, "What brings you here at this fine hour?"

"I teach a night class from 4 p.m. to 6 p.m. twice a week. Since I have the day off tomorrow, I had to do a major cleanup which took longer than expected," Connor answers as he looks at his watch.

The sound of a stomach growls. It is so unexpected that we look at each other like a deer staring at headlights. I'm not sure if it was mine or his, but then Connor is the first to react and puts his hand over his eyes trying to hide his embarrassment. "Please pretend you didn't hear that."

The weight of the takeout bag lingers in my hands and an idea forms. "Long story, but I have two roast beef sandwiches from Substation 54. Would you like to eat with me at my studio?"

"Really?"

"If you don't mind cold sandwiches and fries?"

"I would like that, thanks." Connor's smile widens and he offers his hand out to carry the takeout bag. I nod in thanks and give him the food so I can fish out my studio keys from my purse.

"Make yourself at home," I say to Connor as I turn on the lights and plop down on the bench table.

He puts the food down and then sits on the other side of the bench. We take out the food from the bag and start digging in. The sandwich tastes great–not as great as it would have if we ate them earlier–but still really good considering it is not even lukewarm.

"How is it?" I ask in between bites of my sandwich.

Talking with food in my mouth is a bad habit of mine. I want to eat but I want to talk at the same time so I do both. Over the years, I have mastered the genius technique of putting food on one side of my mouth before speaking. Usually, I would never do this in front of anyone except Isa, but for some reason, I find myself comfortable enough with my friend to not be so ladylike.

Connor continues to chew his sandwich and replies, "Good." After swallowing, he says, "Did you say you got this from Substation 54? I've never been there before but I'm definitely going to check that place out cause either this is super good or I'm really hungry."

"Maybe both? I love their sandwiches. Their roast beef is to die for and the bread is so crunchy without being too crunchy. I was going to get one roast beef and one pastrami but they ran out of pastrami."

Connor raises an eyebrow. "You like pastrami?"

"No, I don't. I'm team roast beef, but Reed likes pastrami," I answer before I can stop myself.

My response kind of summarizes my supposedly "long story" of why I have two cold uneaten sandwiches with me in the middle of the night. Hoping that Connor would not ask me about Reed, I dip my French fry in ketchup laughing nervously.

To my relief, Connor just smiles and casually says, "I like

roast beef too. Not really a pastrami fan. Never have been and most likely never will be."

"Right? Roast beef is the best meat for deli sandwiches." I do a chef's kiss gesture to emphasize my point.

Connor laughs spreading the laughter to me. He has a very soft look in his eyes but then it turns serious and softens again.

Before I can ask what's wrong, he clears his throat and says, "Lia, you have a little...may I?"

I'm confused, but trusting he means no harm, I nod. Connor reaches over and swiftly picks a piece of sandwich bread crumb without pulling on my hair. The one time I forget to tie my hair when eating and food gets stuck in there. Nice, Lia. Way to embarrass yourself for the thousandth time. Why does this guy always catch me at my worst moments? If I didn't know better, it's like I'm trying to embarrass myself in front of him on purpose or something.

I shrink back in my seat before saying, "T-thanks. Sorry, I'm a messy eater."

"Don't worry about it. Seeing a girl devour a large roast beef sandwich and a side of extra-large fries with her bare hands, not afraid to get down and dirty is cool. Really cool actually."

I smile and mentally thank Connor again for making me feel less embarrassed about getting food in my hair. Whether he is lying or not, I am relieved I can eat comfortably around him. In the early days of my relationship with Reed, I remember carefully choosing what to eat and how to eat it. I would opt out of eating a Bar Harbor Lobster Bake at Red Lobster and go with the Crab Linguini Alfredo because I was afraid my messy eating habits would show.

But thankfully my skills in using a fork and knife have improved so I can eat the lobster bake albeit at a slower pace and with my hair tied–of course–and a bib. The only one who knows about my secret messy eating tendencies is once again Isa. Isa's the sweet friend who lends me a hair tie when I forget to bring one and hands me more napkins. It's nice in a weird and good way to eat casually with another friend.

Connor pops a fry in his mouth and says looking around the studio, "I know I was here a few times already, but I just want to say this place looks awesome. The color of the walls is really nice and complements the floors. And this bench table is super dope by the way."

He sounds genuinely impressed and I can't help but beam. "Why, thank you! Traditional wood flooring is beautiful and what I originally wanted, but that is not the best idea for an art studio. With vinyl floors, it is more cost-friendly and personally easier to clean." I motion to the area around us and add, "The paint on the walls were expensive, but no other color can do this space justice. Benjamin Moore Snowfall White 2144-70 is very easy on the eyes and gives a very homey feeling. It is also even more perfect since it matches the Benjamin Moore Black 2132-10 casement windows."

Hearing myself babble about Benjamin Moore paint colors makes me realize how lame and ridiculous I sound. If I didn't know better, it seems like I am trying to advertise Benjamin Moore like "Are you in need of MOORE ideas of what paint color you want, then check out Benjamin Moore!"

Feeling horrible that I must be boring the heck out of my neighbor, I say in a more level voice, "Sorry for blabbering. I get really excited talking about the layout of my studio so thank you for taking note of it."

"It's interesting hearing you talk about it. I would love to hear MOORE."

"Really? I though you would be bored out of your–wait, was that a pun?"

Connor grins at me mischievously confirming my suspicions and then says, "Hearing you talk about art and your studio, I can tell it makes you very happy."

I smile. "I've always dreamed about having my own art studio where I can draw webtoons and paint all day long."

Connor looks at me like he's unsure if he heard me right, "Sorry, did you say webtoons?"

I meet his eyes and answer, "Yeah, webtoons. Web comics

online."

Connor's eyes widen and a huge smile appears on his face, "I love webtoons! I read them on my phone all the time."

"No way, me too."

"To meet an actual webtoon artist in real life, that's insane! Can you tell me what webtoon or webtoons do you draw?" Connor asks leaning forward on the table.

"Well, I used to help out with a bunch of sketching, line art, base coloring, and shading for various webtoon artists from WEBTOONS.com. Then I got an offer to be the webtoon artist of a new Webtoon Original. It updates every Tuesday and is under the romance genre called *When Plum Blossoms Grow.*"

"Shut the front door! Are you talking about the story about the Water Goddess who has been crushing on the almighty Heavenly Emperor because she's been his right hand for thousands of years and then she ends up being stuck with the fearsome Demon Lord in the Demon Realm and they fall in love, but they can't really be together because of the whole conflict between the Heaven and Demonic Realm?" Connor manages to say all in one breath making me bubble with laughter.

I finally nod and smile at his funny yet accurate summary of the story. "Yup, that's the one. Two years ago, the author of that novel emailed me that she loved the art I posted on my socials. She asked me to be the webtoon artist for the webtoon adaption of her story and I, of course said yes."

When Plum Blossoms Grow is similar to hit Xianxia novels that later became adapted into Chinese dramas like *Three Lives Three Worlds: Ten Miles of Peach Blossoms* and *Ashes of Love*. Because of the success of the novel and webtoon adaptation, there are rumors of a live-action adaptation coming out in the next few years.

As an avid C-drama watcher and a huge fan/webtoon artist of the novel, I'll be lying if I said I didn't have any opinion on who should play the female protagonist. Being the stupendous and versatile actress she is, only Yang Mi can capture the beauty, elegance, and natural allure of the Water Goddess.

Connor gasps in surprise, "On the webtoon credits page, it shows ZIA as the webtoon artist. That's you?"

"Guilty." I raise my hand in a small wave.

"Hold on a minute...ZIA as in Z for Zhang?!"

"You got me," I reply with a small shrug.

I publish my webtoon art under an alias because I want to keep my life private. I'm semi-paranoid about keeping the fact that I'm the webtoon artist behind *When Plum Blossoms Grow* a secret. When my fans request for behind-the-scenes footage of creating the chapters, I make sure to only show my hands during the video.

Coming up with an alias is a lot harder than it looks. It took me weeks to think of it. I got inspired to simply combine my name after watching Kirito from *Sword Art Online* which is freaking genius by the way. I watch as Connor gets up from the bench and walks in a small circle before sitting back down again.

"What was that for?"

Connor straightens his posture like he's getting ready for an interview. "I'm trying so hard not to go complete fanboy on you right now." I burst out laughing and he says, "I'm being serious, Lia. Getting to meet the webtoon artist of one of my favorite webtoons? This is a big deal. You're practically a celebrity!"

I playfully roll my eyes, "That's a bit of an exaggeration, but I get your point." Connor looks at me in awe and I can't help but crack a smile. "I didn't expect you to read webtoons much less be a fan of the one I draw. I love being a webtoon artist so thank you for reading and showing interest in my art."

"I said this the first time I saw you, but I need to say it again. You're amazing, Lia."

Not knowing how to react to my neighbor's kind praise, I go with the laugh it off "haha" response. We spend another hour chatting about what webtoons we like and don't like. Due to Connor's really easy to talk to nature, my sadness over how I never got to give Reed the grand tour of my studio almost fades, almost. I don't know Connor all that well, but it feels strangely really nice and refreshing just to be myself and talk to him.

Instead of eating a cold sandwich trying to find something good to watch on TV, I ended the night laughing and smiling with my new guy friend.

Chapter 5

"Reed, you should have told me you were stopping by this morning. It's cold in the morning. You must be freezing!" I scold as I touch his hand which is missing his usual warmth.

He grazes his lips against my fingers and then frowns like he's troubled. "Lia, about yesterday, I'm sorry. Our group meeting took longer than expected and I got pulled into a mandatory work dinner with my colleagues. I wanted to text and call you, but my phone died on me and I couldn't charge it until later that night. But that's no excuse. I'm sorry for standing you up."

I shake my head and place my hand on his cheek. "It's alright, Reed. I get it. I'm glad you're ok and you're here now and that's all that matters."

Reed pulls me in a hug. We are silent and I know he feels genuinely sorry and I hug him tighter to show everything is ok between us.

"I bought strawberry banana Nutella crepes from your

favorite café," Reed says lifting the brown takeout bag he's holding.

"Aw, Reed, that's so sweet. Thank you, but isn't there usually a long line in the morning?"

"It's the least I could do after missing dinner yesterday."

I smile up at my boyfriend appreciatively and open the door to my studio. He walks in and gapes, "Lia, this place looks phenomenal. You really made this your own."

"Thank you. We can tour the place later. Let's eat before the food gets cold," I reply with a smile as I lead Reed to the bench table. We sit across from each other and begin to eat.

He smiles at me jubilantly and says, "I have big news. You know how I mentioned a few weeks ago that our editorial director announced he plans to have a senior editor take over his position during his nine-month break?" Still chewing my crepe, I nod and Reed continues, "Last night, he told me I'm one of the candidates for the position."

"That's wonderful news, Reed! Congratulations!" I clap my hands excitedly.

He sighs. "It's not for sure I am guaranteed the spot since there are other qualified candidates who have been at the company longer and have more experience than I do, but my boss said I have what it takes. This temporary promotion also comes with a higher salary and a few other benefits. So for the next few months, I'll be a lot busier with work."

My earlier smile falls and I can't force another to take its place. Of course I'm excited my boyfriend is in talks of a promotion. As much as Reed loves his job as an editor, I know he also wants to someday jumpstart his writing career. This new job will most likely help him be one step closer to reaching his true dreams, but the idea of not spending as much time together is heartbreaking.

He reads my solemn expression and puts his hand on mine saying, "But I promise to still make time for us. I'll miss you too much if I saw you less."

I set down my plastic fork taking Reed's hand in both of mine. Both my hands are enough to cover his entire hand but I know he can easily slip away from my grasp if he wanted to.

"I don't want to be the type of girlfriend who stops you from doing what you want especially after how much support you've given me. I'll always cheer you on no matter what, but just remember not to overwork yourself and neglect your health, ok? Promise me you'll take care of yourself too."

Reed leans close to me and gives me a quick peck on my lips. It happened so fast that I didn't get the chance to react.

"I feel so lucky to have you in my life."

I let go of Reed's hand pulling away from him and say in my attempt of a stern voice, "A warning next time, please!"

"Sorry." Reed looks at me apologetically before smirking.

"You were so cute I couldn't help myself."

I slap Reed's arm but can't hide the laughter from my voice as I say, "I'm serious, Reed. Promise me that you won't work too hard and stress yourself out too much."

"I'll be fine, I promise. After all, I have you by my side."

I've known Reed for a while now, but his smile still gets me every time. I wonder when I will not have butterflies in my stomach and smile like a goofball at the thought of Reed. Being in love is so crazy sometimes.

Unable to contain my excitement, I also tell him, "I have good news too. I got contacted by another author who wants me to be their webtoon artist!"

Since I drew a majority of the chapters of *When Plum Blossoms Grow* prior to its launch date so readers can fast pass to read ahead, I am taking a short break before finishing the final season. The new author I am in contact with has been greenlit by WEBTOON to join Webtoon Originals. I'm so thrilled to get another opportunity to be someone else's webtoon artist!

Reed takes my hands and waves it around with so much pride in his eyes. "Lia, that's splendid news!"

"The author requested me to send a few of the main characters' design sketches so she can peruse them and tell me what she wants to be changed. I was wondering if you had some time today to model for me?"

"I have to work overtime tonight. Does tomorrow work?"

"The story writer wants it done next week. That's usually no problem, but I am a bit tied up managing my art class and the new painting request I received so I wanted to get a head start today. But no biggie. Isa said she'll model for me and I'll search online for other references I need."

Reed's eyebrows furrow together as he asks, "Are you sure?"

"Mhmm. Totally ok." I put my hand on his forearm reassuring him and then ask, "Did you get the ticket I sent you for the art exhibition this weekend?"

"Yeah, I have it on my phone. I can't wait to see your art displayed in the art gallery again this year! I don't get off until 5 p.m., but I'll try convincing my boss to let me off earlier so I can be there for the entire event."

"You don't need to be there the *whole* time. I'm just happy you're coming." I tuck a strand of hair behind my ear hoping he wouldn't notice my blush.

"Two of my girlfriend's art pieces are being displayed in the city's annual art exhibition. How can I not attend the whole event?" Reed says as he ruffles my hair.

Getting up from my side of the bench chair and moving next to Reed, I kiss his cheek and lean on his shoulder. "I'm so excited for you to be there!"

"I wouldn't miss it for the world." Reed holds me closer

to him and I melt into his body wishing that this moment would never end.

"Can you sit down on the chair and pretend you are typing on the keyboard?"

My best friend follows my instructions and effortlessly gets into position. "Is this good?"

"Perfect, thank you."

I spent years honing my drawing skills, but having references always helps. I can draw without references but with them, it is easier to get the body proportions right. Online references are great but there are only so many poses you can find and models that fit the character's descriptions.

"And done!" I say putting my pencil down. "Thank you for modeling for me, Isa."

"You help me design cute new merch for my Isa-Bells all the time. This much is nothing." Isa puts the laptop down on the table beside her and stands up to stretch. "And you know how much I like posing for my fans."

My best friend starts doing a ton of Vogue-worthy poses and I pretend to take pictures with my fake camera. The chime in my studio interrupts our laughter and we both direct our attention to the door.

"Jax, you're here!" Isa excitedly runs to hug her boyfriend.

"Hey, Iz, I missed you." Jackson hugs her back and it makes me a little sad that the pure happiness on his face is only apparent on my side. This tender moment warms my heart and I also internally laugh at how tiny my best friend looks next to those twin towers.

"Hey, guys," I say feeling the need to greet people out of habit and courtesy.

Jackson gives me a smile with his eyes and Connor waves. "Sorry to stop by uninvited, but Jackson told me Isabel was here and wanted to talk."

"Don't be. You're always welcome here, Connor."

Isa laughs and says, "I still can't get over how you two coincidentally met. Talk about a small world." I plaster a sweet smile on my face and communicate to my best friend to get to her point with my eyes. Isa gleams knowingly and says, "But anyways, yes, I wanted to talk to you, Connor. I was wondering if you had time next week for a vlog? Many of my fans loved the videos I did with Jackson and they've been requesting me to do some more videos of you cooking."

"Yeah. Just let me know what day," Connor answers crossing his arms with a thoughtful expression.

Isa claps her hands together once and says, "Great, thank you! I'll text you the details later." My best friend's stare lingers on Connor before diverting it to me. "Hey, Connor, do you have any plans right now?"

"No, what's up?"

"How do you feel about modeling for Lia?"

"Huh?" Connor says confused.

"Lia needs a guy to model for her. Reed's busy and I would offer Jax but we're off to a romantic moonlit night stroll. All you need to do is stay in one position for a few minutes and let her draw you," Isa delineates with a brilliant smile.

I widen my eyes at my best friend and then to Connor, still not believing she suggested that. "No, that's ok. I can search for references online."

Connor gives me a kind smile and puts his hands in his front pockets. "I'm up for it if you're ok with me as your model."

"Fantastic, then it's settled!" Isa good naturedly pushes Connor towards me before intertwining her arm in Jackson's. "We'll see you guys later. Thanks again, Connor!"

Jackson waves goodbye and then he and Isa are out the door leaving Connor and me alone. While I appreciate my best friend's determination to help me in whatever way she can, it is Connor I'm imposing on this time so I can't easily accept it.

I regard him warily, "Are you sure about this? I don't want you to feel obligated to agree to this. I'm just sketching a few character designs so it's nothing too major."

Connor bounces on his toes and says, "Yeah, it's all good. I don't have anything better to do. And not gonna lie, it would be such an honor to be one of ZIA's models."

I mentally take note that this new friend of mine has a knack for making his simple acts of kindness seem minor when in reality it is a big deal.

"Well, thank you, Connor. I'm going to take you up on your offer then. If you want, you can put your jacket and stuff on the table." I rest my notebook in its usual crook of my left arm and grab my pencil. "And when you're ready, can you pretend you are holding a gun and about to shoot someone?"

"How interesting," Connor says in an amused voice as he places his jacket on the bench and proceeds to get into the stance.

"You assumed that position quite naturally. Should I be worried that you're some kind of secret serial killer?"

Connor's mouth quirks into a smile before dropping into a neutral expression. Through the corners of his mouth, he asks, "Can I talk while modeling?"

Still sketching, I answer with a laugh, "As long as you don't move your body too much, it's fine."

"Whew." He lets out an exhale of relief as he opens his mouth to talk. "I am not a serial killer. Then again, that's something a real serial killer would say. I watch my fair share of James Bond and *Mission: Impossible* so I might have picked up a thing or two, just putting it out there."

I walk behind Connor to sketch his backside as well. Even though he can't see me roll my eyes and smirk, his quiet chuckle hints otherwise. "Ok, I'm done."

Connor drops his arms back to his side. "You're fast."

I chuckle and say, "Not really. It's easy for me to sketch when I have a still model. I'll fill in the details later since this is just for me to reference when I draw the characters with these poses."

"What pose next?" my friend asks and stretches his arms.

I grab three black pens from my desk wrapping them together and hand them to him along with a handkerchief-sized hand towel. "I don't have a bloody knife so we'll just make do with this makeshift weapon prop. Can you look down at the knife as you wipe it with the towel?"

My friend gets into position and stares at the towel he's holding with the "knife" in between it as I begin sketching.

"I can't imagine what other makeshift props you come up with," he comments.

"I'm all about being resourceful," I reply in a half-whisper.

"Your parents must be so proud of you."

My pencil halts abruptly causing a line where there isn't

supposed to be. Luckily, the sketch can still be salvaged but it takes my hand a few seconds to recover. Through the warmth in Connor's words, I know he means well but maybe because it is so far from the truth, a coldness envelops my heart.

"What makes you say that?"

"Their daughter is such a talented artist. How are they not proud?" he states without an ounce of insincerity.

"I'm done with the sketch," I announce curtly.

A little too curt.

As if picking up on my weird behavior, Connor simply hands me back the towel and pen knife prop before asking in a gentle voice, "What's the next pose?"

I place the props on my desk, using those few seconds to get a grip on myself. As I flip to another page of my notebook, I soften my voice in an attempt to make up for my earlier rudeness. "This is the last pose. Can you sit on a chair and get in a lost-in-thought type of position?"

My friend pulls out one of the chairs set up for my art students and then sits down hunching over with his hands folded. He rests his forearms on his thighs and lowers his head as he asks, "Like this?"

"Mhmm."

I start outlining–falling back into a familiar groove–which in turn calms my nerves and eases my tension. We are silent for the next few minutes until I finally say, "I'm finished. Thank you so much for all your help."

"No problem." Connor gets up and pushes the chair back to its original position. "Can I ask you something, Lia?"

Oh no.

He's going to ask me why I was being so weird earlier. To prevent the panic from showing on my face, I harden my expression as I await the impending dooming.

"Do you mind if I take a look at your sketches?"

It's been years but I can still remember showing my drawings—a part of me—to my parents and their responses. In general, my dad was too busy to look at any of my sketches but when he did see it one time, he said it was cute. My naïve younger self did a mini victory dance after hearing his compliment. Now that I'm older and wiser, I realize he probably said that since everything I did in his eyes was "cute" because I was his daughter versus it being anything of significance.

And my mom never praised me except this one time when she thought one of my classmates' drawing was mine. I don't take any offense to this though. My drawings as a kid weren't the best—to put it nicely—but it still hurt knowing my parents didn't like them.

I never wanted them to lie to me or say my drawings were good either, but I just wanted to hear a different response from them...at least something other than what they gave me.

I know Connor is not my parents. He is different and mentioned he is a fan of my art, but to show him it in person–on the spot–is a whole new story. It took me a few months before I even let Isa and Reed look at them when I'm in the room so I can't help but feel anxious. The urgent necessity to decline his request fills me but remembering he did do me a huge favor and didn't question my strange behavior, guilt weighs heavy on me.

I flip back to my first sketch convincing my hands to stop shaking and hand him my notebook. "They're just sketches for me to reference so don't expect anything. It's nothing remarkable."

Connor delicately takes my notebook with two hands as he scans through the pages. Unable to stomach watching his reaction, I face away from him pretending to tidy something on my desk. Centuries seem to go by as I wait to have my precious sketch pad returned back to me. In reality, it might just be a minute but waiting in this agony feels like an eternity.

"If this is your definition of 'nothing remarkable', I can't even imagine what remarkable looks like. Your art on paper is just as good as your digital art."

I turn around and see Connor's eyes browse over my sketches in awe. Even though I literally see him smiling in amazement in front of me, I still can't process my new friend's admiration for my drawings.

He hands me back my notebook with a radiant smile, "You're seriously insanely good at drawing, Lia. I'm sure the new author will love your character designs too."

Not wanting him to know how much I am internally drinking in his compliments, I only manage a small smile. "Thanks."

Connor walks over to the white board I had installed on the wall and studies a newspaper pinned there. "What's this? I didn't know San Willmore has an annual art exhibition."

"It's where the board of art directors, the coordinators of the exhibition, decide a different topic every year and feature art pieces based on that selected theme. Many artists submit their work but only one hundred of them are accepted so getting chosen is a really big feat," I answer closing my notebook and placing it on my desk.

"Did you submit anything?"

"I submitted two." My friend looks at me expectantly waiting for me to say more and an image of a cute puppy pleading with its adorable eyes conjures in my mind. Thanks a lot, Isa. It's hard not to smile at his eagerness. "Both of my art pieces were accepted to this year's exhibition."

He breaks into a wide grin. "That's awesome, Lia! Are your submissions here? Can I see them?"

"The board of directors collected them a few weeks ago."

"Oh, I see." Connor practically deflates next to me and something inside me fuels the need to turn that frown upside down.

"I still have my submission from last year. Would you like to see that instead?" I offer hoping I wouldn't regret this a second later.

"Can I?" he asks, eyes once again sparkling.

"Last year's theme was love or more specifically, your definition of love," I elucidate to Connor as we make our way over to the paintings resting on easels. I remove the cloth over the third painting revealing a nighttime beach setting with a couple gazing lovingly at each other as they hold hands. There are a few shadow silhouettes of the sample couple around the pair but in different poses of them happy in love.

"This is so beautiful," Connor utters as he studies the entire painting.

When I first heard about last year's theme, I had so many ideas of what to draw but none of them seemed good enough. But then one day, when I was brainstorming with music to drown out the world, a picture of a beach popped up.

"The ocean beach scenery is really nice and kinda reminds me of the Kahala Beach in Honolulu, Hawaii," Connor notes as he removes his gaze from the painting and then directs it to me.

I raise my eyebrow. "Yeah, that's exactly where I based it off from. How'd you know?"

"I go to Hawaii at least once a year with my family. We love eating shaved ice and this place with the best Huli-Huli chicken. I cook for a living so I can testify that their Huli-Huli chicken ranks top five on the 'best chicken I ever tasted list.' I can still remember the chicken's tender meat roasted perfectly and that delicious coat of salt seasoning," Connor describes with a dreamy smile and his eyes closed like he can taste the chicken in his mouth which makes me laugh. "Have you ever been to Hawaii before?"

"Yeah. I've been there," I answer, playing it off cool.

The truth is, I've been there at least five times. As a middle schooler, my family and I often went on trips during my school breaks. Most of my happiest memories with my parents were spent at the Kahala Hotel & Resort Beach where we would search for fake seashells, build sandcastles, and eat grilled cheese sandwiches while drinking the most delicious mango and strawberry smoothie I ever had in my life.

But we stopped visiting there and all our other little trips after I graduated middle school due to their busy schedules. At least that's what they told me. I learned too late that it was because they already started to have marital issues then.

Despite everything, I still want to go back to Hawaii someday. I always pictured the next time I go, I'll be walking barefoot on the Kahala Beach and taking in the sight of the vast ocean hand in hand with Reed. Come to think of it, it was that single thought and desire which sparked the whole idea for this painting. I'm so caught up in my own head, I barely hear my friend's next words.

"A lighthouse? I don't remember seeing one at the Kahala Beach."

"To be honest, I just felt like adding a lighthouse because during that time, I watched the movie *Nerve* with Emma Roberts and Dave Franco. There's no special meaning behind it except for the aesthetics. But I guess there is some kind of symbolism going on with the shadowy figures and lighthouse combo." I gesture to the respective parties on the painting.

Connor puts a hand to his chin like he is thinking about it and says, "Oh, yeah, for sure. And I love that movie by the way. The lighthouse you added, that's deep."

"This is actually one of my favorite paintings I ever painted because it was my first submission that got accepted to the exhibition. Having my art piece accepted felt like I finally made it as an artist," I share before adding, "I had the honor of having this painting displayed at the gallery last year and on their website for everyone to see. I'm actually a little sad but mainly happy my baby will have a new home now."

Connor cocks his head. "What do you mean?"

"I'm selling this painting to someone. The board of art directors informed me many people gave good offers to purchase this painting and I refused, not wanting to part ways with it. But then I received an email and call from some guy called Vincent Krause. He wanted to gift his wife, Nadia, this painting because she completely fell in love with it during the exhibition. Vincent asked if I could sell it to him and would pay double the amount I was originally offered, and more if I wanted. Hearing his reason and knowing he wanted to make his wife happy, I finally agreed."

"This sounds like some kind of grand romantic gesture from a movie or something," Connor observes with a skeptical look.

"I know, right? But I promise it's real. Vincent is actually picking up the painting tomorrow morning just in time for Nadia's birthday, so I already said my goodbyes." I give my precious painting one last meaningful look before covering it back up.

"I think Nadia will love her gift. The painting is absolutely breathtaking," he says brightly before changing the subject. "Hey, Lia, the flyer says the exhibition is this weekend. Do you know where I can get a ticket?"

"You want to go?"

"Yeah. I've never attended an art exhibition before so I think it would be really fun and exciting. I also want to see your submissions this year in person."

"Since my art pieces are part of the selection, I got two extra tickets. One's for Reed and both Isa and Jackson insisted early on that they would buy their own tickets so I have one extra ticket. Would you like it?"

"No, I also want to buy my own ticket." Connor waves his hand in front of him like he is refusing my offer.

"The tickets this year sold out really fast. I have an extra ticket that wouldn't be used anyway and I'd feel awful if you paid a ridiculous amount for resale tickets. Can you type in your phone number so I can send it to you?" I ask handing my phone to him.

"I promise to make it up to you somehow, thank you." Connor smiles and begins typing on my phone.

"It's fine, Connor. I should be the one thanking you, not the other way around. You're always helping me out so it's the least I could do." I click send and a ding sounds soon after.

He briefly checks his phone and then looks up at me, "Still, I appreciate it. I have a late-night class scheduled, but I'll most likely be there before 6 p.m."

"Looking forward to see you there."

Chapter 6

"Thanks so much again for coming," I say to Isa and Jackson at the gallery entrance.

A few people come in and out around us as we stand at a corner where we're not standing in the way. We have a thing about not blocking people from entering and exiting the premise. Kinda like how in Hong Kong when you ride escalators, people who stand still on the escalator stay on the right and the left side are for people who want to walk up.

"Congrats again, Lia." Jackson holds his fist up for me to bump and I tap my fist against his.

"Are you sure you don't want us to stay with you until Reed comes?" Isa asks as we share a hug. "Did he text you back yet?"

I look at my phone and shake my head. "No, but it's fine. He's probably driving or his phone's out of battery again. He said he'll be here so I know he will. You guys can go first. Don't mind me."

"Ok, but text me if you need anything." Isa interlocks her fingers with Jackson's and they both wave goodbye.

After returning their wave and waiting until they are out of sight, I let out a heavy exhale. Reed texted me earlier he's running late and he'll be there as soon as he can. He liked my last message about our current location before the line went cold. I texted him a few times later but with no luck. I sigh again before taking another lap around the enormous art gallery.

Putting aside my sad feelings that Reed is not here, seeing everyone's artwork displayed is simply astonishing and helps improve my mood. When you look at someone's art, you can pick up traces of the creator within it. We may or may not know the artist on a personal level, but seeing their creation is in a way even more intimate. We get to see the individual more than surface level deep even without words. That's actually my favorite thing about art.

When too many or no words appear in my brain, I can just pick up something to draw with and my hands automatically move on their own. Through art, I feel like I can truly express myself comfortably and be me.

I finish touring the entire exhibit faster than I want and end up circling back to where my art pieces are located. Because one of my paintings is a panoramic painting, it needs a wall of its own to fit the entirety of it. My panoramic painting hangs on the wall at the end of the gallery and my other submission is displayed on a separate wall nearby. I'm about to head to the front entrance to see if Reed is somehow there until I spot Connor.

As an artist who loves feasting their eyes on beautiful specimens, I can't help but soak up his current appearance. And apparently, I'm not the only one since there are a few other girls gawking at him. Connor is wearing a black turtleneck underneath a dark gray overcoat extending to his knees with black pants that only make him appear taller. His clothes suit him and underline his already evident good looks.

Connor's original "cinnamon roll boy-next-door" vibe just converted to "boiling hot boy-next-door" vibe. When my friend and I lock eyes, he hurries towards me and I see a yellow bouquet in his hands. I recognize them as alstroemeria flowers since I remember reading about them many years ago in science class.

"Hey, Lia." Connor sounds breathier than usual like he was jogging or something. "I wasn't sure what people normally give to artists at an exhibition so I went ahead and bought this. I hope that's ok."

I take the flowers from Connor and smile at their beauty, "They're lovely, thank you."

Connor returns my smile and examines the labels on the bottom of the art pieces around us before looking back at me, "Are these yours?"

I nod and point at them with my hands. "This is a drawing I drew and the other one is a panorama painting."

I remember my frugal side telling me there was no need for the fancy expensive Stonehenge poster and how it was a better choice to use a cheaper poster instead, but I'm glad I talked myself into splurging. As I scrutinize my charcoal drawing decorating the wall, I am pleased to find immense satisfaction with my work.

The drawing is entirely black and white with the same indistinct person's face drawn seven times. Each face is drawn wearing a different expression conveying happiness, sadness, jealousy, anger, boredom, being in love, and numbness. I positioned the faces with two on top, three in the middle, and the last two on the bottom in a diamond shaped pattern so it can haunt—I mean, greet spectators from almost every angle.

Connor walks closer to the drawing and he's silent for a while. His eyes explore the drawing like he's taking everything in before saying anything.

"The expressions are so clear and defined. You can easily tell what each expression shows and the dark color really makes the whole thing pop. I can't imagine how long this took you," Connor says with his eyes still glued to the drawing.

"It took me a total of one week, from coming up with the idea to making it happen. This was my first time using black compressed charcoal sticks instead of charcoal pencils. It was pretty messy in the beginning with all the smudges and my fingers turning black, but it was a lot of fun."

"Words out of a true artist." Connor grins at me before moving towards the painting on the wall.

Starting from left to right, the four seasons are depicted on the panorama painting. For spring, there are trees with dark green leaves and daffodils in full bloom surrounding a bunch of smiling kids playing together. Nearby the elated children, there's a girl sitting alone on a swing set. During the summer season, the bright sun shines over teenagers having fun at a pool party and that very same girl, now a little older, stares at them with her hand on the window from inside the house.

When fall comes around, the identical girl in the past two seasons, is all grown up as she carries an umbrella to shelter herself from the rain. Maple trees surround her and she outstretches her hand as an orange leaf falls in front of her. In the winter, a family's backyard tree is completely barren except for the spots where snow covers it. Inside the house is that same girl throughout the entire season, finally smiling and happy in a crowded room.

Painting this took a span of two months. I wasn't planning on entering another piece, but one night, I couldn't sleep and the concept of seasons changing ran through my mind. I woke up early the next day and sketched the basic concept in my notebook. After fully fleshing out my idea, I was determined to submit this painting and make the deadline.

"It's interesting how in your charcoal drawing, the theme of change is easily seen through the broad range of human emotions. But for this one, it is shown through the alternating seasons and how much can change in the span of a year. Yet at the same time, I don't think that's all. I feel like there is more to the story, but I can't seem to put my finger on it," Connor notes fixing his eyes on me.

I smile but focus my attention on the painting in front of us. "It's all in the eyes of the beholder. I didn't want there to be one specific interpretation. It's meaning comes from however you want to see it." Connor studies me with a curious expression and I ask, "What is your take?"

He gazes back at the painting and replies, "I'll go for the straightforward answer first. As each season goes by, the girl's life changes with it."

"Yes, that's the main message I wanted to portray."

"I noticed a twist in how the girl's happiest moment is during the winter as opposed to spring or summer. There seems to be a lot to decipher from that alone." Connor rubs his chin in the famous thinking position and I hold in a snort. "I have two theories about that."

"Be my guest."

"My first theory is the girl finally found her happy ending at the end of the year during the winter season. Second theory is that the girl's happiness was stolen by spring and summer and only started finding it again during the last two seasons."

"Which interpretation are you leaning towards?"

Connor shrugs. "Both don't change how the girl had to go through a rollercoaster of ups and downs."

I let out a hollow laugh. "You make a good point. Seasons and people changing are normal so there's nothing too special about that concept. I think the easiest way to see the change is not just by looking at the change itself but at the things around them. It's the things that accompany them during the change that really show the differences. That's the theme of change I wanted to portray."

I pause to take a moment to breathe before continuing, "I want people to focus on how it's the seasons and things around her that stick with her throughout the change. Sure, everything else is changing as well so people can argue that that makes no sense. But instead of interpreting the changing season and other objects literally, it can be seen as the people who care about you that will always be there. That there will always be someone or something there for you during all the changes, good and bad."

I snap out of my post-speech daze after rambling for so long and feel Connor's stare. Turning to face him, instead of finding eyes looking at me like I'm delusional or out of my mind, I see true understanding and empathy from my friend. There's not a single trace of pity in them and for a moment, I find myself lost in his warm brown eyes.

This year's San Willmore's Annual Art Exhibition theme is change so all the art submissions should depict change, but to spice things up a little, I included a mini paradox in my painting. At least that's what I think I did since the whole paradox concept still makes my head spin. The obvious illustration of change in my painting is the constant alternating seasons and the girl's life.

Yet the one thing that never changes throughout each season is the fact that the girl herself never changes. She may grow older and experience more things, but the girl was and is always the same. She's still that same lonely little girl who longs to be surrounded by people who love her.

Connor is looking at me with eyes that know being loved was what the girl always wanted. He is looking at me like he knows all that girl wanted, all I ever wanted, was to be loved by the people around me.

Every cell in my body is screaming at me to laugh and make up a random joke to change the subject, but instead, I am guiltily reveling in the joy this brings me. Being acknowledged–no, understood by someone so immensely brings up emotions in me I thought I long locked away. My whole life, it was easy to fall in the familiar rhythm of bubbly facades and reflecting what people expect from me back onto them.

But the eternal truth, my undoing, lies naked in front of me. All my creations end up revealing little dark truths I bury in the deepest part of my soul and having someone look upon them with so much sympathy and understanding renders me completely vulnerable. Tears well up in my eyes from my raw defenselessness and I quickly rip my gaze away from my neighbor friend.

Hoping to distract him with my hand gesturing to the other paintings around us, I clear my throat and say, "We only have less than an hour left before closing. Do you want to go browse around?"

There's a delay in Connor's response but he finally answers in his usual amiable voice, "Yeah, sure."

The two of us casually stroll around the gallery and make small talk about each artist's creations. We just barely manage to finish perusing through all one hundred of them before the exhibit is over.

"We will be closing in the next five minutes. Please start making your way towards the exit. Thank you to everyone who attended this year's San Willmore Art Exhibition and we look forward to seeing you all again next year!" a jolly voice proclaims from the speakers.

A quarter of the original attendees have already left, but a good portion of the crowd still remains. Swarms of human bodies start making their way to the main exit all at once. Connor and I are near the back of the line trying our best to avoid bumping into people. I check my phone for new text messages or a missed call but it comes up clean. Reed never texted or called back and the event is already over. The unease in my heart worsens and it feels like a big rock is slowly sinking down to the pit of my stomach.

"I had a lot of fun tonight. Thank you again for inviting me," Connor says. His gentle voice reminds me that there is an audience here so I can't break down into tears yet. I smile without looking up and continue to take small steps forward with the exiting horde. "You know even after looking at the whole gallery, my favorite is still yours."

I raise my head to look at his face and am greeted by his boyish grin which makes me roll my eyes. "I'm glad you had fun. You don't need to compliment me as compensation."

"I'm not. I promise." Connor lifts his right hand and does the Scout's Honor sign. "I don't know much about art, but both your pieces stand out to me more than the rest." He lets out a chuckle after he sees my deadpan expression. "Hey, hear me out."

Sighing, I cross my arms and shoot him a quick glance to

let him know I'm listening.

"Everyone else's submissions are all astounding. But when I look at yours, I can really see the passion, heart, and soul from them. It's like they speak to me. I can stare at them the whole day and find things I didn't see before and then fall in love all over again."

When I showed Reed my submissions for this year's exhibition, he told me they were very beautiful. He applauded me for the hard work I spent creating those pieces, but I don't think he ever explained what exactly he liked about them. I never pressed him further for his reasons and I'm sure he would have told me, yet sometimes I do wonder what exactly he liked about it. The way Connor easily puts it all out there in the open surprises me. I haven't known Connor for too long but I trust in his words and am really touched by what he said.

We finally make it out to the front entrance of the gallery where we walk to the side where there are fewer people. My mouth feels dry making it difficult to say something back and thankfully Connor doesn't expect a response from me as he simply asks, "Is your car close by?"

"Jackson and Isa picked me up from my studio so my car is there...Reed was originally going to drive me back, but I'm not sure when he's coming since I can't seem to get ahold of him." I try not to let on the disappointment and bitterness I feel but fail miserably judging from Connor's worried expression.

"I'm sorry."

"It's not your fault. You don't need to apologize."

"I'm sorry to hear that," he amends.

I lift one side of my mouth so it looks like I'm attempting for a smile. "Thanks again for coming, Connor. I also had a lot of fun tonight. You don't have to wait for me, you can head home first."

"I can drive you."

"I don't want to impose. I can just call an Uber."

"You're not imposing. It's the least I can do and I'm going to pass by your studio anyways when I drive home."

I check my phone again only to see the selfie of me and Reed at the mall photo booth laughing together as we pose in front of the camera staring back at me. Still nothing.

"If you don't mind, that would be great."

Connor points to the left, "I parked that way. It's not a long walk but it's kinda windy. Do you want to wait here while I get the car?"

"No, I'll go with you. Thanks."

Connor nods and I follow him as we make the way to his car. A few minutes later and we reach his vehicle, a beige Lexus SUV. He unlocks the car and I hop in the passenger seat. The leather seat feels comfortable and nice. I didn't peep in the back, but his car looks relatively tidy in the front. Besides a red envelope and tangerine next to it, there's no loose trash or empty bottles in the cup holder. The hygiene state is the first thing I notice about a person's car.

Everyone has their own phobias. Mine, unfortunately, is sitting in dirty cars because that's gross. The feeling of being in a confined space that feels nasty and icky everywhere sends shivers up my spine. So it pleases me to know Connor keeps his car clean and I'm able to enjoy the ride without having to worry about how to properly sanitize my clothes and myself later.

My friend waits for me to buckle my seatbelt before shifting the gear to drive. After a few minutes of driving in silence, he asks, "Do you mind if I turn on the radio?"

"I don't mind."

With his eyes glued to the road, Connor presses the media button and adjusts the volume at a decent level before putting his hand back on the wheel. The chorus of "Kiss Me More" by Doja Cat ft. SZA plays on the radio.

Ah, that's my favorite Doja Cat song with its catchy tune and cute lyrics. But that's the type of song I would listen to with a casual girl friend or my romantic partner. Not with my boy friend, as in boy that is a friend who is driving me home from a special event after my boyfriend ghosted me. I love this song but it seems kind of wrong and borderline inappropriate to have this song play over our cordial tranquility.

Seeming to read my mind, Connor presses the next button somewhere on his steering wheel and the song switches to "I'll Never Love Again" by Bradley Cooper and Lady Gaga in the movie *A Star is Born*.

Oh my God is the universe doing this on purpose?

I feel like Judy from *Zootopia*. The chorus is playing and now I feel like I'm using Connor as my rebound but I'll never love him as much as I love Reed. This is more than a tad absurd and the complete opposite of the song's actual meaning, but my stressful long day has led to my already overthinking brain go on overdrive. There is nothing going on between Connor and me, but I admit, I'd be semi-jealous of a girl if she and Reed were alone in a car together listening to romantic love songs in the middle of the night.

My friend clears his throat and hits the next button again on the steering wheel. I bite the inside of my cheek trying to contain my laughter at how it's not just me feeling awkward. Connor is just a friend that's a guy. He's cool. We're cool. And there's not the least bit of sexual tension that a guy and girl might feel in a closed space together like in those rom-com movies going on here. Connor is not interested and I have a boyfriend.

It's cool. We're cool.

Even so, I still appreciate him for switching the song because he knows how to keep boundaries and things on a friendly level. Though it might actually be even more awkward if we skip every love song, but all the radio tunes remind me too much of how it is not Reed with me in the car.

The beginning of "Unchained Melody" from The Righteous Brothers sounds from the speakers and before Connor changes the channel, I ask, "Can we listen to this?"

"Yeah," he responds, eyes still focused on the road.

This love song might arguably be the worst amongst the romantic love song selection earlier, but this song is special to me. My parents blasted this all the time when I was a child and I fell in love with the lyrics when I was old enough to understand them. I remember watching the movie *Ghost* with them as an eleven-year-old. Probably not the most age appropriate for a kid, but hey, it was a good movie.

It was nice to be like a real normal family watching a movie and stuffing popcorn in our mouths, even for a little while. Things are so different now that it replaces the joyful feelings of reminiscing about happy moments with my parents to aching for rare, good times we will never have again.

In a blink of an eye, a pleasant more recent memory overtakes that older memory. During my third date with Reed, we planned to watch a movie. Since the movie theater was only a few blocks from his apartment, to save us the hassle of finding a parking space, we decided to walk there. But then out of nowhere, rain started pouring down on us non-stop. The unexpected weather change caused us to run back to Reed's apartment and take refuge there until the rain died down.

Reed changed clothes and I changed into one of his over-sized T-shirts which almost fell to my knees. My undergarments and the spandex I wore underneath my skirt did not get too wet–thank the Lords–but it was still kind of cold. Reed's apartment is fit for only one person to live in, given the one room and bath, but it still felt homey with the addition of an electric fireplace he had in between the kitchen and living room.

As an editor, it made sense to see Reed's apartment filled with shelves of books wherever there was space. That was why the small shelf of records with an old-looking record player on a table next to it caught my eye. Probably seeing me stare at it, Reed turned the record player on. "Unchained Melody" started playing and Reed put one hand behind his back and offered his other hand to me.

"Miss Zhang, would you give me the honor of having this dance?" Reed asked with a heart-stopping smile. "I hope this dance can give you a taste of how prom should have been like."

I couldn't trust my mouth to say anything equivalent to

the smoothness of what Reed just said so I let my hand do the talking. The minute Reed caught hold of my hand, he pulled me closer to him and wrapped his arm wrapped around my waist. My heart fluttered and I was no doubt blushing hard. Reed smiled at me again and I couldn't help but be mesmerized by him.

I rested my free hand on his shoulder and leaned closer to him. I had never been this close to a boy and could smell the aroma of cedar wood mixed with rain from him. I'm still not sure if cedar wood is Reed's natural scent, but it's a smell my olfactory sense can't get enough of.

Reed and I were close enough that our lips could touch at any second. My first kiss and our first ever kiss, in his apartment with a warm fireplace dancing to a good song, take a snapshot of that, BOOM, perfect couple moment. I would have loved to kiss Reed that moment and I think he felt the same way too since I caught him sneaking glances at my lips a few times.

But us not kissing that moment was actually more romantic. We stared into each other's eyes and then leaned against each other, swaying left and right. If a meteor came crashing down on us or a zombie apocalypse happened, I think I would have died with no regrets. I got to have my most ever romantic dance with the perfect boy. I could peacefully die the happiest girl in the world.

Every time I hear "Unchained Melody", I can't help but think of Reed. Dancing together barefoot in his living room in front of the fireplace. That moment was so perfect and even though the heavy rain derailed our original plans, it seemed like it happened so we could have an even more blissful moment. I know I asked Connor to stay with this song, but I kinda regret it now since my brain is reliving one of my best memories with Reed and it hurts to think about him. I'm mad at him for flaking on me, but I miss him.

I miss Reed.

The car comes to a stop and I can feel Connor look over at me. "Are you okay, Lia?"

I slap a smile on my face and say, "Yeah, I'm ok. I just got lost in the music."

Connor scrutinizes me like he knows there's more to it but doesn't pry. He nods thoughtfully and plays along, "Yeah, it's a good song."

I open the car door and get out. Rotating back, I see that the passenger side window is already rolled down. I bend my knees so Connor can hear me better. "Thanks for dropping me off. I really appreciate it."

"Yeah, it's no problem. Have a good n—" I hear Connor saying before another voice catches my attention.

"Lia."

I whirl to see Reed behind me like the thought of him

willed him to appear out of nowhere. It's dark but I can immediately tell that he is not ok. My boyfriend's brown hair that usually looks good without trying appears sort of messy like he was running his fingers through it a lot. He looks paler than normal and there are dark circles under his eyes.

All the anger I felt towards Reed for standing me up is gone in an instant. Seeing him in this state feels like needles stabbing into my heart and I want to throw my arms around him and ask if he's ok. But remembering we're not alone, I rein myself back in.

"R-Reed," is all I manage to say.

He reaches for my hand and I let him take it easily. My boyfriend gives me a smile and it's handsome as always but he looks drained like he'd probably collapse if he's not holding onto me.

"Hey, Connor. Thanks for driving Lia back," Reed says.

"It's nothing. I had a great time tonight. See you, Reed. I'll catch you later, Lia." Connor waves his hand as the window rolls back up.

I hold one hand up to say goodbye to Connor before he drives away. When we're alone, I twirl back to Reed and look at him. "Reed, what's wrong? Are you okay?" I put my free hand on his forehead to check if he has a fever and fortunately, his forehead is not hot.

He puts my hand on his chest and says in a low voice, "I'm

sorry, Lia. I let you down."

I shake my head and say, "It's cold, let's go back in first."

We walk inside my studio and I hit the lights. I place the flowers Connor gave me on the bench table and Reed and I sit down next to each other. He touches my face and his hand feels colder now, sending goosebumps down my skin but I don't pull away. I learned from a public speaking class I took in my freshman year of college that sometimes we feel uncomfortable looking at people's eyes when we speak in front of them because it is a very intimate gesture.

Eyes are very revealing since you can see the inside of a person just by looking at them. As Reed's glassy and bloodshot eyes peers into mine, I can tell he is searching for any sign of anger I may have.

My boyfriend stood me up even though he knew how important this event is to me. Him not being there with me took away a small part of tonight's greatness. It's not like I need Reed's presence to know the value of my achievement. I am still proud of myself and am really thankful to all the love people have shown my art, but I also want my boyfriend to be there too.

I just wanted to share this major accomplishment with him next to me. But even if he is scanning my eyes for another five minutes, he won't find any residual resentment I have. I was sure Reed had a good reason why he didn't show and right now, I'm more than certain. I stare into his eyes to gauge how bad the situation is and if he is really ok.

Before I can say anything, Reed pulls me close to his chest and hugs me. He holds me like I'm his lifeline and says, "I'm sorry, Lia. I'm so sorry for not showing up. I'm sorry."

I pat Reed's back and console him in a soft voice, "Hey, it's ok. It's ok, Reed. It's ok."

"Work has gotten so busy, and today, when I thought I could leave early, my boss told me that an author I was managing did not send in his finalized manuscript. The last time I spoke to him, he told me he had sent it. Today was the deadline to submit the final manuscript but he didn't pick up any of my calls. The situation was pretty dire so we had to pull that author out and deal with the aftermath. I'm sorry it was a work emergency. I'm not saying this so you can forgive me, but I'm truly sorry for missing out on a special night for you. I'm the worst boyfriend, I know. No matter how many times I apologize, I can never tell you how bad I feel for missing tonight. But I'm sorry."

I pull back from Reed to cup both of my hands on his cheeks—which are missing their usual glow—and put my forehead to his.

"I'm not mad at you, I promise." He smiles at me gratefully and I feel my eyes getting teary. "But I am worried about you, Reed." His eyebrow lifts and I continue, "Earlier this week, you told me how much this promotion means to you. I meant what I said about supporting you in whatever way I can, but it is talking a toll on you. You must be exhausted working so much that you're not getting enough rest and taking care of your health. Is there something go—"

Reed cuts me off and shakes his head, "I can't slack off. I need this promotion and all the benefits that come with it. I know it's hard right now, but I promise I'll get myself together."

During the many years I've known him, I've never seen Reed this stressed out and haggard. I'm scared it would not get better but worse as more time goes by. I'm hesitant to persist in arguing how overworking himself is not the solution and I don't know what else to say to convince him otherwise.

Reed gives me a weak smile before leaning on my shoulder. "Can I rest here for a bit, Lia?"

One thing I know and love about my boyfriend is his dedication to things, especially his work. Since Reed has set his mind on it–that lovable determination of his which I'm half resenting right now–the best thing I can do for him is be whatever he needs from me. I shift my position a little so Reed can lean on my shoulder easier. I'm not sure what happens next. If we stay quiet or chat.

All I know is how that night, for the first time in my life,

I understood what it means to miss someone even though they are right next to you.

112

Chapter 7

Isa and I usually buy groceries together because it is more fun to do so in a pair. But since she is currently vlogging her road trip and won't be back until three days later, I'm shopping solo.

As I push my cart down the canned food section aisle, my mind can't help drifting back to Reed. He's been so busy lately, I haven't had the chance to see him since the night of the art gallery. We still text every day but the time span between his responses are getting longer than before. I want to visit him at work, yet I worry I'll be a bother to him instead. Seeing how tired Reed looked that night still concerns me. I want to do something for him. Something that would hopefully make him feel better.

Wait, that's it.

I'll cook a homecooked meal for him! On our worse days, warm home food usually does the trick. I take out my phone and text Reed.

Me: "Are you by any chance free this
week?"

I am about to shut off my phone screen, but surprisingly, three dots appear and for a second, I think my eyes are
deceiving me. Even after five blinks, the dots are still there.
Reed's texting me back. He's texting me back right after I
text him. That hasn't happened since I don't even know
when.

Reed: "I should be free Thursday night."

I immediately type back in case another work emergency
comes up and I won't be able to text him anymore.

Me: "I have a surprise for you. Isa's out of
town for a few days so we can"
"hang at our apartment. What time good?"
"Is* good?"

Reed: "Does 6 work?"

Me: "See you Thursday at 6."

I add the heart and kiss emoji at the end. Reed loves my message and sends me the same emoji as well. I put my phone close to my chest and smile. Reed and I are going to see each other in person again and I'm going to surprise him with a delicious homecooked meal. But there's only one problem.

What is something I can cook that he would like?

As I continue wandering through the lanes in search for another epiphany, I freeze when a voice calls out my name. Connor pushes his bountiful cart closer until he's directly across from me.

A playful grin spreads across his face as he teases dramatically, "I know what you're thinking, but I go to Safeway at least three times a week to buy ingredients for my cooking class. This time I feel like I have the right to ask if you're following me."

I laugh with my voice dripping in sarcasm, "Sorry to disappoint, but no, I'm not following you. I might not go here three times a week, but I do visit once a week."

My friend smiles at me as he leans his surprisingly well toned forearms on the cart.

"It's funny how we tend to know the same people and go to the same places, but never ran into each other. I guess our timing was always off." His eyes are looking straight ahead but they seem so distant. He dons an unreadable expression but before I can say something, Connor smiles at me asking,

"Are you almost done shopping?"

"I got everything I came here for, but it's just..." I trail off and sigh in defeat.

Connor knits his eyebrows together. "Is everything alright?"

"Reed has been swamped with work lately and I'm worried about him. I don't think he's taking care of himself properly so I want to surprise him with a homecooked meal, but I have no idea what to make him. Or more like, I have no idea what I can make him." The truth spills out of me at 1.25 speed and I pray Connor got all that since I don't think I can be vocal about my problems again without crying.

"How about what do you want to make him?" he inquires with more patience than I deserve.

My right hand automatically goes to my go-to thinking position when I'm stumped on a hard question. I pretend I'm stroking my imaginary long white beard and something like a choke snort laugh comes out from my friend.

"What? That's how I think. Don't judge."

"Not judging." Connor's eyes look innocent but the smirk he can't seem to wipe from his face gives him away.

I bite my lip to prevent my mouth from daring to quirk up. Things have been a little lonely without Reed that I forgot how good it felt to smile freely. Everything lately has been either me working or stressing over Reed's well-being.

He says he's fine and there's nothing to worry about, but I know better. I want to talk to him about it–press him for answers–yet there never seems to be a right time.

And that's what hurts.

It hurts to know he's hurting deep inside and I want to help him, but he won't talk to me and I can't force him too. I'm powerless and there's nothing I can do about it. I really want him to be ok. I want us to be ok. I—

"Lia?"

Connor's voice catches my attention and I'm out of my own head. Realizing I left him hanging for however long, my cheeks redden. "Sorry, I was lost in thought."

"It's alright. Take your time."

I smile at my friend's understanding. Taking a deep breath, I clear my head from those dark thoughts and focus on the task at hand. And that's when the epiphany I was waiting for partially occurs.

"Chinese food," I finally answer.

"Ok, that's a good start. What type of Chinese food?"

I shrug. "I'm not sure, but I'm picturing five dishes including rice. Maybe one meat source, two vegetable courses, and some kind of other staple food?"

Connor is quiet for a moment before saying, "I'm not sure if you or Reed have any food allergies, but how about hairy melon glass noodles, boiled mushrooms and choy sum for the veggies, and lastly fried chicken wings for the meat source? That's only a suggestion, though. You don't have to go with it."

When I was younger, my parents and I used to eat at my grandparents' house almost every day. I went grocery shopping with my mom and grandma so I am familiar with the food Connor mentioned. They all sound great but hard to make. Let's just say my expertise lies in the eating versus the cooking of the meals.

I tap my fingers on the cart and reply, "That sounds perfect and I think Reed will like it. It's just my culinary skills are quite lacking and I'm not sure if I can cook...well."

"I can teach you."

My eyes meet Connor's, needing to make sure I didn't hear wrong. "Really?"

Connor eases my anxiety with a gentle smile. "I'm happy to help. Take this as me thanking you for the art gallery ticket. Are you free tonight or Thursday night? We can go to my place to cook and have dinner."

"I'm planning to surprise Reed on Thursday. Can we do tonight?"

"Does 4 p.m. work? I'll have all the ingredients ready, but it does take time to prepare so the earlier the better."

"Yeah, that works for me."

"I'll text you my address in a bit. I have more shopping to

do so I'll see you tonight."

"Ok, thank you."

He waves goodbye and as I watch his figure disappear down the aisle, I send a silent prayer of thanks that Connor showed up when he did.

#308. I double check my phone to make sure I'm at the right place before ringing the doorbell. Thankfully, it wasn't much trouble getting here since I still remember the roads from when I drove Isa here a couple times. Jackson and Connor live in the same condo building with Jackson being in #318. The fact that both their apartment numbers have the number eight in there is totally not a coincidence.

Eight is a lucky number in Chinese culture so we like to have that number in everything such as phone numbers, license plates, and mailbox numbers. I find it cute whenever I see other Chinese Americans share the same fondness for that number.

After a moment, Connor greets me with a dazzling smile, "Hey, Lia, come on in."

"Thanks." I step inside the doorway as he closes the front door.

Connor takes off his sandals and puts them on the shoe rack against the right side of the wall. He walks with his bare feet onto the clean polished wooden floor before turning around to face me, "Feel free to take off your shoes and make yourself at home. I also have some hotel slippers too, if you want to wear them instead?"

I bend down to untie the shoelaces of my combat boots. "I'm good with my socks. Thank you."

Connor smiles before doing a double take and asking in an incredulous voice, "Is that SpongeBob SquarePants on your socks?"

"Yes, yes that is," I reply like it's the most normal thing on earth.

Connor doesn't say anything as he walks forward but I think I see him bob his head with an approving nod. I follow him in and can't help but notice that his apartment is very large and spacious. At the end of the room, there is a gigantic floor to ceiling window overlooking the city. The curtains are drawn back letting the natural sunlight illuminate the entire space. Near the window is the living room area with a big dark gray sofa and a medium-sized glass coffee table in front of it.

A black TV hangs directly across the sofa on a wall that separates the living room and kitchen. Underneath it, there is a TV stand with a few picture frames lined up. To the left of the sofa is the dining area with a long rectangular table able to seat at least eight people. In the middle, in between the dining and living room, lies a small hallway with a few rooms which I presume to be the bedroom and bathroom.

Connor must catch me looking around since he says, "I live alone, but Jackson likes to hang and crash here a lot. We live directly across from each other but it seems like he spends more time here than at his place. And my family comes over for dinner a few times a month so I like to make sure I have enough room for everyone."

I nod. "That's nice of you."

Connor smiles warmly and says, "My family lives by the motto: the more the merrier."

I give a half smile in response, hating how I'm always at a loss of words whenever conversations about families are involved. He leads me to the kitchen and I trail behind.

"You can put your stuff down wherever and we'll get started."

I take off my jacket and put my purse on one of the five bar stools in front of the kitchen island. In front of the island is a six-burner gas stove with a silver hooded convection system above it. A stainless silver fridge freezer stands a few feet to the left of the stoves. Close to the doorway are two ovens stacked over each other. Similar to what I've seen so far, Connor's open kitchen exudes elegance with its design and how the grayish-white granite countertops matches well with the white drawers and light gray walls.

I don't cook but if I had Connor's kitchen, I would totally cook every day. His open kitchen, no, his entire condo, reminds me of those famous celebrities' homes in Architectural Digest videos I binge on YouTube. I know Connor's space is relatively a lot smaller and not a mansion, but his condo is FREAKING AMAZEBALLS and I would so picture a rich CEO in a webtoon living here.

Given Connor's background, this is probably what I should expect. But still, simply being in his luxurious condo, it takes all my self-control not to just stand there and gape at the place. Connor puts a black apron over his dark grayish blue sleeve shirt rolled up to the elbows and hands me a similar black apron. I thank him and adorn the matching apron.

"Are you ready to get started?"

"Quick comment / question. I'm really forgetful so would you mind if I take notes and pictures of the ingredients during the lesson?" I ask as I line up to wash my hands after him.

"I can text you instructions on how to make everything afterwards and send you a detailed list of where to buy the ingredients and pictures of everything too. You can text me if you have any questions."

"That would be really helpful, thanks." I let out a relieved breath as I wash my hands with soap.

"Cooking is easy once you get used to it, but if you don't do it often or after a long time, it's easy to forget. I recorded all my mother's recipes because even though I remember them by heart, there's a chance one day when I'm older, I'll forget."

I nod and ask, "Is your mom a chef too?"

Connor opens the refrigerator and answers, "My mom, dad, and older sister are all part of the family real estate business. When I was a kid, we ate together every day and it was usually my mom who cooked for us. I wouldn't say she loves cooking since it's a lot of work and takes up the whole day, but she's happy to cook as long as we enjoy her food. Which we always do."

Connor's words jog up memories from my own family. After my grandparents decided to permanently move back to Hong Kong, my dad–although he never said it outright–missed his parents a lot, especially his mom. My mom knew how much he yearned for her cooking so she would try mimicking Grandma's recipes.

I can still remember the way Mom's shoulders hunched ever so slightly, her hands glued to her lower back when she thought no one was watching, and how her legs took smaller steps down the stairs. Dad never knew how much effort and time she put into making those dinners.

All he did was arrive when the food had been set out for at least five minutes and proceed to spend the majority of the dinner sharing his opinions, or more like firing off criticism after criticism hidden in the guise of simple commentary. Mom, however, followed his advice and kept trying again and again to please him, but Dad never even once appreciated her efforts and kept comparing the dishes to Grandma's cooking.

Mom's food never tasted exactly like Grandma's and it didn't need to because it was delicious in its own way. Call me crazy but every time I ate my mom's homecooked meals, I could taste her love in them. I told my mom how much I loved her food every time she cooked and she would always smile at me, yet I knew the only thing she would be taking from that night were all the words Dad said, never mine.

My voice comes out a little stiff as I respond, "Your mom sounds really sweet."

"She's the best. My mom's the one who taught me about my heritage, inspired my love of cooking, and gave me a lot of good advice on running a restaurant business," Connor explicates and I can see the love he has for his mother through his happy smile. Despite hurdles with my own mother's relationship, I can't help but think how adorable it is that Connor is such a mama's boy. "I am very grateful to my mom and my entire family. They weren't angry at me for not wanting to follow in their footsteps and instead encouraged me every second of the way. They even told me I could always come back to the family business if I ever wanted to. Jackson's family were also very supportive of him so C&J's would never have existed without them." Connor shakes his head, "You came here for a cooking lesson not to hear my life story. Sorry for talking so much."

I wave both of my hands simultaneously to communicate that it's fine. "No—I mean yes, I came here for a cooking lesson. But don't be sorry for telling me that. I like hearing you talk about your life. Thank you for sharing."

Connor gives me a bashful smile before clearing his throat and says, "So first things first. Let's start the prep work."

Since there is only one sink in the kitchen, I finish washing all the veggies as Connor sets down the rest of the ingredients we need on the counter.

"After you're finished, we need to peel the skin of the jeet gwa for the fen si—the hairy melon for the noodles, I mean." Connor lets out an embarrassed laugh, "Sorry, the names of food come easier to me in Chinese."

"If it's easier, you can speak Cantonese to me if you want. I'll understand you." I smile at him, proud of my ability to speak two languages.

"You can speak Cantonese?"

I peel the jeet gwa as instructed and reply, "I learned it from my family at home. You?"

Connor leans his back on the kitchen countertop as he answers, "Cantonese is my native language. I learned it from my family and studied English in school. And since my mom and older sister loved watching C-dramas, it was easy to pick up Mandarin too. Even if I can't speak it as well as they do, I can get by and understand what they are saying."

"Wow. I took four years of Mandarin back in high school and binge C-dramas all the time, but I could never watch them without subtitles."

"You're able to speak Cantonese though, arguably the harder one amongst the two so that's already really impressive. And don't take this the wrong way, Lia, but I think it's very cool how you didn't turn your back on your Chinese roots despite growing up in America. The people I know, well..." He hesitates and then finally says, "Not many people embrace both their Chinese and American sides."

I wipe my hands on the hand towel attached to the dishwasher rack and say in a quiet voice, "I like being Chinese and I like being American. But sometimes that makes it hard to find people to connect with. In school, even though there were other Asian girls in my class, we weren't friends. We shared different values and interests, to say the least."

I begin cutting the jeet gwa in strips and continue, "And

whenever I visited Hong Kong, I never fit in either. It's like people there could sense I was not from there despite looking Chinese and speaking Cantonese fluently. I was too Chinese to be American and too American to be Chinese. Always somewhere in the middle and never really falling into one distinctive category. That's why when I met Isa, it was nice to find someone who speaks Chinglish and really vibes with me. And maybe because I'm a total homebody, it's genuinely almost impossible for me to make real friends."

"I feel the same way. It's hard to find people who you can connect with. Jackson and I only had each other during our entire school life. There were other Chinese American kids like us but we were never close. Most of them ignored their Chinese side like it didn't exist," Connor laments as he turns on the stove. "But beyond that, I guess since my family and Jackson are such a huge part of my life, I never felt the necessity to expand my social circle."

"Hey, Connor."

"Yeah?"

"I'm glad we're friends. Not just because you keep helping me or because you're a fan of my art, but it's nice talking to you. Thank you for being my friend."

He gives me a warm smile. "I enjoy talking and hanging out with you too."

Before I know it, all the ingredients have been washed and

cut so all that's left is waiting for the water to boil.

"Can I ask you something, Connor?"

"Of course."

"How'd you know you wanted to be a chef? Own a restaurant that specializes in prime rib and not something else?"

My friend crosses his arms and stares at the pot with a gleam in his eyes. "My parents taught my sister and I the family business as toddlers. When I started working full-time for my family, I started doubting if this is what I wanted to do for the rest of my life. My sister is a natural at it and she enjoys her job, but I didn't love it as much as she did. And one night when I was flipping through the channels, *Ratatouille* was airing again on TV. Did you watch the film? Is it ok if I spoil?"

"Totally, I love that movie."

"You know that scene with the food critic, Anton Ego, eating Remy's Ratatouille and having a nostalgic flashback with his mom's cooking?"

I let out a mini squeal. "That's my favorite scene! Ever since then, eating Ratatouille has always been part of my bucket list."

"Whenever I eat chicken bits with rice and sautéed beans with a side of canned chicken soup, it reminds me of that scene. That is my own Ratatouille dish that makes me feel nostalgic and warm."

I raise an eyebrow teasingly, "Canned soup?"

"That must sound weird since I'm a chef, but after a long day, that stuff really works its magic," Connor responds in a jesting defensive tone.

I let out a laugh. "I like it. That actually sounds really good. I don't have my own special dish so I'm kind of envious."

"I can make that dish for you next time. And if you like, I can make Ratatouille too. I've been meaning to share that dish with someone since I spent three months perfecting it."

I nod fervently and say, "Oh my God, yes please. I've always wanted to try it."

A soft smile materializes on Connor's face as he continues, "But going back to your question, when I saw that scene in *Ratatouille* that night, it felt like a sign. The family business is great but it's not my passion. I want to make people happy and feel a multitude of emotions when they eat my food. So the next day, I talked to Jackson about opening up a restaurant and he was fully on board. While I cooked with my mom and played around with different recipes as a hobby, Jackson became obsessed with baking sweets ever since he watched the anime *Yumeiro Patissiere.*"

I almost double over laughing but hold myself back since I don't want to ruin the moment. I also had a phase of wanting to be a patisserie; however, that dream died the moment I made my first mille crepe.

"Jackson and I went off on our own and opened our first restaurant. Business was slow at first and when we finally received some traction, there were some internal issues going on. Out of nowhere with no explanation at all, a few of our kitchen staff quit on us and then a few weeks later, a new Chinese restaurant opened up a few blocks away that serves food similar to ours."

"No way! Those jerks copied you?" I gasp in utter surprise.

"They did but we couldn't say or do anything about it without proof. But funny thing was a year later, that restaurant was temporarily shut down due to a health violation. And when they opened back up, business was very slow since people were still afraid to eat there after what happened. Not sure how the health inspector got tipped off to visit that day and time." Connor's tone is coated in false ignorance accompanied with an all too matching half-smirk.

"The health inspector showing up? What a total coincidence." I play along feigning innocence.

(Note to self: Do not get on Connor's bad side...add Connor's name to list of confidants when I'm in need for some much-needed revenge payback.)

He grins, "Even though we eventually closed our first restaurant since we weren't profiting enough, it was satisfying to see some type of karma—whether it be natural or manmade–fall upon those copycats."

Now that the food is done, we begin transferring every-thing onto plates and bowls.

"Jackson and I were really bummed after our first attempt to make a successful restaurant failed so we went back to working with our families for a few months. And during a two-day business trip to San Francisco, we stumbled upon a restaurant called House of Prime Rib. It occurred to us that we could try opening up a restaurant specializing in prime rib since there's nothing like it back home. With my mom's help, we developed a good recipe for cooking the prime rib along with other menu items and Jackson created the perfect dessert selection to go with it. We ended up getting nomi-nated and winning Best New Restaurant in our first year."

Connor takes out a few trivets and asks me, "Do you want to eat at the dining table or the kitchen island?"

"Island," I answer immediately. I've been eyeing those bar stools the moment I came here and was waiting for a chance to sit on them.

He lets out a soft laugh. "You got it." Setting down the trivets, he continues, "After the massive success of our sec-ond restaurant, Jackson and I also opened a few other restau-rants that focus on Chinese and other Western food. They are not as popular as C&J's but it still makes money and people post good reviews on them. Our team knows how to run the restaurants and entire operation so well, Jackson and I only stop by to help when they get really busy. We took some time off and then needing a change of pace, I started teaching at the youth center."

We sit down on the stools and they are as comfy and snug as I thought it would be. I lift my cup of water to Connor's and say, "Hearing the whole backstory to C&J's is so inspiring. You and Jackson didn't let your first setback stop you and got to where you are today through all your hard work and perseverance. Seriously, you guys rock."

Connor raises his glass to mine with a laugh, "Thank you, but we also had a lot of good people helping us. It wouldn't have been possible without them."

We sip our glasses of water and begin digging in. I take a bite of the boiled mushrooms first because I've been anticipating putting that in my mouth after its aroma dominated every other delicious scent in the air. The chewy texture matched with the saltiness from the mushroom makes my taste buds tingle in delight.

"These mushrooms are literally the best mushrooms I ever tasted. They're SO GOOD!" I beam.

Connor grabs some jeet gwa fen si in his bowl and comments, "I'm glad you like them. I learned how to make those mushrooms from my mom."

"Your mom is a genius. These mushrooms taste so heavenly. If I could eat one last meal before I die, it would be these mushrooms," I say stuffing another one in my mouth.

Connor laughs. "I'll let my mom know. She'll be ecstatic to hear that."

I take a bite of the jeet gwa fen si and the rest of the food. The jeet gwa fen si tastes wonderful without the noodles being too dry. The choy sum is cooked just right with the stems being crunchy and the leaves easy to chew. The crispiness and salt level of the chicken wings suits my taste perfectly. In front of guests, I try not to eat with my fingers as much as I can, but all etiquette is gone and squared away when it comes to these wings.

We eat in silence since I am too busy devouring the food around me to start up and engage in any conversation. When the dishes are close to being cleared, Connor tells me he is full so I can have the last piece of everything if I wanted, though I'm pretty sure he is just being nice letting me eat the rest of it. I thank him and finish everything, leaving only empty bowls and plates in front of us.

I stretch my arms and sigh happily. "This is one of the best meals I've ever had in my life. I don't remember the last time I ate something this good and satisfying."

Connor cocks his head and asks, "What do you usually eat on a normal basis?"

"Reed and I normally go to different restaurants, buy

takeout, or sometimes cook pasta. If it's just me and or Isa, we usually make salad and eat it with any kind of meat and call it a day."

"How about when you eat with your parents?"

Every hair on my body stands up. I have to send gentle reminders to my body that there's no need to panic before I can answer his question.

Breathe, Lia. Breathe.

After a moment, I reply, "I don't eat with them. My parents are divorced and we're not close."

Connor doesn't respond and I give into my nervous habit of fidgeting with my hands. Way to go, Lia. You just ruined the moment with your stupid family baggage.

Again.

Before I could think of something to clear the air, Connor speaks. His voice is soft and gravelly like he's afraid he'll cross a line as he says, "Your painting with the seasons changing. Was it her parents' love that the girl always wanted?"

Our eyes meet like many times before, but this time, I feel rigid and cold. My guard goes up whenever I hear words that trigger memories of my family. Having a conversation that relates to them, especially with someone who is not Isa or Reed, makes me anxious and tense all at once.

When I don't say anything, Connor adopts back his usual friendly demeanor. "I'm happy you enjoyed tonight's dinner. Let me know if you would like to come over again to eat or to learn how to cook something else."

There's no pity in Connor's eyes and he is being kind like always. He's not changing the subject because I'm being weird, but rather, he's respecting my boundaries and not pushing for information I'm not comfortable with sharing. He's about to step down from his stool and I feel myself fall into turmoil.

I'm tired of carrying the burdens of my past. I'm tired of having to let my family problems consume me. I'm tired of having to push away good people because of my inability to talk normally about anything related to my family. I'm tired of all of it. And maybe today, just maybe this time, I can let my guard down in front of someone else and they'll understand. It can end up bad and destroy everything, but I'm tired of running.

Tired of hiding.

"The girl might have wanted her parent's love, but she never got it. It was never within her reach. Never was, never will be." My harsh words catch Connor's attention and the filter over my mouth completely disappears. "It didn't matter if she worked hard in school to impress them, followed all their rules and instructions to please them, or went out of her way to make them happy. None of that mattered because her father spoke more words to his brokerage clients than his own daughter and her mother was blind to everyone except her husband."

Voicing everything out loud, it's funny how I don't even remember when was the last time I actually had a real conversation with my father. When we lived in the same house, I mainly saw him in the mornings before he left for work. He always asked me how I was and I would always answer I was ok because any other response would mean I have to explain things he wouldn't understand or he'd have to spend more time than he was willing to give to try and understand me. All of which left me sadder than when the conversation started.

Connor is already fully seated back in his chair with his undivided attention directed towards me.

I avoid looking at him as a dry chuckle escapes my mouth, "My dad does have good points though. He's excellent at his job and there was a time when he was a good father to me. As a kid, he would piggyback carry me around the house and I remember feeling like I was on top of the whole world. But as I grew older and more opinionated, the appeal of raising me completely faded away. When I was fourteen, my dad told us he was busy with work so he would be eating dinner with us a lot less."

To be honest, part of me was relieved. I wouldn't have to suffer my dad's unnecessary comments about Mom's cooking or how to mix rice from the rice cooker properly. There's no correct way to mix rice because everyone likes their rice differently. Some people like rice mixed and others like it not mixed–aka me–so the rice would be more condensed. And that's just one example.

There are more stupid little things he comments on that don't even matter and I can't help but remember all the bad feelings associated from those conversations. It wasn't even a big deal until he started getting defensive about nothing and when I tried explaining to him my point of view, he would always mansplain and say I was wrong.

I let it go–not because I concluded he was right and I was wrong–but rather, there's no winning with my dad. Dad was always right and that's the end of the conversation. I know my dad also has his own problems from his past causing him to act the way he does since his generation wasn't taught how to handle mental health issues as well as it is being addressed nowadays.

That's why I always bit my tongue and told myself to let it go. It was the best solution I learned when dealing with stubborn people.

My arms automatically cross itself making the next words come out easier, "And when I was fifteen, my dad stopped eating with us entirely and a few months later, my mom told me she would work longer hours at her journalist job so she would not be able to cook dinner anymore. I told her that's ok because I didn't want to be a burden to my mom and hold her back from doing what she wanted. But little did I know, it was because there was a bigger issue going on I wasn't aware of at the time."

Taking a deep breath, I tell Connor one of the worst days of my life. "On the night of my seventeenth birthday, when we celebrated my birthday–birthdays and special holidays being the only days we ate together as a family–I woke up in the middle of the night hearing my parents fight. I never heard them fight before or at least I never knew they fought prior to that night. Their voices were loud in the living room and I overheard my mom being upset at my dad for seeing another woman. She yelled at him, not for cheating on her, but the fact that I could have seen my dad with the other woman. He yelled back how he was sure I wasn't there."

Recounting this memory aloud is harder than I thought. The rattling sound I heard for the past minute but have been unable to pinpoint finally strikes me when Connor's knee bumps mine. My legs resting on the lower bar of the stool have been intensely shaking the poor chair. My friend has been silent the whole time, giving me the room and space to talk as he listens. The simple gesture of having our jeans touch and reassuring me I'm not alone gives me the strength to keep going on.

"It seems like sometime between when I was fifteen, my dad fell out of love with my mom and even though they tried working it out for a year, things were still not working out. My mom convinced my dad not to file for a divorce because I was still in high school so she was afraid it would affect my studies. In the end, my dad agreed and they settled with divorcing when I moved away for college."

A hollow mocking laugh comes out of me as I say, "When I overheard them fighting that night, everything started making sense. My dad being too busy with work to eat with us. My mom working more because she had to distract herself with something. The fact that my parents began sleeping in separate rooms out of nowhere, and when I asked about it, my mom gave me her most serene smile and said, 'Your dad snores really loud. Mommy needs her beauty rest and Daddy doesn't want to always tiptoe out of bed every morning so he won't wake me.' And I–as the world's biggest teenage idiot–naively believed what my mom told me and didn't think it was a big deal."

The tears I've been fighting back all this time are getting harder to ward off as I near the worst part.

"Furious after the fight, my dad stormed out of the house and did not return until late the next day. And my mom, she started drinking from a bottle of red wine I didn't even know we had. I wasn't sure what I should do. My parents clearly did not want me to know they were having issues, but halfway when I noticed my mom drunk in the living room, I went downstairs and tried getting her to stop drinking and go to bed. But she wouldn't listen and still managed to protect the bottle from me."

My voice cracks despite my inner protests. "I pleaded with my mom to stop drinking. I remember telling her she could divorce my dad. She deserved someone better who would love and appreciate her for all her greatness and how I would side with her no matter what. All my mom needed to do was say the word and I would be ready to leave my dad and the house with her right that moment. But instead, she shoved me aside and I fell to the ground right next to where she's sitting with her glass in hand. She told me that my dad still loved her and he just needed to temporarily date that other woman to remind himself how much he loves her."

I close my eyes and lower my head to my lap, holding onto the last straw before I completely bawl my eyes out.

"My mom was never mad at my dad for almost getting caught with his mistress like she claimed. She was jealous of her. My mom still loved my dad deeply and was heartbroken he didn't feel the same way."

This horrible truth dawned on me and I could never see my mother the same way ever again. She used me as an excuse to shackle my father down as long as she could as she tried salvaging whatever they had left. My mother would always love that man and I could shower her with all my love but it was only my father's affection that she wanted.

No matter how much I loved her, she always put her cheating and undeserving husband first.

Always.

I keep the next part to myself because this is a detail I can't bring myself to speak aloud and it horrifies me to even think about it. My mom drank even more so I settled with getting her upstairs so she wouldn't catch a cold falling asleep on the living room floor. As I tried putting her arm around me, she suddenly grabbed onto my shoulders and violently shook me.

Goosebumps form on my skin as I remember how her warm motherly hands became like hawk talons as she clutched my shoulders and cried hysterically, "Why couldn't you be more useful and convince your father to stay with me? I didn't want children in the first place but your dad wanted one so I did it to please him and his parents. What's the point of having you if you're not going to keep him from leaving me?"

It wasn't the alcohol talking.

It was her. My mother's words stung because she had spoken the truth. It is a lie to say that she didn't love me at all, but her love for me was nothing compared to her love for my father. But I couldn't abandon my drunk mother despite everything that happened so I hauled her back to her room, turned her sideways on her bed, and left after setting a glass of water on the nightstand.

My voice trembles ever so slightly but I'm grateful I managed to keep my tears in check.

"The next morning, it was like nothing happened. My mother acted like everything was normal and the scariest part is—to this day, I don't think she was pretending. Her meltdown the night before must have been too much for her to handle and the alcohol must have helped her forget. I pretended that night never happened as well because it was best for her and it temporarily closed the can of worms I wasn't ready to have opened."

My parents poured more of their time working, if that was even humanly possible. I started applying to jobs at fifteen to gain experience and to also start saving up for college because I didn't want to always rely on my parents financially. But after overhearing my parents' fight on my birthday, I worked even harder.

If people were looking for me during that period of my life—not like anyone would though—they could find me either at school or work. When I was at home, I put on my headphones and blasted BEAST's "Suite Room" and "Will You Be Alright" on repeat as I drew. It was the only way I could ensure being able to focus on my drawings and fill the silence of our once happy family.

My vision is a little blurry but I still see Connor sitting next to me and feel the warm sensation from his knee.

"When I was about to move away for college, my parents sat me down and finally told me they were going to get a divorce. They told me–lied to me, it was for the best since they had some irreconcilable differences but they would always love me."

I feel my mouth finally tug into a small smile as I say, "I went to live in my new dorm and met Isa. My parents sold our old house we lived in for eighteen years and moved to different homes. We texted occasionally when I was in college and one night I asked them to meet me so I can tell them I wanted to quit school to pursue my art dream."

From the lightness in Connor's eyes, it seems like he's holding out hope that there is a good part to the story. But as my face darkens, Connor's expression follows suit.

"Of course they disapproved and gave the speech of how being an artist doesn't make money and many jobs require a college degree. My dad threatened that even if I begged and cried, he would not give me a single penny if I went through with my plan. My mom didn't say anything but her face told me I had no one on my side. We fought and it wasn't pretty. We erased ourselves from each other's lives. End of story."

That is me putting it nicely. The most messed up part was how during the confrontation, my dad somehow had the audacity to transfer his rage at me to my mother. He bellowed at her for teaching me badly and blamed her for my choices. They raised me to stay mute my whole life–when the adults were speaking–but I finally snapped. Everything I kept bottled in completely poured out of me like a tsunami.

I got up from my chair and finally had the guts to talk back to my dad. "You don't have the right to be mad at Mom, Dad! You're always so busy that you're more like a stranger to me than a father. You only provided for me financially but it was Mom who raised me well. *She* taught me how to do my homework back in middle school, *she* drove me to and from school, *she* attended every parent-teacher conference, and for God's sake, she's the only parent who took the time to teach me how to drive. You were never a good father to me so don't you dare blame Mom!"

"Lydia Zhang, watch your mouth!"

It was like someone had stabbed me with a knife only to take it out and then stab me again but twisting it in the process. I shifted my body slowly toward her and it took all my willpower to hide how much her words hurt me.

"You're still defending him, Mom?"

My parents gazed at me wide-eyed and I let out a bitter laugh.

"Mom, why do you love Dad so much? He cheated on you! He doesn't love you as much as you deserve to be loved. Why did you put up with him for so long? I'm sorry he fell out of love with you, but how could you use your daughter for your own personal gain and get angry at me when it didn't work out the way you wanted it to?"

This was probably the only time I ever saw my mom's jaw drop and my dad look the most confused he's ever been in his life. If things weren't so serious, it'd probably be comical.

I don't stop and continue talking back, "I asked you guys to come over so I could tell you my plans. I knew you wouldn't support it, but I was hoping we could at least come to an understanding. But instead, you guys start fighting again. I'm sick of all the fighting. Even though you guys are my parents, what gives you the right to dictate my life when you are the ones who hurt me the most? I'm an adult so I can make my own decisions. And from this day forward, since we're all grown adults, just pretend I'm not your daughter like you both always wanted."

I finished saying everything I ever wanted to say to my parents. An invisible weight lifted off my shoulders and it became easier to breathe. My parents called me something along the lines of the swear word version of a disrespectful ungrateful brat in Cantonese–which hurt a lot since every-thing in Chinese hits somehow worse than English–before they proceeded to argue with each other like I wasn't in the room.

It was too much for me to bear. Having already given the restaurant my credit card beforehand, I exited the private room I specially reserved for tonight. I didn't know where I was going but I couldn't take being in the same room as my parents any longer and they didn't chase after me. I recall hearing the quiet echoes of their raised voices and the restaurant chatter before that all faded together.

Connor does not speak or move. I'm not sure what's going on inside his brain and I don't blame him. Even if I lost a friend from what I revealed, I don't regret it. I want Connor to know this about me. He's a new friend I made—someone I thought I could show only my good parts to—but that was foolish.

That night at the art gallery, he managed to see through me and all the ugly parts of me reflected in my art. That day, I was scared.

Terrified.

Not of Connor or how he knows one of my darkest secr ets...but how the trauma from my parents will always show no matter how hard I try to paint over them.

More time goes by and I don't dare check my friend's face for any clues of what he's thinking. Instead, I fidget more with my hands and continue to babble. "If I think about it, I shouldn't really complain about any of that though. My life was pretty great. I never needed to worry about money with all my school tuition paid for, food on the table, and a roof over my head. I was—am, grateful for all of that. What most kids struggle with was the least of my worries...I'm just a bad kid who hates her parents."

"No." Connor speaks for the first time after my long speech. His voice is deep and serious, almost angry.

When he doesn't say more, I finally move my eyes to his. His puppy brown eyes now look slightly glassy and his face looks stiff like he's holding himself back.

"The girl's desire to be loved by her parents never changed throughout the seasons and she never once stopped loving them despite all the crap they put her through." Connor's voice goes quieter as he repeats himself, "As much as she could have–should have, she never stopped loving her pare nts...not once."

I hear every word he uttered, but besides the small parting of my mouth, I'm still. Of all the things he could have said, Connor spoke the words that struck my heart the most. My dad was not ready to be a good father or husband, but he wasn't all bad. He bought me toys whenever I wanted them and always remembered my birthday despite his busy schedule.

There is a good part of him–somewhere inside–but that

doesn't make up for all the damage he'd done. And a small stupid part of me, no matter how much I try to deny it, will always love my dad because he's my dad.

As much as my mom prioritized Dad above all else, I can't hate her. I can't hate how she wanted to eat together with him even when he nitpicks about her cooking and made hurtful jokes. I can't hate how she always diligently reminded him about work stuff he often forgot even when he says he doesn't need them. I can't hate how she massages him after his long workday when she is in no state to do such herself.

I can't hate her for doing everything to benefit him even at the expense of herself and her own daughter. I can get angry at her, but I can never hate her. Sometimes people do things that hurt themselves because they care too much about the other person. My mom chose to do so and it was insufferable to bear witness to that. But I understand why she did what she did. She wanted him to love her.

She wanted his love.

And I know how that feels, wanting to be loved by the person you want to love you. Wanting something so bad, every other pain seems trivial to the result. That sounds so toxic and it probably is. But that's the ugly truth.

In one way or another, we all want to be loved.

A genuine smile spreads across my face. "From the last time I stalked my dad on social media, he seems blissfully happy married to the woman I think is the one he cheated on my mom with. And from the travel blogs my mom wrote and photos she posted online, I think she finally moved on from my dad and found the right guy for her."

"You're happy for them," Connor says as more of a statement than a question.

"I am."

My parents were good to me, even if the bad outweighed the good. The part of me that will always love them is happy that they are happy. Even if I'm not part of their lives and it's too late for them to enter back mine, I'm glad they found their happiness.

Connor stands up from the stool and stacks all the dishes together as he heads over to the sink. Holding the remaining empty plates, I follow behind him and set them in the sink.

"I'll wash the dishes," I volunteer as I roll up my sleeves.

Connor smiles at me appreciatively. "I'll use the dishwasher later. It's getting late. You should get going."

I look at my watch and realize he's right. It's 8 p.m. and the sky is already really dark. The drive back home won't be long but I still like to get home early given that it is a little scary walking back to the apartment myself at night.

"I feel bad for having you cook and clean up after me."

"Maybe because I like to hang out with my family and Jackson so much, it sometimes gets lonely eating alone. So you don't need to feel bad at all."

I smile and bounce on my socks. "Then I guess I'm going to get going now."

"I'll walk you to your car."

"No, it's ok. I don't want to take up any more of your time."

Connor gives me a polite smile like I can say more but it will be futile to argue. I relent since I know he's not being overprotective or anything as he simply wants to walk me to my car because it's dark. In the elevator, we are silent and I finally say something when I can't bare the silence any longer.

"The meal was really delicious. I don't think I can cook it for Reed as good as it was today but I'll do my best."

"You'll do great, Lia. I'll text you all the information tonight so you can look it over. I'm sure Reed will be more than happy you made something for him. It's really the thought that counts."

The elevator arrives to the lobby floor and we step out. I parked on the street close by so Connor follows me as I lead the way. Nearing my car, I stop walking and turn to my friend.

"Thank you so much for today, Connor. You're such a lifesaver. I would be in a pickle if it weren't for you."

Did I just say pickle? I know that's an expression, but I

don't even eat pickles so I rarely ever say that word. What the heck is going on with me? I walk toward my vehicle–finally making a good decision for once today–as I wave goodbye. But my escape plan gets thwarted when I hear Connor's words.

"Just to be clear, Lia. Your parents are awful people and the way you turned out to be such a good person has nothing to do with them."

I want to respond to his blunt statement but my mind goes blank.

Maintaining eye contact is all I manage to do as my friend continues speaking, "We make the decision of who we want to be. Not our environment or the people in our lives. They play a part in shaping us into who we are, but in the end, it is up to us, as a person, to decide. And because you make that decision every day–to be the sweet and kindhearted person you are–it is a pity your parents will never know how much of a positive impact their daughter brings to the people around her. They will never know how much you matter to people."

I'm as unmoving as a statue and my heart aches. I want to tell him how much his words mean to me. How thankful I am to hear him say that and truly mean it. But since I have been way too honest today for my comfort, I voice out another thought I have instead.

"I know I made things kinda weird after telling you about my family drama, but I told you because I wanted to warn you about what type of person you are befriending. Only Isa and Reed–the two people closest to me–know about my poor relationship with my parents. I don't want you to regret becoming friends with someone as messed up as me."

"I don't regret it. I will never regret being friends with you. I like talking to and being around you. And whatever you tell me about your family or you will never change that. I promise you." Connor's eyes are resolute and his voice is so confident that I'm a little intimidated.

We are at least a good seven feet apart but his firm steady gaze towards me still manages to thaw a part of my icy heart. Unable to stand hearing more of his heartfelt words, I mutter a quick "Goodnight", hop in my car, and drive away without looking back.

I am well aware of my habit of keeping my guard up around people to protect myself from getting hurt. But with Connor, I don't know. My walls crumble and I find myself sharing a lot of personal information about me with ease. Just being around him draws out my honesty and things I've hidden deep down. Yet as truthful as I have been, there are still pieces of me I keep from my friend.

Especially how the worst night of my life–my breakup with my parents–ended.

I ran out of that restaurant with no destination in mind and before I knew it, I bumped into someone. Concern written all over his face as he took in my tear-stained face and red eyes brimming with fresh tears, Reed asked me what was wrong. Instead of answering, I leaped into his arms like a little kid and hugged him. I wrapped my arms tighter and refused to release my grip on him. He was left with no other choice but to take me back to his apartment because we might have frozen to death standing outside in the cold.

Reed held onto me as I cried until there were no more tears left. He kissed my head and then handed me a cup of warm milk to drink. After taking a few sips, I finally calmed down enough to talk. Reed listened as I told him everything that happened with my parents. He pulled me in a hug and shared he also had family issues of his own and how it would be ok.

He told me we could lean on each other for support and I could stay over at his place as long as I needed. I leaned my body against him and he held me closer. I looked up at him and our eyes met.

My boyfriend tenderly caressed my cheek and then said in a soft voice, "I love you, Lydia Zhang. Can I kiss you right now?"

I probably looked really ugly with my puffy eyes and face swelled from crying so much but for some reason, Reed still wanted to kiss me. I have never been asked to be kissed before so that made me feel nervous and excited at the same time. I couldn't trust my voice so I simply nodded and closed my eyes. A few seconds later, Reed's lips met mine and we shared our first kiss. My first ever kiss, in his apartment.

With a single kiss, he made me forget all the bad memories of that night and held all my broken pieces together. Reed filled the emptiness in my heart with those magic three words I always longed to hear.

Chapter 8

Operation: Surprise Boyfriend with Delicious Homecooked Dinner is about to be put to the test in the next three minutes.

Before turning off the fire, I sprinkle some more salt on the chicken wings and let them sizzle on the pan a minute longer so the skin would darken to a crispy golden color. The chorus of Taylor Swift's "Lover" plays as I set the plate of wings down on a trivet next to all the other dishes.

"Are you ready for your surprise?" I ask as I answer the call, unable to contain my excitement. When there is no response, I get the hint some bad news is coming my way. My voice lowers to an almost whisper as I try again, "Reed?"

"My boss announced I'm one of the last two candidates in line for the promotion. He wants to take us out to dinner tonight so he can make the final decision and I think I've got a good shot at getting it. I'm so sorry, Lia. But could you show me the surprise another day?"

"Of course. Go get that promotion, I'm rooting for you!"

"Really, you're not mad?"

"No worries, there's always next time."

"Thank you, Lia! I'll make it up to you," Reed promises and I can hear the joy in his voice.

"Good luck!"

We hang up and I put my phone down on the kitchen table. Aside from the kitchen convection system, no other sound livens the space. It kinda makes me miss the earlier bustling of steaming pots and sizzling pans. I smile at the food prepared on the dining table and then frown when I see a drop of liquid ruining the perfect display.

I rip a piece of napkin to wipe it away, only to find a twin droplet right next to the spot I just cleaned. My eyebrows crease and I lean my head backward to see if our apartment has a water leak before realizing tears are trickling down my face. I dab at them with the back of my hand but they keep falling.

Why am I even feeling sad?

Reed's been very busy lately so I shouldn't even have hoped that I could present him with a special homecooked dinner. Guess I really should have given him a heads-up and visited him at his workplace instead. If I showed up unannounced–knowing my luck–it might have been one of those good intentions gone wrong moments where the surprise for my boyfriend somehow goes up in flames.

After splashing water on my face a few times, I use a hand towel to dry off and proceed to give my cheeks a few slaps. My cheeks burn from the hard smack of my palms but the pain reminds me there's no use being sad and dwelling over things that can't be helped. Instead of crying, I should be eating the good food–or hopefully good food–in front of me. Walking back to the kitchen, my phone dings with a text.

> Connor: "When you get the chance, let me know how the dishes went."

I don't know what makes me do what I do next, but the next thing I know, I'm dialing Connor's number. I put my phone to my ear and after the second ring, he picks up.

"Hey, Lia. Sorry to bother you. I just wanted to check in and see how's everything going." Connor sounds a little flustered which makes the corners of my mouth go up.

"Reed called saying he can't make it today."

"Oh." That's all my friend says which I oddly really appreciate. No words of comfort can change the fact that my boyfriend isn't here right now. Connor seems to understand how I feel and patiently waits for me to explain the reason for my call.

"I already finished preparing all the food and I remember

you saying you were free today so I was wondering if you wanted to come over and eat with me?" I ask running a hand through my hair, hoping he wouldn't hear my unspoken plea. He doesn't say anything for a while and I add, "You don't have to or anything. It's just if you're not busy. But that's silly, sorry for calling you."

I'm about to end our call with a quick goodbye but Connor responds, "Where should I meet you?"

"Huh?"

"Where should I meet you?" Connor repeats in a gentle voice.

"Oh, I'm at my apartment I share with Isa. I'll text you the address." My phone fumbles in my hands as I press the speaker button so I can multi-task between texting and calling.

A beat goes by and then he says, "I'm nearby. I'll be there in the next five minutes."

"Ok, see you in a bit," I reply in a small daze as we hang up.

I can't believe Connor said he'd come over. I didn't expect him to say yes. I mean I can't believe I called him in the first place. If Isa was here, she would be the first person I'd invite to eat with me. But since she's still on her road trip, I don't want to interrupt her with my melancholy when she is having fun. The only other friend I have is Connor.

It's probably wrong of me to celebrate my surprise I originally planned for my boyfriend with my guy friend, but the truth is, I really don't want to be alone tonight.

The doorbell rings shortly and I tiptoe to peek at the small hole in the door to see who's there. I unlock the door and open it. Connor is really here–in the flesh–and I mentally exhale in relief. Part of me wonders if my friend was in the middle of an important event since he's dressed in a white T-shirt underneath a black blazer jacket–that fits snugly onto his Pacific Ocean shoulders–over dark blue jeans.

I am about to ask if I disrupted his plans tonight but forget to when I notice Connor's cheeks are flushed with pink and his chest is subtly rising up and down. The cute goofy smile on his face confirms my suspicion he jogged here and my brain tallies this is the second time my new friend rushed here to see me. I move aside and open the door wider for him to walk in, "Hey, Connor, please come in."

"Thank you," he says with a nod as he enters the apartment.

"I don't have any fancy new unused hotel slippers so feel free to just take off your shoes and make yourself at home," I tease.

Connor smirks. "I didn't expect to visit someone's house today so please pardon my plain white socks."

I playfully roll my eyes at his comment. "You're pardoned. Now, let's eat before the food gets colder."

My friend follows me as I lead him to our dining table which can seat up to four people. As we pull out our chairs to sit across from each other, he tilts his head towards the vase of alstroemeria flowers he gave me on the night of the art gallery where it sits on the window.

"You still have them?"

"All the flowers in this apartment are alive and blooming well because of Isa. She's the plant whisperer and I'm sort of, oh who am I kidding, I'm a total plant killer. Those flowers are so pretty and it'd be a waste if I leave them at my studio to wither away so I brought them back home. Isa is helping me take care of them while I get to sit back and enjoy the view," I answer uncapping the two lids I put over the boiled mushrooms and jeet gwa fen si.

Connor smiles sweetly at the direction of the flowers and I scoop a paddle of rice in my bowl. He takes a bite of the food I prepared as I nibble on a piece of rice in anticipation. He has on a neutral expression and I can't tell what's he thinking.

After waiting in agony for what feels like an eternity, Connor finally speaks, "I'm usually the one staring and making it hard for people to taste the food properly. This is a nice change."

"So what's the verdict, Chef?" I ask trying not to sound impatient.

Connor takes another bite of the choy sum he's holding

with his chopsticks. "Try it yourself and tell me what you think."

I sigh disappointed with his answer and set down my bowl of rice. I grab a piece of all the dishes and sample them.

Connor continues to eat as he watches me evaluate my culinary skills. I finally meet his eyes and he looks at me expectantly, "Well?"

"Not as good as when you made it, but it's not bad," I confess.

"You're being too hard on yourself, it's good." He gathers more food in his bowl and continues, "The jeet gwa fen si is on the drier side due to the lid covering it too long, but you probably did that to preserve the heat so that doesn't count. Other than my own personal preferences of boiling the vegetables longer and having less salt on the food, everything tastes great."

"Reed likes salty food so I added more salt to the chicken wings. And he likes the chewy texture of veggies so I boiled them a minute less," I answer with a tiny smile.

Connor nods in agreement. "Everyone has different tastes and the key to making good food is to know who is eating it so you could cater everything to their taste buds. Exactly like what you did today. I think you're well along your way to becoming a master chef."

I laugh. "I only know how to cook these four items. I can't

cook anything else."

"You know how to cook an entire meal."

"I guess so, but I can't take all the credit. I had a good teacher."

He grins. "I just gave you the recipe. You cooked every-thing yourself. It was all you, Lia."

"Still, you helped a ton so thank you, Connor. Really, thank you."

A brilliant smile crosses his face and the lump in my chest from my earlier phone call with Reed gradually lightens. We continue to eat without talking until Connor asks, "You play mahjong?"

I look up and see him eyeing the mahjong set on the coffee table. "Isa and I play at least once a week. Do you play?"

"I know how to play from parties my family used to host when we invited friends and business partners over to eat at our house," Connor replies and from the spark in his eyes, I could tell those are fond memories.

"Do you want to play mahjong with me?" I blurt without fully thinking my sentence through.

Connor's eyes widen at my random question and I want to rewind time back before I asked. I only invited him over for dinner so playing mahjong out of nowhere is totally not part of the plan. After we finish dinner, there'd be no reason for my friend to stay longer and I don't want that. I don't want him to leave yet.

I don't want to be alone just yet.

"I haven't played mahjong for some time so I might be rusty. But I would love to play," Connor answers with a broad smile.

"Great! Give me a few minutes to wash the dishes and I'll be right out."

"I can wash the dishes," Connor offers and immediately gets up from his seat to gather the rest of the empty plates.

I give him my teasing version of the polite smile he once gave me before and say, "I'll do it. I would feel bad if you helped me clean up when I didn't last time."

I slip on the pair of pink dish washing gloves and begin scrubbing a plate. Luckily, I washed most of the dishes earlier when I waited for everything to cook itself so there's not much to wash. Connor brings over the rest of the used utensils and whispers in such a low voice I have to strain my ears to hear him, "I know I wasn't the one who should have been here tonight, but I still enjoyed myself. Thank you for inviting me over."

His dark brown eyes are looking at me with so much warmth and sincerity. It makes my heart feel uneasy. Since the first time I met Connor, he's been there for me whenever I was alone and needed a friend. He's been nothing but nice to me without expecting anything in return.

No one is obligated to do anything for anyone.

People don't need to help others just because they need help. People choose to help others because they care. That's why every time someone is being nice to me, I feel so grateful to them from the bottom of my heart. Having two people in my life do kind things for me is more than enough and adding Connor to that list, I don't know. It's sometimes hard for me to believe.

He literally went out of his way to support me at the city's art gallery, helped me with my surprise with Reed, and was the perfect listener when I info dumped him with my unnecessary family history. Like do I even deserve to have such good people in my life?

As I rinse a bowl, I finally give into my curiosity and ask, "Why are you so nice to me, Connor?"

"Hmm?"

"You say you like being friends with me, but what about it? You are always helping me out and I don't really do anything that is particularly helpful to you. So why?"

Connor furrows his brows closer together like he's deep in thought and considering what he should say. After a minute, he speaks up, "Let's make a deal. I'll answer your question if you beat me in mahjong. Two out of three games. No gai-wu. We play big and win with the good cards. If I win, you'll answer a question I want to ask you."

I wasn't expecting this. I thought Connor would simply deflect or give me an unclear answer, but instead he suggested a cordial mahjong showdown to ease the intensity of the topic. I have no reason to refuse since I love a good challenge. We are just playing a friendly game of mahjong to learn more about each other. I'm not sure what my friend wants to ask me, but I already spilled my guts to him once so what the heck.

I take off the dish washing gloves and pretend to crack my knuckles like I'm about to fight someone. "Deal, let's do this."

Connor and I sit down on the wooden floor so we are around the same height as the mahjong set. Mahjong usually has four players, but since it's the two of us, we'll adjust the rules of four people to fit our two-player game. Everyone plays mahjong differently, but we agreed to play the style we know: Hong Kong Mahjong. I hand Connor the three dice to roll and he nods in thanks before rolling them.

Seven.

That number is supposed to determine which of the four diagonal sets of double-stacked eighteen tiles or pai–as we call it in Cantonese–we get our thirteen cards from. Since the number is seven, we start counting from the right side of the person who rolled the dice. Due to our seating arrangements, we will get our pai from my side. From my side of the stacked tiles, starting from the right, we count to seven.

Connor grabs two stacks of pai over each other making it a total of four pai from the left side. We continue doing this two more times until it's time to "tew-pai" or when the roller stacks their next tile over the adjacent one and takes both those pai making their tile collection a total of fourteen pai. As the roller, Connor gets fourteen pai and commences the game by throwing out the tile he doesn't want.

We take a minute to rearrange our pai and check if we have any flowers. Connor has two flowers and I have one so we flip our flower tiles over and set them aside in a separate row near us. I wait for Connor to grab two tiles to replace his flowers before I take one pai from the right side where we first drew from. After a few seconds, he tosses out a tile with two circles on them, "yi-tong."

From my speculation, this indicates either Connor is not planning to win with the circle patterned pai or he has too much of them so he doesn't need it. But there's also the possibility he wants me to think he's not going to win with the "tong-gee" pai by throwing one out. There's so much thinking involved in a mahjong match, I sometimes forget how stressful it is. But at the same time, there is a certain thrill to guess the reason for your opponent's every move.

I take a moment to ponder before making my first move. Mahjong is all about luck and strategy. Sometimes I'm lucky and am blessed with good pai right from the beginning. But most of the time, I have a bunch of random tiles. Since Connor and I are not going for small chicken wins, I can only win with a solid set of tiles.

My winning fourteen pai must include the same one to ten set amongst the three types of patterns: circles / "tong-gee", sticks / "sock-gee", or ten thousands / "man-gee". I also must accompany that pattern with a pair of eyes–or two of the exact same tiles–which can consist of the same patterned tile I decided to go with, the legendary big three tiles, or the four directions.

I don't have any direction tiles much less my own direction tile which would have added some bonus points if I did have them, but I'm not too bitter about it. Instead, I have one of each legendary big three pai: a tile with a blue rectangle or "bak-ban", a tile with a Chinese character written in red or "hong-zhong", and another tile with some other Chinese character written in green or "fat-choi." Those are the pai I usually keep the longest in hopes I could find the matching pair to be my eyes. But due to the limit of four of the same exact tile in the game, that's often easier said than done.

Most of my pai this round consists of a lot of the same "man-gee" pai so my best solution to win this round is to "dui-dui-pong." I can just constantly "pong" or take the matching tile–of the two I already own–thrown out by

Connor and switch it with a different pai I have but want to discard. This way, I can get the upper hand by getting the tiles I need while quickly removing the ones I don't need. I draw a new tile and the four sticks pai stare back at me.

I put that tile in the center and it's Connor's turn again to pick a new pai. This goes on for another two turns before I say "pong" and grab the eighty thousand tile he tossed out. Since I can't sacrifice any of my other pai, I say good-bye to my "fat-choi" and pray that another one doesn't show up soon after.

Connor still has not revealed what pai he is planning to win with, but I think it's maybe with "sock-gee" since he threw a few "man-gee" and "tong-gee" tiles already. He didn't "serng" me yet so I know for certain that he doesn't have a consistent set of three consecutive pattern pai like one, two, three or six, seven, eight.

A few more turns pass by and I do my best to hide my smug grin that my theory about Connor planning to win with "sock-gee" is right since he said "pong" to a few of the sticks pai I threw out. Our duel continues to lengthen and I'm worried he's going to win until I draw a "hong-zhong" and exclaim, "Zi-mo!"

Using both my hands to push the last two pai at the end of the row together, I ultimately lay my victorious pai set flat out to see. I have two "hong-zhong" as my pair of eyes and the rest of my pai are "dui-dui pong" of other "man-gee" patterned tiles. Connor eyes my winning pai set and then shows me his pai which involves a bunch of "sock-gee", two "bak-ban", and the north direction tile.

His pai is pretty good and he was close to beating me. If another "bak-ban" showed up for him to "pong" and another north pai appeared to be his eyes, he would have secured his victory. It takes all my self-control not to jump up and down like a kangaroo to contain my glee that I won by "zi-mo" since a player drawing out their winning card themselves further increases the greatness of the win.

Connor lifts his hand for a high-five. "Nice job."

I high-five him and then smile. "Thanks. I think you would have won if the hong-zhong I was waiting for never showed up."

"That was an intense first game. I got a bunch of patterns in the beginning so I had to throw a lot of random pai out before settling on the sock-gee pai," Connor remarks as we flip all the pai to the blank purple side.

As we shuffle the tiles, I comment with a small laugh, "I was lucky to get good pai in the first round. I hope the next two rounds are the same."

We finish setting up and dividing our pai for the second round. Since I'm the one who rolled this time, I throw the eight sticks pai out. This time, my pai contains a "fat-choi", two different directions, and a lot of "tong-gee." Guess that means I will try to win by using either the "fat-choi" or one of the two different directions as my pair of eyes and have the rest of my pai be "tong-gee."

After a few rounds, I throw out the sixty thousand pai and Connor says, "Serng."

He takes the sixty thousand tile and reveals he has a consecutive set of sixty thousand, seventy thousand, and eighty thousand. Connor must be near winning since he openly disclosed his plan to win with "man-gee." I'm close to winning as well since I have two potential pairs of eyes and just need to get one more of that same pai to win.

Two turns later and I throw out ten thousand and then Connor calls out, "Sik!"

He takes the pai I threw out and shows me his winning pai. As suspected, it consists of all "man-gee", three "bak-ban", and two "hong-zhong". I show my own pai to him and we both analyze each other's tiles.

I pretend to wipe sweat off my brow and mutter, "I'm glad we are not betting money on this because I would have lost a good amount for throwing out the pai you needed."

Connor chuckles as we shuffle our pai and set it up for the final game. "Whoever wins the next round can ask a question the other person must answer. Isn't that scarier than betting money?"

"Surprisingly, no."

Connor glances up at me before bringing his eyes back to the pai and a placid smile tugs at the corners of his mouth. I think I've reached the stage where I accepted how I don't need to be so "put-together" in front of my friend. He's seen me at my most embarrassing moments and doesn't seem to mind. Connor knows about my difficult relationship with my parents and didn't judge me for it. I want to win our mahjong duel so I can hear Connor's answer to my question, but part of me is curious–not scared–about what he wants to ask me.

Since Connor is the roller again for the final round, he begins the game by throwing out twenty thousand. I don't need that tile so I draw a new pai. My tiles this round are really jumbled up and I'm not too confident I can win. I have an equal amount of the same patterned pai of "tong-gee" and "sock-gee."

Great.

Now I need to choose a pattern and hopefully not choose the wrong one. I have a tendency to pick one pattern and then after I throw out more of the pattern I don't choose, I start drawing all those pattern pai I tossed out. Fingers crossed this doesn't happen tonight, but knowing me, it will.

During this last round, Connor has only "pong" one of

the big three and a direction. I don't know what pattern or tactic he's going with, but his pai seem pretty good. At this rate, Connor will win. I try not to let defeat show on my face because mahjong is also all about having a poker face so your opponents can't tell what you're thinking. This is one of the many reasons why I don't gamble with mahjong since I break under pressure.

When it's my turn to draw a pai, I get six sticks which is exactly what I need. Feeling a little more relaxed after organizing my pai where I just need to find a pair of eyes to win, I let out an inaudible sigh and throw out seven circles.

"Sik!" Connor rejoices and reveals his winning pai of "tong-gee" making me want to facepalm my forehead for assisting with his victory once again.

My gut told me Connor was collecting a bunch of "tong-gee" so it's inevitable I throw out what he needed. If I threw that pai out earlier, then he probably wouldn't have been able to get it yet. There's no way I could have known he needed that specific "tong-gee", but still. I am not a sore loser or anything. It's just defeating to know right when I was finding my rhythm, the game is over.

I sigh in acceptance and put my hand out for Connor to shake, "Great game."

We shake hands and Connor nods in unison, "Great game. That was really fun."

I flip the pai over and rearrange it to set up for the next time we play mahjong. Connor helps me finish stacking the pai over each other and then we both get up from the floor to stretch a bit. The lightish gray three-seat sofa Isa and I bought feels smaller now that it's me on one end and Connor at the other.

I turn to him crossing my legs in crisscross applesauce position before saying, "A deal is a deal. Ask away."

Connor takes a deep breath and starts, "The last time we saw each other, you told me you didn't want me to regret being friends with 'someone as messed up as' you." I nod to show him I remember and he continues, "In the beginning, I thought you meant about your past and what your parents did. But the more I thought about it, I wondered if there was a double meaning behind it?"

Shoot.

I really underestimated my neighbor friend's perceptiveness. Connor's comforting words about choosing who we are consoled me that night, but in retrospect, it makes me feel like a phony. I'm not as good of a person he said I was. I wish I was, but I'm not. Even if it's all in the past, it's still not something I'm proud of. I hate myself for what I did, but I hate myself more for not regretting it. I try to find words to say yet nothing comes to mind.

After a while, Connor shakes his head and says, "Never

mind, Lia. Forget I asked. Sor—"

"You're right," I cut him off before he can apologize for something he shouldn't be apologizing for. "I did mean something else."

Maybe it's my weak heart being fragile at the moment from tonight's events or the intensity of Connor's gaze filled with so much compassion, but I finally let down all my walls and come clean.

"When I was little, the only friend I had was this girl called Ami. We weren't close enough to text and keep in contact outside of school, but I still cried when I found out she was transferring schools right before summer vacation started. And then in fourth grade, Angelica, a girl who has been in my class since kindergarten, and I got close. We became pretty good friends, but she had to move away after that year ended."

I swallow and go on, "And then in sixth grade, there was this new student named Sierra. We bonded over watching the same anime and became friends, but then halfway during the school year, she transferred schools too, leaving me friendless yet again."

I let out an empty laugh. "You're probably wondering where I am going with this story besides sharing how none of my friends seem to ever stay with me. I mean it's middle school so it's not like we were super tight or anything. We never kept in contact so I don't even know their where-abouts or what they're doing now, but it was just hard to lose one friend after another."

I'm not even halfway done telling the story, but I'm doing that thing again. Our apartment echoes with my feet bun-ny-tapping the wooden floor. Connor doesn't comment on my nervous shaking and gives me an encouraging smile, the type of smile I wish was present in the audience during all my public speeches.

His reassuring smile reinvigorates my drive to continue and I still myself to take a shaky breath before speaking, "Then in eighth grade, our latest transfer student, Callie, arrived at our school. She reminded me of Sierra since she was nice, soft-spoken and liked watching anime too. I ap-proached her and then we started hanging out. A few weeks later, one of my classmates asked me where Callie was be-cause he thought I would know since we hang out together so much."

The air conditioner is set to the normal cool temperature but it feels extra chilly. The next part of the story haunts me even after all these years and I want to go back to pretending it never happened. I want to forget it, but I can't. It did happen and I can't forget it.

I don't deserve to forget it.

Clenching my fists so hard they turn white, I force myself

to talk even when my voice wavers. "Right after he said that to me, it's like I internally flipped a switch. The next day during lunch, Callie followed me to hang out like we usually do. I don't exactly recall what I said, but the next thing I knew was she walked away from me and didn't turn back. For the rest of the school year, Callie hung out with Emilia and I sat alone during lunch. Besides having to interact with each other during school projects or events, we never spoke much afterward. But even during then, I could feel her guard up around me the whole time."

I stare at our polished wooden floor but everything blurs together making it look like a puddle of mud. "I hurt someone on purpose, Connor. I broke off my friendship with Callie to protect myself from getting hurt first. And the worst part is I knew Callie was never going to switch schools or leave until we graduated, but I still chose to direct all my anger and pain onto her because I was sick of being the one hurt and left behind."

"You were just a kid, Lia. You can't blame yourself for that your whole life." Connor's tone is soft and soothing and I want to relish in that comfort but I can't.

I profusely shake my head. "I knew better, but I still went and did it anyways because...the one who loves more is always the losing party. At least that's what I learned from watching my parents."

My parents' marriage is probably one of the worst examples of love, but I didn't know that at the time. They were the closest thing I had to love, even if it was the bad kind.

My mother would place Charmin toilet paper on the toilet paper holder for Dad to use while she put the one she preferred more in the drawer further away. She often held back from eating another bite of dessert to save more for him. She would immediately drop everything to purchase new slippers and undergarments for him whenever they were worn out, but never bought anything new herself even when she had more holes in one of her pajama shirts combined. Her selfless devoted love to my father and his numbness to it are memories I want to claw and whisk away from my mind.

My voice wobbles more but I trudge on, "Because of them, there was a time I thought love and any relationship was like that. Being close to someone is like fire. It tricks you with its false blanket of security making you feel all warm and happy, until one day, you get too close to the blazing flame and get burned."

I annoyingly brush off the tear that fell from my eyes with the back of my hand.

Dang it.

I was hoping I could at least keep some of my pride and dignity in front of Connor but guess that's all down the drain now. Blinking back more tears as I tilt my head upwards, my mouth forms a smile that doesn't reach my eyes.

"But I know better now. Reed and Isa taught me there are people who love each other equally, and genuinely enjoy being in each other's company. My love life and all my other relationships doesn't need to be like my parents'. I thought I wasn't meant to have friends and shouldn't have them because I hurt Callie. I never apologized to her which probably wouldn't have made what I did any better, but still."

This was once a secret I thought I would take to the grave. Not even Isa knows about this. And now, my new neighbor friend, knows all my inner demons. I never shared this with anyone because I didn't want to fully acknowledge that there were—are messed up parts of me that stem from my past. I didn't want to tell this to anyone because I didn't want to admit to them–to myself–that I'm just like my parents.

"This is the real me, Connor. I want to say I came out unscathed from my parents' marriage, but I'd be lying. I swore to never do it again, but I did hurt someone before and I don't regret it. The relief of knowing I wasn't going to be the one hurting that time overpowers any feeling of guilt I have. I am not the good person you think I am."

Instead of responding, Connor scoots one seat over and pulls me in a hug. His body feels really warm. Aside from my father and Reed, I've never hugged a guy before. I guess it's true that all males naturally radiate a lot of heat. Warmth envelops me as I lean against my friend's chest which is shockingly as sturdy as it looks.

The scent of citrus and lavender exudes off him and it's a very pleasant smell. If I wasn't so caught up with his close proximity and the seriousness of our conversation, I might have asked what type of cologne or detergent he uses.

Connor lowers his voice close to a whisper and I can feel his breath tingle my hair, "You might not have apologized to Callie, but the fact you still remember the incident that happened nine years ago, I think that means more than an apology. And it's not like Callie ended up friendless. You said she became friends with Emilia so it's not all bad."

More tears drip from my eyes and I want to back away from Connor so I won't dirty his clothes, but he doesn't release his hold like he knows exactly what I'm thinking.

"You are different from your parents. You acknowledged what you did wrong and learned from it. We all make mistakes at some point in our lives, but it's how we use those experiences to help us be a better version of ourselves in the future. Your past actions do not sum-up if you're a good person; your current actions matter too. You are a good person, Lia. You are."

My hands are still squeezed shut resting on his chest so it's easy for me to push him away if I wanted, but I don't move and he doesn't let go. Being engulfed in Connor's embrace and hearing his words replay in my mind makes me realize how long I've been underwater. How long it's been since I've been able to really breathe.

And I'm desperately clinging onto that first breath–the first gulp of air I inhale–after having my head under the water too long. Oxygen fills my lungs and revives my whole body back to life.

My past will forever be seared into my memory and I will never be able to change it. But that doesn't take away my right to let go of all the guilt, anger, and resentment from it. I've been carrying the weight of my mistake for so long and maybe I needed to suffer that pain to amend for it.

Yet at the same time, it's not wrong for me to live my life being a better person without that weight on my shoulders. It's ok to accept my past and move on from it. I don't need to allow these negative emotions to consume me any longer.

I can be ok.

Chapter 9

With a bouquet of red roses and a small gift bag in hand, Reed stands at my studio front door with such an endearing smile that reminds me why I fell in love with him in the first place.

"Hey, beautiful, I got these for you."

Reed holds out the flowers to me and it takes me a minute to convince myself I'm not hallucinating. There's only so much texting and talking on the phone can communicate about how well we've been doing. Taking a closer look at him now, the dark circles under his eyes have disappeared and his face looks more well-rested. Relief floods through me to know Reed's more or less back to his usual self.

I'm not sure how long he can stay or when is the next time I can see him again so it takes all my self-restraint to stop myself from wrapping my arms around his neck and glue myself to him. Fearing I will overwhelm him with my neediness, I opt for taking the roses from him like a normal person and respond, "They're beautiful, Reed. Thank you."

I set down the red bouquet on the bench table and scribble a note for myself to put them in water later. The flowers my boyfriend bought for me look nice, but roses tend to have a short lifespan and it might be even shorter under my care. I have to ask Isa for a few pointers on how to keep these roses alive as long as possible.

Reed takes out a small square shaped black case from the bag he's holding and puts the bag on the table. He opens the box revealing a necklace with the letter "R" on a rose gold chain. I let out a gasp as I notice the "R" has a yellow-ish green stone next to it.

"It's a peridot which is one of the birthstones for August, your birth month. I know it's nothing too big. I promise I'll get you a bigger stone next time, but I hope this can do for now." Reed steps behind me moving my hair to one side and clasps the necklace around me.

I spin around to face him with my hand on the necklace. "How much did this cost? It must be really expensive. I can't accept this."

"I can afford it, don't worry. I'm sorry I haven't been able to spend much time with you these days. But you're always on my mind and I wanted to splurge on a gift for you the minute I received a raise from my position as the new editorial director!" Reed says cheerfully.

"Oh my God, congratulations!"

Reed hugs and whirls me in one full circle before putting me back down. "I'm the new editorial director, at least for now. If I do a good job, they might let me keep the position since my boss was in talks of transferring to a different department. Nothing's set in stone, but I'm just thrilled to get the promotion."

I lean back so I can peer at my boyfriend's handsome face. "Reed, that's amazing! I'm so happy for you. I knew you could do it!"

Reed caresses my cheek with his hand gently like he's savoring every second his skin is on mine. "I'm sorry I let work come between us, but it won't happen again. Now that I got this position, I'll be able to buy you more things and make you even happier."

"I'm grateful for the gift, but you know I don't need fancy necklaces or other expensive jewelry. I just need you, Reed. I'm always happy when I'm with you." I touch his hand on my cheek and press my face closer.

"You make me so happy, Lia. I feel like I have everything I've always wanted when I'm with you," Reed whispers in my hair before kissing my head. We snuggle closer and he asks, "Do you have any plans tonight? I want to take you out to a dinner party my colleagues and I are having to celebrate my new promotion."

"Are you sure? Is it ok for me to tag along?"

During our entire dating timeline, my boyfriend and I only introduced each other to people we are really close with. On my end, Reed's been acquainted with my best friend and her boyfriend. Since Isa's my only friend and Jackson is her boyfriend, they are the few individuals who account for my extremely small circle of friends.

Well, now there's Connor too, I guess. And Reed knows him so that's pretty much it.

On the other hand, I only met a few of Reed's closest friends but not any of his co-workers since it's usually all about work with them. I really want to spend some quality time with my boyfriend, but I'm worried it would be awkward for me to show up at the dinner party as the only one not working at their company.

"Of course it is fine for you to come, Lia. I told my colleagues about you and they said they would love to meet you."

"Ok, then. When's the party? I want to make sure I have enough time to go back home to change first."

Reed heads to the front door and says, "It's at 6:30 p.m. I'll pick you up and we can go there together."

"That's soon, I better hurry." I get on my tiptoes and place a goodbye kiss on his cheek.

He graces me with a tender smile and murmurs in my hair,

"I miss you already" before leaving again.

"You look superb, Lia! Sooo giving off 'I'm the girlfriend of the new editorial director' look," Isa rejoices as she princess waves to her non-existent subjects.

I laugh and assess myself in the full-length mirror in my room. The dress I'm wearing is black minus the white collar and the one button shirt cuff embedded on each sleeve. From the waist down, the garment flares out extending to the knees. The weather is cold today so I have leggings underneath and plan to match the look with my two-inch heeled black boots. My hair is styled in a high ponytail to highlight my small white globe earrings. Isa comes up behind me in the mirror and we smile at each other through our reflections.

"I know it must have sucked not being able to see Reed for so long. Have fun tonight, Lia. But not too much fun since you have an early meeting with a webtoon story writer tomorrow morning," Isa reminds me as she rubs my shoulders.

I sigh. "You're right, I almost forgot. I need to get a good night's sleep today so I won't be a wreck in the morning."

"You'll do great as always. Now get going or else you'll be late." Isa navigates me to the front door and hands me my brown over-the-shoulder purse.

After my boots are on, I twirl around and give my best friend a hug. "Thank you for helping me choose my outfit tonight on such short notice. I don't know what I would do without you."

Thinking back to my most recent conversation with Connor, I remember yet again how lucky I am to have Isa in my life. I never thought I would be able to make a real friend given what happened in the past, but she proved me wrong. Isa changed my life for the better and I thank the universe every day for giving me the chance to befriend her.

Isa squeezes me back and says, "You also helped me pack for my yacht cruise with Jackson. That's what besties are for, girl. I won't be back until the day after tomorrow so don't miss me too much."

I smile and we say our goodbyes. Reaching the last step of our apartment building staircase, I see Reed waiting for me in the parking lot. His brown hair is neatly gelled up and he is wearing a dark gray suit jacket with matching gray pants. His dashing smile and straight posture really give off boss vibes, and I'm one hundred percent digging it.

"Did I say beautiful earlier in the day? I meant gorgeous." I blush at my boyfriend's words and playfully punch his chest to hide my embarrassment. Reed makes my heart flutter with a winsome smile before covering my eyes with his hand. "I want to show you something. It's sort of a surprise."

"Another surprise?"

Reed guides me forward and then after a minute, we stop. He drops his hand and I see a shiny silver car in front of us. I don't know too much about cars but I can tell this is definitely a luxury car.

"Ta-da! This is my new car!" Reed cheers excitedly. "It's the 2022 Audi A5 Sportback I mentioned I wanted before. Do you like it?"

My gaze relocates from the car to Reed trying to decide what to say. "It looks nice, but how did you manage to afford this? And what about your old car?"

"I sold it. I have a new car now. Well, I'm loaning this car for the time being but when the loan expires, I'm planning to officially buy it. By then, I should have saved up enough money."

"Is that really ok? I mean the necklace and the car. Aren't they both really expensive?" I ask knitting my eyebrows in concern.

"I'm tired of living on the safe side and waiting for things to slowly change. I want to live a little. Getting a small gift and a new car is just the beginning. I am the new editorial director and I plan to take full advantage of all the financial perks of it." Reed winks at me.

Before I can say anything else, he changes the subject and

nudges me towards the driver's seat, "This car is so fun to drive and the engine sounds great. It has a nice roar to it, but it's not loud or flashy enough to get you pulled over. You have to try it."

I want to protest and say more, but I don't want to spend the only alone time I have with Reed talking about things that might lead into an argument. I get in the driver's seat as my boyfriend puts his hand on the car to protect my head and closes the door for me. His gentlemanly gestures reassure me he's still the man I fell in love with and all my feelings of unease vanishes.

I buckle my seatbelt as Reed jumps in the passenger seat. He teaches me how to turn on the ignition while he buckles his seatbelt. I adjust the chair and mirrors and then we're on the road in no time.

Reed's right.

I'm not a huge fan of fancy cars, but driving this car is nice. The steering wheel feels smooth against my hands and has a nice grip to it too. The gas pedal and brake are very easy to maneuver and I feel like I have full control of the car. I spot an available parking space near the restaurant the party is being held and pull over.

"So, how was the drive?" Reed asks with an expectant grin.

I hand him back the car keys and reply, "It was good. I can see why you like it."

He offers me his arm to loop around and smiles at me. "I'm glad you like it. You can drive this car whenever you want."

"Thank you," I answer putting my arm in his. "Oh-Reed, I forgot to mention I have an early meeting tomorrow morning. I need to head home right after dinner is over. Sorry I can't stay longer."

"Not a problem. I'm pretty sure the party won't go on too long since we still have work tomorrow."

Reed's colleagues booked a private room at the back of the restaurant. By the time we walk in, there are already seven people seated at the round dining table. At the sight of Reed, everyone in the room applauds, "There's our new editorial director!"

Reed laughs and does a bro-hug with a guy two inches shorter than him wearing a polo T-shirt with khakis. Khakis claps my boyfriend on the back and whistles. "The man of the hour is finally here! Let's start partying!"

An older man a few inches taller than me with a black beard dotted with specks of gray, approaches us. The bearded older man was the first person that caught my attention with his vibrant, maroon-colored suit. If I didn't know better, I would assume he's the man we're throwing the party for.

"Reed, my boy! We're glad you're here but hurry and introduce us to your lady. You didn't mention how pretty she was. Where have you been hiding her all this time?" The bearded man says as he not so subtly does a whole body scan of me.

Reed steps closer to me placing his hand on my lower back. "You can't blame a guy for trying to keep such a beauty to himself." Everyone laughs good-naturedly and Reed proceeds to introduce me. "This is my girlfriend, Lia."

I force my most natural smile and wave at everyone as they direct their attention to me. I can handle my fair share of false flattery, but having everyone's eyes on me is a different story. Their scrutinizing eyes judge me from head to toe and size me up as if I'm really all that. I get it's normal to want to look at the new arrival, but it still does not make it any less uncomfortable to have random strangers stare at me. My mind is going into full panic mode and I rub at my dress sleeve to calm the goosebumps forming on my arms.

Thankfully a second later, Reed leads me to the two empty seats left at the table. We sit down and I say a silent word of thanks I'm seated next to Khakis on my left instead of the maroon suit man. I just met him like a second ago, but I don't have good vibes from him. He gives me the creeps and it's not just him. Everyone in the room doesn't make me feel comfortable except for maybe Khakis, however, it's too soon to be sure.

My legs are getting antsy and I want to leave this stuffy

room, but I remind myself why I'm here. Not wanting to ruin my boyfriend's special night, I do my best to maintain the smile already plastered on my face and get into the role of Reed's girlfriend who totally enjoys being the prey in a cave full of hungry lions.

Khakis leans forward so he can speak to both Reed and me at the same time. "We've already ordered so the food should be coming shortly." He turns his face to me and then says, "I'm Luke by the way."

I raise my hand to say hi and then Khakis—I mean, Luke, points to everyone at the table one by one telling me their names. Turns out the creeper old man is Alan, Reed's boss and the previous editorial director. It's so obvious now that I know. I should have put two and two together earlier, but I'm going to be lenient on myself and say it was hard to process everything with so many new faces in the room.

The girl with the shoulder length braid and pink long sleeve is Ava. The preppy looking guy wearing a red sweater over a collared shirt is Walter. The only other girl in the room is Ivy. She's wearing a collared black dress that matches the darkness of her hair tied up in a top bun. All the Ivy's I met aren't pleasant people to talk to, but I won't assume anything with this Ivy since I don't want to let my previous bad encounters cloud my judgement.

But as soon as that thought crosses my mind, Ivy rolls her

eyes at me before studying her fingernails like I'm not even worth her time.

Um, ouch?

I'm sorry to all the good Ivy's out there but so far this Ivy isn't really cutting it. The last two guys at the table, one is a curly blonde guy with a green striped tie and the other a black-haired guy with glasses wearing a gray vest over a black shirt. One of them is Briven and the other is Dylan, but I don't know who's who.

My minimal interaction with people in school which extended to my adult years has only degraded my ability to memorize people's names and faces. I simply nod and smile at them since they all already know who I am.

"Here's a toast to my short break and my boy, Reed's promotion as the new editorial director!" Alan bellows as he lifts a shot of whiskey.

Everyone follows suit and raises their own alcoholic drink in toast before sipping. I guess it's just me weirded out by why Alan keeps calling Reed "my boy." If he's anyone's boy, he's his own boy and my boy too, since I'm his girlfriend. I take a sip from my water glass to stifle a laugh from my hilarious mini joke to myself.

As if he was staring at me from the corner of his previously wandering eyes, the creeper immediately takes note and points out the absence of an alcoholic beverage in my hand.

"We are toasting. Why aren't you drinking?"

I try not to break my fake jolly girlfriend smile at the disapproval in his tone as I respond, "I have an early meeting tomorrow so I can't drink."

Alan frowns and pours a glass of red wine holding it out in front of me. "That's no fun. You should celebrate your boyfriend getting promoted with a proper toast."

I've never been a fan of alcohol. Maybe I have not drank it enough, but I dislike the strong scent and bitter taste. And I know it's already been a few years but memories of that night still crawl their way from the back of my mind every time I see any alcoholic beverage, especially red wine. I don't mind if other people drink it, but I just can't.

Right before I'm debating whether or not I need to pull the liver card, my boyfriend comes to my rescue and takes the glass from his boss. "No can do. Lia is the DD tonight so I'll drink for the both of us."

Reed taps the wine glass to Alan's before drinking. Satisfied he got someone to drink, Mr. Creeper spots his new target, Walter, and begins his pestering. After making sure the ex-editorial director is preoccupied with someone else, Reed looks over at me and places his hand on top of mine.

We don't say anything but I can tell from my boyfriend's expression he is apologizing for what happened. I respond with an "it's ok" smile and a light squeeze. I won't let my dislike for some of Reed's colleagues spoil the night. I'm a tough cookie. I can deal with these suckers–ahem–people for one night.

Pretending to smile and have fun for a few hours, yeah, piece of cake.

When the food arrives, I almost cry tears of joy as I finally have a reason not to sit there awkwardly and pray no one talks directly to me. Everyone continues to chat amongst each other and I excuse myself to the lady's room after the second course is served. I don't have to go or anything, but my reclusive self will leap at any opportunity to exercise my legs and take a breather.

Turning on the faucet, I scrub my hands with soap even though they aren't in need of sanitization. I just enjoy the sensation of cool water trickling down my hands, like it can also wash away the stuffiness of that room. Taking a few deep breaths and calming myself, I think I'm ready to head back out there. I'm about to pull the door open but someone from the other side pushes the door with so much unnec-essary force, it swings the door right to my face.

My reflexes are fast and I dodge a gruesome smack to my face. To my surprise–or not–it is Ivy standing in front of me. She walks past me, ignoring the fact that she almost crushed me and doesn't even look apologetic about it.

Seriously, what does this woman have against me?

I'm not really good with faces, but I'm one hundred percent sure we've never met before until tonight. Many nasty words come to mind as I itch to confront her about her rude behavior, but I hold my tongue. It's not worth my time and I have better things to do.

I leave the bathroom with my head held high and make my way back to Reed. He's engaging in a conversation with Briven/Dylan but he gives me a bright smile as I walk back in the room. After I'm seated again, his hand finds mine underneath the table. My spirits are immediately lifted and it sort of balances out my earlier dreadful encounter with Ivy.

When the waiters bring in the second to last round of food, everyone is engrossed in their conversations, giving me the luxury of immersing myself in the food minus the occasional bobbing of my head to show I'm listening. But the minute Ivy shoots me a wicked smile, I knew I was too relaxed. Even though my heels give me an extra two inches and our table is on even flooring, I can practically feel her glaring down at me.

She's finally going for it. She's finally coming at me. I swear this woman is a b—.

"So Lia, what do you do for a living? Reed never told us," Ivy asks as she bats her eyelashes innocently at me. Ivy is the type of girl most men would probably find sexy. I try not to barf as I link the words "sexy" and this Ivy together. I mean she's not particularly unattractive, but her personality is, at least from what I've seen.

She purposefully–maybe even orchestrated–this moment to happen. At this point, I'm not even being paranoid. Ivy just had to open her annoying little mouth right when the room took a pause in their loud conversation. And she had to ask me, of all people, a question, so that everyone's eyes and attention would once again be on me. It's like she wants to emphasize how I'm the odd one out of the group and don't belong here.

Remembering that the faster I respond, the faster the spotlight will be removed from me, I set my fork down with a pleasant smile. "I'm an artist."

"Wow, that's so cool." Ivy's voice sounds sweet but I could sense the underlying malice. "It must be fun drawing pictures all day. If I had known being an artist was that easy, I would have done that instead."

A few people laugh, but I'm too distracted by Ivy's smirk on her way too dark of a shade purple lips, to identify her co-conspirators. My new archenemy is obviously trying to undermine the importance of my job with her over-the-top commentary. Is that the best she can come up with?

What is this, high school?

Does she think she can low-key make fun of my occupation and hurt my feelings? I've heard way worse before and

I almost laugh at the ridiculousness of this situation. I dab my napkin lightly on my mouth and am about to make her rue the day she messed with Lydia freaking Zhang, but stop myself when Reed puts his arm behind my chair.

My boyfriend gazes at me lovingly as he says, "Lia always makes everything she does look so effortless. That's what makes her even more astonishing."

At his classy rebuttal, the room explodes with heart emojis in their eyes and an "Awwww." I can't tell if Reed is doing this to get Ivy off my back or because he genuinely means it, but either way, the butterflies fly wild in my stomach. I mentally shelve this moment in my life as top ten moments when evil girl tries to make Cinderella look bad, but it backfired when the prince turns the table around. I spend way too much time watching those clickbait C-drama titles on YouTube, but I can't help it, they are hilarious.

Luckily, Reed's intervention sizzles down the unspoken impending showdown between Ivy and me. He takes this time to make his own toast and share how much Moon Bay Publishing means to him. During his whole speech, everyone is captivated by Reed's natural charisma.

But that's nothing new.

Reed's charm is part of the many reasons why I'm so drawn to him. It's like when he's speaking, all other chatter and murmurs are muted. All I want to see and hear is Reed.

However, the way Ivy's eyes trail my boyfriend's every move and her mouth is actually smiling a real smile throws me off. Her happy smile is such an unusual and unappealing sight–if I'm being honest–but that's not what's bothering me. Now that I use my brain a little more, aside from me receiving Ivy's side eye glare for almost the entirety of the dinner, there were a few times I caught her glancing somewhere near my side of the table with less hostility.

Oh my Lords.

It all makes sense now. Ivy has a crush on Reed. She is jealous of me dating him so she tried to stir trouble just to spite Reed's current girlfriend, aka me. Never in a billion years did I think I would be the subject of someone's envy. Either I'm overthinking or it's the bad juju from my last year's "Fan Tai Sui" going over to this year.

Since last year, I carry an amulet in my wallet every day for protection but maybe it is wearing out. I probably need to ask Isa to help me ask Jackson about this. My consistent weird encounters and things happening to me as of late can't be a freaking coincidence.

Aside from my superstitious theories, I'm surprised at myself for not being more angry at Ivy for liking Reed. I mean I totally get her. I'm his girlfriend so of course I know why she would fancy him, but she should be ashamed of herself for letting her jealousy do the talking. Because of girls like Ivy, we females, are given such bad reputations.

Can't she just be happy for me and Reed? Or at least make her hatred for me a little less obvious? But whatever, she doesn't intimidate me. This only gives me more juice to spill to Isa.

After Reed concludes his speech with how he hopes with their united hard work Moon Bay Publishing can be listed as part of the top ten instead of top twenty best publishing houses one day, everyone claps and toasts again. We finish eating dinner and move onto dessert without any more hiccups. The clock hanging on the wall show it's already 9 p.m.

I tug at Reed's sleeve signaling him with a friendly smile I need to get going now. His face is a little red from drinking but through his eyes, I can tell he's still sober enough to think clearly.

Reed stands up from his seat and says, "Thank you everyone for the party. I had a lot of fun, but we need to go now so I'll see you all tomorrow morning."

To my utmost displeasure, Alan puts an end to our escape when he wiggles his stubby index finger in our direction as he slurs, "Y-you can't l-leave yet. T-the party can't end s-so soon."

"We're not fully drunk yet," Walter unhelpfully chimes in.

"The night's still young and we have more time to party," Luke agrees.

"We also start work later tomorrow too," Ava pipes in as she sways around in her seat.

Everyone else nods in agreement and starts drunkenly chanting, "Stay! Stay! Stay!"

My boyfriend looks at them and back at me like he's wondering what to do. As the new editorial director, he probably doesn't want to disappoint his co-workers. Reed is their new boss and I'm sure that must be a lot of pressure on him. I can probably go catch an Uber right now and leave myself, but he has been drinking so he can't drive back home.

Reed is sober enough to look out for himself, but I'm worried if I leave him with his co-workers, they might get him even more drunk and he couldn't get back home safely.

To my utmost displeasure, Ivy joins the bandwagon and offers her unwanted commentary, "If you need to leave, Lia, you can leave. We'll take good care of Reed."

She has on an angelic smile, but I know she's triumphantly smirking from the inside. Now I, for sure, cannot abandon my boyfriend to the clutches of this woman or his colleagues. I bite the inside of my cheek and say to Reed in a low voice so only he can hear me, "I guess we can stay a little longer."

"Are you sure?"

I nod and lower my body back onto the chair hoping I did the right thing. Reed glances at me and then his colleagues before sitting back down. The whole room erupts in another cheer and thus begins yet another round of drinking.

By the time I manage to haul a fully drunk and chatty Reed to his apartment, it's 11:30 p.m. He leans on me mumbling something along the lines of, "Don't ... no ... home. Bad... no..."

I'm not sure what exactly he's saying because I'm too focused on opening the door to his apartment while not dropping the keys I so painstakingly pried from his coat pocket. "Yes, we're almost home."

I get Reed inside and manage to lock the door without further difficulty. He unexpectedly contributes more of his weight on me and I almost collapse from his sheer heaviness. It was exhausting enough to get him to walk with me to the car and up the stairs to his apartment, but I did everything in high heels. Yes, they are thick-heeled two-inch boots so it could be worse, but heels are still heels.

"Reed, honey, I love you but you're really heavy," I chide pushing my boyfriend away causing him to make a whimpering sound as he rests against the wall.

Since I don't usually drink, Reed accompanies me in drinking non-alcoholic beverages. He told me he is definitely not a habitual drinker, but he does drink a little when he is with his co-workers. This is the first time I've ever seen Reed full-out drunk. I guess he's the type to get clingy and whiny when drunk. Despite the trouble this brings me, I have to admit, it is kind of adorable to see Reed like this.

I switch on the apartment lights and gasp at the untidiness of the space in front of me. There are unwashed dishes piled up on the sink, dirty clothes about to tip over in the laundry basket, and loose papers scattered everywhere on the floor. I've been to Reed's apartment multiple times before and it is always clean and tidy. The last time I was here was around the same time Reed got even busier with work and the promotion.

"My bad...no...clean...sorry," Reed mutters.

I turn back to look at him just in time to catch my boyfriend from losing his balance in the midst of taking off his shoes. I steady him and make sure he won't fall before removing my own shoes. My feet are killing me, but I bear with the pain as we slowly make our way to his bedroom with Reed's arm around me and my arm around his waist.

"Reed, you need to change and brush your teeth before sleeping. Can you do that for me?" I ask as I hold his shoulders so he can look at me.

He nods and slurs a little as he says, "I'll d-dooo a-aanything fooor yoooou."

If he wasn't slurring so much, I would smile at him but instead I laugh. Happy to hear me laughing, he wraps his arms around me and giggles. Oh boy, I can't wait for Reed to sober up so I can tell him how he is when drunk. I help him undress but thankfully he is able to change his pants on his own.

Under my supervision, he brushes his teeth without much assistance and then he is finally in bed. I flip my boyfriend over to one side in case the wine decides not to stay down and pull the blankets higher to cover his shoulders. When I set a glass of water on his nightstand, Reed grabs my hand with his.

"Stayyy here with meee, Liaaaa," he pleas as he tugs at my hand gently.

I brush his hair out of his eyes and say, "Sorry, not today, Reed. Soon, ok?"

He swings my hand like a pendulum as he begs, "Pretttyyy pleaseeee?"

I bend down until we are level and tuck his hand back under the sheets. I kiss his forehead and murmur, "Good night, Reed. Sweet dreams."

He says my name one more time before drifting off to sleep. I tiptoe out and close the door to his bedroom as quietly as I can. It's late and I should call an Uber to drive me back home to get as much sleep as possible. But the second

I walk to the living room and eye the mess—I can't bring myself to leave.

The sight in front of me is too much for me to sit by and do nothing. Having no spare clothes or wanting to borrow one from Reed–only to contribute more to the laundry pile–I roll up my dress sleeves and begin cleaning. Like Isa and my apartment, Reed also has an in-unit washer and dryer. A little pricey but worth every penny. As I am sorting out Reed's clothes, I calculate it should only take three loads to wash everything. I put the clothes in the washer and add detergent, letting the machine do the rest.

After clearing out the mountain of dirty dishes, I start tidying the apartment floor. Most of the papers are random magazines, advertisement flyers, and other mail. A postcard falls out from one of the magazines and I pick it up. It's a postcard of a family photo with a small message on the side. Looking at the picture, I immediately know that the post-card must have been intentionally shoved in the magazine.

I recognize the two older folks to be Reed's parents and the younger couple standing next to them as Reed's older brother and his girlfriend. They're all smiling at the camera which gives the impression they are smiling at me. Which is honestly really scary because I've met them before and they definitely never smiled at me like that. Reed's apartment window is open for ventilation but that's not the breeze making me shift uncomfortably.

One long miserable night ago, I had the pleasure of dining with Reed's family for a family get together. Reed warned me about his difficult relationship with his family and although I believed him, I was fooled in the beginning.

When a black-haired woman with streaks of white wearing a brown polka-dotted dress that highlighted her killer legs greeted us at the door–Reed's mom–she welcomed us with open arms and a kind smile. Mr. Wang, who had the same shade of dark brown hair and defined jawline as Reed's, waved a hand to us but never took his eyes away from reading his newspaper.

Ok, nothing too abnormal.

The action started when we were sitting at the dinner table and Alexander and his girlfriend, Cheryl, arrived. Alex is a few inches taller than his younger brother and more lean but also lacking the muscles he has. And all of Reed's time in the gym was definitely not a waste because I can proudly announce to all the ladies and gents out there that unrealistic ideals for boyfriends with six-packs are not just in fiction.

But on a different note, Alex has their dad's face structure and nose but his eyes and smile gives me their mom vibes. Cheryl is a very pretty girl with her sharp nose, plump red lips, and sleek black hair pulled into a loose ponytail. I didn't mind trying to talk to her thinking we could bond over being girlfriends of the Wang brothers but her straight as a ruler posture made her look like the type of girl you need to be at a certain level to talk to.

During dinner, Reed's parents wouldn't stop talking about how Alex makes the family so proud by graduating at the top in med school and how he is now one of the top cardiothoracic surgeons in his field. Reed wasn't kidding when he said his brother was the golden child. And the fact that Alex is dating a lawyer from a well-known law firm was like the cherry on top.

Mr. and Mrs. Wang's attention and interest were all directed towards Alex. Reed and I were kinda like extras in a movie. Maybe even cannon fodder, but that was actually more preferable and bearable than what came next.

"At least someone in the family did not waste his years in college and actually got a real job," Mr. Wang said clearly throwing shade at Reed.

That jab was the first thing Reed's dad said about Reed and I give my boyfriend so much credit for not even flinching. I was taken aback but I still managed to keep my face neutral. Even if Reed never let it show in front of his family, I could tell it hurt him that his parents never gave him as much love and praise as they did with Alex. And the saddest part is how Alex was not a very good brother to Reed either.

In front of their parents, Alex would act like the kind

helpful older brother. But the second they were out of sight, he would ignore Reed like he was invisible. Whenever I asked Reed about his family, he would answer all my questions but never say more than necessary. I can relate and sympathize with Reed's family situation.

I was lucky to be an only child, but it was work and another woman who stole my father's attention and it was that same cheating father that overshadowed me in Mom's eyes.

We just want to be loved by the people who should love us, but sometimes even that is too much to ask.

When the tension in the room became even thicker, Reed's mom steered the conversation towards me and asked me about my life. I told them about my current situation which was me quitting college two months ago and working miscellaneous jobs to keep afloat until I can become a full-time artist.

The entire room except Reed started laughing and they continued to laugh until they realized I wasn't joking. Their heads turned to Reed and he put an arm around me saying he fully supported my decision. Everyone looked at us with disapproval in their eyes before resuming to focus on Alex and Cheryl for the rest of the dinner.

When I glanced at Reed, he gave me a pained smile and patted my knee affectionately. It became clear he knew this was going to happen, but him not reacting showed he did not care what his parents thought of me. Because we've been dating for some time now, Reed thought I should meet his folks at least once since it was a rite of passage of some sort.

After meeting them, that was crossed off the to-do list and I wouldn't need to see his family again unless I wanted to. It still breaks my heart how Reed doesn't have a good relationship with his family. I want to be like those female main characters who enters the male lead's life and mends the broken bond between him and his family, but this is real life. No amount of my meddling can mend anything if the other party is too stubborn to change their ways.

The only thing I can do for Reed is to love him with all my heart and hope that that will be enough to make him happy.

Chapter 10

Closing my laptop, I let out a relieved sigh. The Zoom meeting call just ended and thank the Lords it went well.

In the next few days, I would be receiving the entire season one script outline for me to sketch. As I finish marking up my calendar for deadlines I need to meet to keep from falling behind schedule, a knock sounds from my studio door. When the bell chimes, I see Connor walking in.

It's been a while since I've really spoken to him. We still wave to each other during our morning jogs, but I never linger long enough to say more than hi. The last time we hung out and played mahjong together, I bawled my eyeballs like a little kid. Not my best moment in life, but I stick to my word. My neighbor friend whom I haven't known for too long now knows practically everything about me. I don't particularly feel uncomfortable around Connor, but I needed some time away from him. He knows too much about me.

I told him too much about me.

Creating distance between him was my way of protecting what scraps of myself I have left. But at the same time, ever since I told Connor my darkest secret, I feel a lot lighter and more at ease. The weight in my heart is no longer there and I feel free. I didn't even know how tied down I felt until I let everything go. As much as I want to avoid getting too attached to Connor, my new friend has already become such an important part of my life that I started to miss him when he is not around.

My brain automatically shifts my thoughts to something else before I can deep dive any longer. That's when I notice Connor is wearing a white long sleeve dress shirt paired with black pants. His clothes fit his tall frame well and wearing this outfit makes him look like he came straight out of a webtoon. But more importantly, how the heck does this guy cook with white long sleeves? It's the equivalent of asking me to paint without an apron. The damage to the clothes will be irreversible and no amount of washing can save them.

"Hey, Lia. I didn't see you jogging this morning so I just wanted to see if everything is all right," Connor says interrupting my train of thought.

Due to yesterday's well, complications, I skipped my morning run to get all the sleep I could. Last night–or early this morning I should say–I left Reed's apartment sparkly clean. The washed dishes were dried and neatly stored back in the cabinets. The laundry was all washed, folded, or hung to dry. I sorted all the miscellaneous mail putting them in piles from newest to oldest on the table for Reed to look at when he has time.

I drove his car to the nearest grocery market that was open in the middle of the night and bought healthier unexpired food. After restocking Reed's refrigerator with edible food, I took the liberty to throw out all the old takeout and expired stuff in there. On my way to lug out three Hefty bags of trash from Reed's apartment, I ended up tripping on the uneven pavement at his apartment garbage disposal area. I didn't fall but my one of my favorite boot heels broke.

It is an easy fix with hot glue but the combo of a broken heel and blistered feet is definitely not something I am thrilled about.

By the time I took an Uber back home, it was 2 a.m. Due to my early meeting and art class being soon after, it was more practical for me to set up everything my class needed and spend the night at my studio. Connor studies my face and I'm sure he can tell I barely got any sleep yesterday—as if my blood shot eyes, dark eye bags, and the lack of color on my face are not obvious enough indicators.

Wanting to spare Connor the long details, I run a hand through my hair and summarize, "Yesterday was hectic and

I had an early meeting this morning so I skipped out on my morning run to get a full almost four hours of sleep. I have art class in the next fifty minutes but I'm getting really hungry so I'm debating whether or not I should forgo sleep to eat. So to answer your question, everything is as okay as it can be."

"How about doing both?" Connor suggests with a grin. "You can take a quick nap right now and I'll be back with the food."

Of all the things he could say, I did not expect Connor to say that. That honestly sounds great, but I'd feel awful for imposing on him for the umpteenth time.

As if reading my mind, he says, "Don't worry, Lia. I have some ingredients leftover from my class yesterday so it's not an inconvenience. I'll call you once I'm at your front door."

Before I can argue, Connor jogs back to the youth center and his figure disappears from sight. A wave of exhaustion crashes over me and I decide it's best not to resist any chance of rest I can get. After locking my studio front door, I set my phone alarm for twenty minutes and sit on my chair. Once I close my eyes, it only takes a few seconds to drift off to sleep.

Somehow in the span of twenty-five minutes, Connor prepared me a full-course meal. He presented me with sautéed green string beans, chicken bits with rice, and chicken soup. I recognize this meal to be Connor's version of Ratatouille. The blend of rice and chicken bits are perfectly balanced and taste so good. The beans are crunchy and cooked to perfection where it's not too dry or undercooked. And Connor was right about the canned chicken soup.

There's something so pleasantly satisfying about the delicious taste of MSG.

The nap did not remove all my fatigue but having warm delicious food in my stomach fuels me with enough energy to survive a few more hours. After I finish savoring all the food, Connor takes out three small packs from one of the lunch bags he brought and hands them to me.

"In case you feel tired later, here's some candy to give you some energy."

"I love gummy bears! They're my favorite," I squeal as I take a bag and tear it open.

"Really?"

"When I was younger, my dad and I used to share a big pack of Goldbears as we waited to board the plane for our family trips. It was kind of our tradition to eat candy at the airport. I loved eating gummy bears so much he gave me the nickname Lia Bears," I tell him as I pop a green gummy bear in my mouth.

Connor rests his chin on the palm of his hand with an amused expression. "I didn't know you loved gummy bears so much."

"I love all the flavors, but green is my favorite. I think it's all in my head since I'm pretty sure I can't taste the difference if I close my eyes."

Remembering my manners, I offer my friend some of the delightful treat. Connor nods his head in thanks and takes a red gummy bear out of the pack. "The color does make a difference. My favorite is red."

We raise our gummy bears like we are toasting and then eat them. Gummy bears are naturally yummy but they somehow taste even better when it's shared.

Connor eyes his watch and says, "Your art class is almost starting. I better get going." As I clean the table, he packs back up the multiple thermoses he brought over.

"Thank you for the meal and the sweets. I don't know what I would have done if you didn't help me out today," I say to my friend hoping he knows just how thankful I am for him, once again.

"No problem. And I didn't forget."

"Huh?"

"We'll schedule a day for you to try the Ratatouille next." He smiles at me and waves a hand, "See you when I see you, Lia Bears."

I laugh. "See you."

Connor has his hand on the doorknob, but before he opens it, he pauses. He turns back around and strides toward me until we are a foot apart. The intensity in his usual soft brown eyes startle me, but I stand my ground as I brace myself for his next words.

"About the other night, I never got the chance to thank you for your candidness. I know it's not easy to tell someone what you told me so thank you for trusting me enough."

"We had a deal and you won fair and square. It was only right I answer your question. And to tell you honestly, I feel a lot better after talking about it. So I should be thanking you, again," I reply with an appreciative smile.

"Do you still remember the question you wanted to ask me?" Connor asks in a low voice like he's uncertain whether or not he wants me to remember.

I nod but don't speak. For some reason, my palms begin to sweat and I'm nervous to hear what he has to say.

"The answer to your question...what you want to know. ..the reason why..." he starts before sighing and then finally says, "I like you, Lia. As more than a friend..."

Connor's words completely take me by surprise and all I can manage is a mumble of "What?"

"I know you have a boyfriend and I must have crossed a line, but I don't think it's fair if I continue to keep this from you. And just so we're clear, none of my previous actions had any ulterior motive. I never expected anything from you and never will. I simply like having you in my life as neighbors, friends, or in whatever way I can."

My mouth parts but I'm speechless. I did not have the proper amount of rest to handle such an honest confession this early in the morning.

Seeming to realize it would only be a one-sided conversation from here on out, Connor continues to talk. "I'm sorry for putting this all on you now. The last thing I want is to lose my friendship with you and make you feel uncomfortable around me."

I bob my head like an idiot since that's the only thing my body can do and a small boyish grin forms on Connor's mouth before he grimaces.

He takes a step back from me and doesn't meet my eyes as he goes on, "There are days when I find myself wishing you met me first and...it is me in that big heart of yours. You deserve better than someone who breaks their promises and makes you cry. You deserve so much more love and happiness than you are getting from R—"

He doesn't finish his sentence, but his implication is clear. Connor begins again but his voice is gentler this time. "I want you to be happy, Lia. And I will always want that for you even if I'm just a friend in your eyes."

He walks toward the front door with his back facing me and I hear him say under his breath so quiet I think I imagined it, "Even if it's not me, I hope one day you'll find someone who loves you as much as you love them."

Chapter 11

"So what happened next?" my best friend asks as her eyes glimmer in anticipation.

"Isa, it's your turn to pick a new pai," I point out rearranging the positioning of my tiles.

"Oh, forget about mahjong, Lia! Tell me what happened next between you and Connor!" Isa demands leaning forward.

"Nothing else happened. Connor left and we haven't talked since," I answer with a small sigh.

"I had a hunch Connor like likes you and I was right! I caught him staring at you a few times in 'not just a friend way' and he tends to smile more when you're there. And what about you, Lia? Do you like like him too?"

I shrug. "I mean Connor is a nice guy and I feel very grateful to be friends with him. Any girl would be more than lucky to have him as their boyfriend. He's polite, good-looking, checks all the boxes of being boyfriend–and even husband–material. But even if Connor likes me, my heart is with Reed."

Isa reels in her enthusiasm and gives me an understanding smile. "You're right, sorry. That was thoughtless of me. It's just Reed has been overloaded with work lately. You look fine on the outside, but I know you are hurting from it on the inside. But on the days you were with Connor, I could see you genuinely happy again. As your BFF, I want the best for you and it doesn't sit well with me when someone is making you sad."

I get up from the floor and hug my best friend. "Thanks for looking out for me, Isa."

"Always." She rubs my back up and down and then asks in a concerned voice, "Do you know what you plan on doing about Connor?"

"Nothing. We're still going to be just friends. Nothing more, nothing less."

"And Reed?"

I lean back from Isa with a confused expression on my face and she strokes my hair with a small sigh of her own.

"I know you like him, L, but Reed has not been a good boyfriend to you these past few months. Bailing last minute on a few dates and being too busy to meet up in person, okay. Life happens, that's fine. But how could he miss your special day at the art gallery? Reed said he would be there and then did not show up. That was such an important event! And the work party where he couldn't say no to his co-workers? He's the new boss and can call the shots without anyone questioning his authority. And don't get me started on that stupid Ivy looking down on you. If you didn't forbid me from doing so, I would have marched straight to Reed's workplace and given that Poison Ivy an earful for that."

I laugh at my best friend's defensiveness over me. She has always been like this ever since I'd known her. Isa could sense whenever something was bothering me and after she fishes it out of me, she says things that make me laugh and I would feel happy again. But don't get me wrong, Isa is not all bark and no bite. She would totally kick someone's behind and front for my sake.

Not only that, she will also get her Isa-bells to back her up as well. Isa has such a loyal massive fan base and she is not afraid to use it to her advantage. As cute as Isa is, she can also be really scary and not someone you want to incur the wrath of. And I love her so much for that.

"The art gallery was a work emergency and the work party wasn't his fault. I chose to stay and do all the stuff afterward," I rebut.

"Would it kill him to send a quick text or call saying he couldn't make it? And Reed should have known you were being considerate of him and stood firm on calling it a night.

He could always party with his co-workers some other time," Isa argues with a bitter expression. "I'm serious about what I said earlier. I know you guys have been together for a long time and you love him, but I'm worried this new promotion won't make things better but worse between you guys." My best friend takes my hands in hers and squeezes them. "I'm all for whoever and whatever makes you happy, but promise me you'll at least talk to him about his absence?"

As much as I love Reed, I can't really refute Isa because it's the truth. Reed really has been MIA this past year. I understand work is making him busy, but it never hurt any less every time he canceled or couldn't make it. I guess part of me was too scared to confront my boyfriend about it because if he had to choose between work or me, I'm not confident he'd pick me anymore.

I know Reed loves me but I can tell his job occupies more space in his mind than it did before.

I never want Reed to abandon his job for me, but it would be nice if he could also prioritize me as well. My feelings are all over the place and it's hard to keep up with them. I should probably talk to him since communication is key, yet I'm terrified of hearing his honest thoughts.

But look what staying quiet lead to.

Everything my best friend said is valid and I'm glad she told me since I think part of me already knew what I should do but was unable to come to terms with it myself.

"You're right, Isa. As always." I sigh. "Reed said he's free tonight and asked me to come over to his place. We're going to have dinner and I'm probably staying over the night. I promise to talk to him about it then."

Isa gives me a devilish look and wags her eyebrows. I push her away playfully and add, "Just to eat dinner, nothing else."

"You can have fun, but remember to talk to him first," Isa teases as she gives me another smirk.

I roll my eyes but my wide smile shows how much I love her humor. Isa places her hand on my arm and says, "But all jokes aside, you are hot stuff and Reed is lucky to have you, Lia. Don't forget that."

I nod and hug Isa again. "I love you."

She hugs me back and replies, "Love you too."

"That is not an option. There are too many things we need to—" I hear Reed talking on the phone through his partially closed bedroom door.

Reed cooked me his famous spaghetti with white sauce and clams. It tasted delightful as always and we were chatting together like old times until his phone rang. My boyfriend gave me an apologetic look as he accepted the call and has been in his room since. It must be urgent since he wouldn't have taken the call otherwise.

Ten minutes later and he was still on the line so I started cleaning up. The walls of Reed's apartment are not too thick so even if I cannot hear everything, I heard enough to know it's not good news. Dinner was going so well, I almost forgot I need to have a talk with him. I convince myself again that even though I might ruin the night, we are in desperate need of a heart-to-heart.

As I finish drying the last dish and put it away in the cabinet, Reed comes back out to the living room. He eyes the clean dining table and then at me with a somber expression. I set the drying towel back down and make my way over to him.

Reed runs a frustrated hand through his hair. "I'm sorry you had to clean up after me again. I didn't mean for us to get interrupted. I know I keep saying it, but I'm sorry, Lia."

I shake my head and brush my hand over his cheek. "It's ok, Reed. More importantly, is everything alright?"

Reed wraps his arms around my waist and he sighs as he says, "Our publishing house has been marketing and hyping the release of five highly anticipated books from our new batch of debut authors. We just got wind one of the books were leaked online. We don't even know how this happened or who would make such a big mistake like this. And despite taking down the book, it was up for two hours so numerous people already had time to read it. It was decided our best course of action is to rush that book's launch to ride the buzz from this mishap. So now we are in charge of finding another book to release with the previous other four." My boyfriend looks away before cautiously meeting my eyes again, "The good news is I already have a new author's book in mind. The bad news is I need to fly over to New York to oversee the preparation of the new author's book. I leave in two days and won't be back until Thanksgiving Day."

My hands automatically drop to my side and I take a step back from him. "That's the day of our four-year anniversary."

Reed closes our distance as he holds onto my forearms and pleads with me, "I know and I'm so sorry, Lia. I tried pushing for an earlier date I can come back, but they wouldn't listen. And since I'm the new editorial director, it's my job to deal with situations like this. I promise I will make it back on time for our anniversary."

My mouth feels dry and I can't even form a fake smile. The part of me trying to be hopeful and positive tells me Reed's right. We might not get to spend the whole day together, but at least we'll get a few hours. Then again, similar to all the previous incidents before, I'm afraid Reed might not arrive back on time.

It is just an anniversary date so it's not the end of the world if he doesn't celebrate it with me. Nonetheless, I have this gut feeling things won't be the same between us anymore if he does not show up and I can't fathom the slightest chance of that happening.

I press my hand on Reed's chest and look him straight in his eyes. "I know you've always been very dedicated to your job and even more so after the promotion. That's wonderful and I will always support you in everything you do. Missing and cancelling last minute on dates is fine as long as you have a good reason for it, which you did every time. I'm not as angry as I am concerned. I'm worried about you, Reed. Are you really ok?"

Reed returns my gaze but his brows are furrowed and his face is angled more towards one side. "What do you mean? Of course I am fine."

I give my boyfriend a knowing yet pained smile as I gesture around his apartment. "You have a whole individual closet dedicated to Mr. Clean and other cleaning supplies. You are not a messy person. I've seen you busy before but never like this. Your apartment was a mess, you lost weight, and there were dark circles under your eyes until recently. I'm scared you are pushing yourself too hard."

My voice comes out higher and more emotional than I meant for it too. I take another step back and cross my arms because I need some physical distance between us for me to be able to say the next words out loud.

"Is there something going on that you're not telling me? You naturally put your all in everything you do, but you've been exhausting yourself to the bone. Whatever the reason is, it's consuming you. I don't know what to do, but I'm here for you, Reed. You can talk to me about anything." I lift up the necklace he gave me around my neck for him to see and continue on, "I appreciate the gift and the Audi joy ride, but I don't want any of those things if it means you aren't here. I just want you here with me. That's all I want. You, Reed."

With a single step, he shatters the gap I created and with his hands–which are almost the size of my face–he wipes away tears I didn't even know were falling. His lips touch mine with care like he's holding a fragile piece of glass that can slip out of his hands at any time.

When he pulls away, he rests his hands on my face as he whispers in a husky voice, "I'm sorry for making you worry, Lia. It's been a rough past few weeks, but I promise to get myself together and I'll be better."

Reed showers me with kisses on my forehead, cheeks, and nose making me giggle uncontrollably. My guard goes down and a few seconds later, he has me in his arms carrying me bridal style. He spins me around before bringing me to his bedroom. My boyfriend sets me down on his bed and kisses me again. This time his kiss is harder as if he's pouring all his feelings into a single kiss before pulling away.

"I love you, Lydia Zhang," he says before kissing me again.

The three magic words that kept me from falling apart a few years back continues to hold me together. In his arms and with his love, I feel so happy and completely at ease. All my previous doubts and worries washes away with my fallen tears.

We spend the rest of the night getting lost in each other's eyes and I forget that despite Reed's sincere apologies, he never actually did give me a real answer or explanation...yet I willingly let it pass without further question.

Chapter 12

Weather Report: Snow comes early this year in New York City. All flights to and out of New York will be delayed. Please sit tight, everyone, until the snow lightens up and stay warm on Thanksgiving evening.

The news app on my phone screen is covered when I receive an incoming call.

"I saw the news," my best friend immediately says the second I pick up the phone. Her voice is coated with worry as she asks, "Do you want company? I can drive back and we can eat another round of Costco chicken at home. Just the two of us."

Every Thanksgiving since Isa and I became the best of friends, we would buy a Costco feast consisting of roasted chicken, cobb salad, pecan pie—along with chocolate chip, white chocolate chip with nuts, and oatmeal cookies–to eat at our home. Even if both of us can't cook, we can still have a festive Thanksgiving dinner. If Reed and my anniversary date ever ended up being on the actual Thanksgiving Day, it became a tradition for Isa and me to celebrate the holiday a day or two early together.

My best friend's thoughtfulness warms my heart and I don't have to try too hard to sound upbeat. "It's alright, Isa. You go have fun celebrating your first Thanksgiving with Jackson and his family. Eat lots of food and enjoy yourself."

"I don't think Jackson and his family will mind if you celebrate with us. I promise you won't be the third wheel or anything."

I laugh at the bizarre yet tempting suggestion. "Nah, I'm good. I think I'm going to head home in a bit. We still have leftovers from yesterday's feast so I'm probably going to eat all of that and rewatch *Turkey Drop*."

"Fine, that sounds fun enough for me to hang up. But don't hesitate to call me if you change your mind. I'm here for you," Isa reminds me and I can practically see her adorable smile as if she was physically here with me now.

"I will. Thank you," I reply and we end the call.

This is not how I pictured Thanksgiving Day to be. Reed and I were supposed to spend tonight throwing darts at balloons full of paint, kinda like the scene in *The Princess Di-*

aries with Mia and her mom. I had everything prepared and was waiting to hear back from Reed, but then he called about his flight being delayed by the snow. The earliest he will be back is tomorrow morning, but our anniversary would be over by then. Reed profusely apologized over and over again, promising he would make it up to me.

The Lia a few months ago would have readily told Reed it was ok and I couldn't wait to see him when he comes back. The Lia now said what old Lia would have said but without any ounce of sincerity. I didn't want Reed to go to New York. I am well aware it was a poor timed work emergency and he couldn't not go, but from the way things played out, I should have known better. I am disappointed in myself for not foreseeing this would inevitably happen and still being miserable over it.

Not wanting my hard work to go to waste, I put on my large plastic poncho–which makes me double over laughing every time I see myself in it–and begin hurling darts. Considering I am only four feet away from the dart board, I would like to believe I have hit a bullseye at least once by now, but no. As I continue to miss the targets, everything on the dart board blurs altogether and I'm not sure where to aim anymore. Giving up my feeble attempt to land a mark, I take off my poncho and set it back on the table before sinking onto the floor.

I should feel angry at the snow for preventing Reed from coming home. Or angry at the person or whatever caused the author's book to be leaked in the first place. But in the end, I can't help but feel the most anger toward Reed.

I am—was worried about him overworking, but all that is long gone. Right now, I am so mad at him for not being here on our four-year anniversary. Throughout this year, Reed has never once kept his word and I let it slide for far too long.

Time and time again, I let him get away with missing dates and still continued to prioritize him in my life when he never did the same. I tried so hard to keep us from falling apart. I loved him with all my heart. I did everything I could. So why isn't it enough?

Why couldn't I be enough?

Tears stream down my face, similar to how the paint would have if the dart hit the balloon. I think I finally reached my limit. I can't forgive Reed another time. Yet the most disturbing sickening part is if I see those dreamy brown eyes and charming smile–that makes me weak in the knees–right this moment, I would forget exactly why I was ever anything but content in the first place.

One look from Reed is all I would need to fall under his spell again and willingly give him my heart to break once more.

My ugly crying echoes across my studio walls so loud, it

takes me a few seconds to realize there is a vague knocking sound on my door. Has the world taken pity on me and finally answered my prayers? Hope rushes through me and I'm up and back on my feet dashing to the door in a flash. My tears still blur my vision but they don't stop me from flinging the door wide open and wrapping my arms around him.

"Reed, you're here! I missed you so much! I'm sorry I ever doubted you," I say as I tighten my grip on my boyfriend.

Reed's here.

He came back to me. Everything can go back to the way it was and everything will be ok again.

The earlier anger I felt simmers down, leaving only relief and joy to have my boyfriend within my reach. He stiffens at my touch and doesn't immediately put his arms around me like I thought he would. He must not want to contaminate me with airport germs, but I couldn't care less. In this moment, nothing else matters except Reed. A few more seconds pass and then I begin to notice my head reaches a little below his shoulders.

That's not right.

Whenever we hug, my head is always aligned with Reed's shoulders. We are on even ground and his shoes are flat too. That's strange. And for some reason, his usual scent of cedar wood is not present. Instead, the scent of lavender and citrus fills my nose.

Oh no.

Panic shocks me from my lovesick daze and I retreat a few steps back. When my vision adjusts itself–to my utter horror–Connor stands before me. I can't even admire the denim over denim look he is rocking–with his denim shirt jacket over jeans–because I'm too busy internally yelling at myself for not realizing my mistake sooner.

Judging from my friend's expression, I don't think he's mad but more surprised and confused? I'm not sure and can't even ponder what he's thinking because all I want to do is slam the door and bury myself in a cocoon. Embarrassing moments are kind of my thing, but this is unbelievable. I've officially hit the point of no return with my cringe-tier level of embarrassing myself in front of this guy. Never in my life did I wish to be swallowed up by the earth more than this moment now.

"Sorry," Connor tells me with apology written all over his face which I can feel deep in my heart.

Why is he apologizing? He did nothing wrong. If any-thing, Connor's the innocent party or more like victim in this. I launched myself at him and being the nice guy he is, he didn't push me away.

I frantically shake my head and say, "No, don't apologize. I should be the one apologizing. I'm sorry. I mistook you for

R—"

Fear and pain are relentless as they come crashing down on me all at once. The fact that it was not my boyfriend at the front door really means his flight is delayed and he won't be back until tomorrow. Which means I really would have to end things the next time I see him. He keeps letting me down and as much as it tears my heart to shreds, I can't keep dragging things on like this. Just the realization of this makes me unable to speak his name aloud.

"Someone else," I continue after a beat. "I'm sorry for assaulting you earlier. That was totally my fault. I'm really sorry."

Connor surveys me like he's trying to decipher the reason for my disheveled and totally not ok appearance before grinning at me. "Don't worry, I won't press any charges. It's Thanksgiving after all."

Laughter erupts from me after hearing his corny joke. I can see him crack a smile from the corner of my eyes and I can't help but be grateful for his presence. After crying so much, it feels really good to laugh a real laugh.

"Thanks." I smile and wipe away the remaining tears from my eyes with the back of my hands. Trying to sound casual, I ask, "So what brings you here?"

"My family and I are celebrating Thanksgiving over at my parents' house. We ran out of chives so I'm grabbing some from the youth center since all the grocery markets nearby are closed at this hour. I saw your studio lights on so I thought I'd drop by and wish you a Happy Thanksgiving," Connor answers as he puts his hands in his back pockets.

I smile and say, "Happy Thanksgiving to you too."

We stand there awkwardly waiting for the other person to make the first move. Connor is being considerate and holding back from asking me the reason for my tear-stained face. I'm sure he's worried about me since if I too, saw a friend in need, I would definitely not leave until I made sure they were ok.

But I can't talk about it yet.

The wound in my heart is still fresh and I'm not confident I can control my emotions well enough to talk level headedly. So instead, I explain what I can. I move away from the door so he can walk in to see the dart board full of balloon paint. I gesture to it and say, "I'm heading back home after cleaning up."

Connor stares at the floor and is silent for some time before asking in a soft voice, "Would you like to come over for dinner by any chance?"

"What?" I say in disbelief even though I heard him the first time.

"My whole family is going to be there. We celebrate and eat Thanksgiving dinner together every year. There is so much food that we usually have leftovers which lasts us for the whole week. You should come."

A small part of me always longed to know how a normal family celebrates Thanksgiving. Hearing how often Connor fondly talks about his family, I am curious how they are in person. But the last time I saw Connor, he basically confessed he sees me as more than a friend. Even though we never overstepped the boundaries of friendship, I'm not sure if me going to his parents' house to celebrate Thanksgiving with his family is a good idea.

As if reading the hesitation on my face, Connor adds, "I promise it's just a Thanksgiving dinner as friends. Nothing more. You can come if you want, but you don't have to if you don't want to."

"Can I really go? Won't I be intruding?" I ask in a small voice.

Connor brightens and replies, "I'll be back here in ten minutes."

Chapter 13

"This is your parents' house?"

Did I say house? That's incorrect. It's a freaking mansion! There is a black gate protecting the entire land and a massive water fountain decorating the front of the building. I thought Connor's condo was nice, but his parents' living quarters are on a whole new level and I haven't even gone inside yet. My mind is still overwhelmed by the fantabulous sight so I almost don't hear Connor's answer.

"Yeah. I used to live here too until a few years ago. Come on, let's head inside." My friend grins as he leads me to the front porch.

"Are you sure it's ok I'm here, Connor? I know I agreed to come and we're already here and all, but this might be a bad idea on second thought. I'm not in the best outfit and I also didn't bring a housewarming gift. What if your parents and family don't like me?" I ask nervously wrapping my cardigan tighter around me.

I dressed to throw darts at paint balloons. The dark blue cardigan was thrown on top of my black T-shirt and ripped jeans to make my outfit look less casual and more casual chic. I am not dressed in the proper attire one would wear to meet a friend's family, much less a rich friend's rich family. And if things couldn't get any worse, I come bearing no gifts and would be imposing on their hospitality instead.

Great, the odds are so in my favor.

Connor gives me a relaxed smile. "I already gave them a heads up I'm bringing over a friend so it's no surprise. And we have so much food prepared it's actually better if you come empty-handed. My family are really chill and they enjoy the extra company. You have nothing to be nervous about, Lia. They're going to like you. You should be more worried if they'll let you out of their sight after meeting you."

Hearing his response–joking or not–my breathing becomes more steady and the tension on my shoulders relaxes. Connor looks away from me and says ever so softly, "And you always look beautiful, no matter what you wear."

Come to think of it, this is the first time my friend ever straight out complimented me on how I look. He usually kept things between us strictly platonic and never once commented on my appearance or anything that implies he like likes me at all. As much as I shouldn't, I blush a little at his compliment. My traitorous heart can't help but skip a beat after knowing that's how he honestly thinks of me.

Before I can go further down the rabbit hole, Connor inserts the key and opens the front door. We walk in taking off our shoes and a woman with a slick black bob and model-like frame greets us.

"Good, you're back. We thought the chives would never arrive." The beautiful woman's tone is light so I know she's kidding as she takes the jar from Connor before giving him a hug. He laughs and hugs her back. The woman and I make eye contact and she raises her eyebrows at him before turning back to me. "You must be Lia. I'm Karissa. Emily's mother and this guy's older sister." Karissa lightly bumps her brother's shoulder and offers her hand to shake.

I shake her hand and say, "Hi, it's very nice to meet you. Thank you for having me over."

"Of course. Emily raves about how much she loves her art class. It's the only class she complains is too short."

I smile at the compliment. "That's really kind of her to say. Emily is a joy to have in class so I'm happy to hear that."

As if on cue, Emily with her braids and checkered red dress comes skipping from the living room and then loops her little arms around her mother. "I caught you, Mommy!"

Karissa lets out a warm motherly laugh—a laugh I think only mothers can make—and says in a loving tone, "Yes, you did, sweetie. And look who's here."

Emily looks up and claps her tiny hands together. "Yay! Ms. Lia and Uncle Connor are here!"

"Dinner's almost ready," Andrew calls out as he walks over to pat his daughter's head.

Although Andrew and I are not well acquainted, I know him because it's usually him who drops Emily off to class. We've never talked to each other individually except the normal formality greetings, but I guess he's the third closest person I know in this family gathering.

"Right. I'll bring the chives to Mom now," Karissa says as she gives us a little wave.

Andrew and Emily lead us to the dining room. Numerous family photographs hang on the walls making the long hallway appear even longer. The savory scent of turkey and Thanksgiving dinner food already welcomed me at the front entrance, but my brain couldn't fully believe it until we finally reach the dining room.

Connor was not kidding when he said there will be lots of food. The round lazy Susan table carries so much food I worry if its legs can hold so much weight. The plump turkey is right smack in front of the table with cream of corn, spinach, bread rolls, green bean casserole, sweet potatoes, and baked potatoes surrounding it. Still on the table but off to the side is a steaming pot of clam chowder and corn bread adjacent to it.

My mouth is practically watering at this point and I try my best not to drool. The sight is so lovely, I think I can die out of pure happiness just by staring at the feast before me. From the corner of my eye, I see an elderly woman a few inches shorter than me wearing the cutest bright purple sweater entering the room. She holds a matching purple scarf in her hands and is about to put it around her neck, but it slithers down onto the floor. I hurry to pick it up and hand it to her before she bends down.

The elderly woman thanks me with a sweet smile and it takes me a moment to realize she spoke in Cantonese. Sometimes because I am so used to speaking Chinese and English interchangeably, I have to make a conscious effort to speak complete English in front of other people. I return the smile and then realize I have yet to introduce myself.

I bow in respectful greeting before responding in Cantonese, "Hello. I am Connor's friend, Lia."

The older woman nods approvingly. "Pretty, has manners, and can speak Cantonese. Very good." She then switches over to English and fluently says, "My grandson is single and ready to mingle."

She winks at me and I manage to keep my snort laugh in. I met Connor's grandma only a few seconds ago but she has so much personality that it's impossible not to immediately adore her. Connor–who apparently witnessed the whole interaction–stands there rigidly as his ears turn a shade of pink.

He interrupts our conversation as he clears his throat, "Ma Ma, we're just friends and Lia has a boyfriend."

"Who has a boyfriend?" A woman who looks only a few years older than Karissa asks as she walks out–of what I'm assuming to be the kitchen–carrying a big glass bowl of Caesar salad.

An older man with a clean-shaven stubble comes out after her holding utensils and plates. They set everything down on the table before walking towards us.

Connor uses his hand to gesture to the respective parties as he says, "Mom, Dad. This is Lia. Lia, this is my mom and dad."

Upon closer inspection, I can see where both Connor and Karissa get their good looks from. Mr. and Mrs. Li are both so good-looking, they practically radiate sunlight when they're together. And I have to say, Mr. Li is fire emoji hot. He has short well-groomed black hair with minor strands of white, a sharp jawline, and dark brown eyes that can practically see into your soul. He exudes so much Daddy vibes and I'm all for it.

Connor is basically the younger version of his father but mixed with his mom's gentle mannerisms and smile which softens his features to be somewhere between a boyish man and not yet Daddy material like his dad. Mrs. Li, like Karissa, can totally be on the front cover of a Vogue magazine. Her voluminous black hair is tied in a loose braid and her sharp nose along with flawless skin makes me wonder what type of products she uses.

The entire Li family are full of visuals and I feel like a freaking potato next to them.

"Hi, Mr. and Mrs. Li. Thank you for allowing me to come to your home," I greet them with a slight bow to show my respect towards my elders.

"It's nice to finally meet you, Lia. Our son and Emily have told us so much about you." Mr. Li nods at me good naturedly.

"We are happy to have you here, Lia dear. Aside from Jackson, Connor doesn't have any other friends so I'm glad to finally meet one," Mrs. Li beams as she pats me gently on the arm.

"Seriously, Mom? Did you have to say that last part?" Connor asks as he covers his eyes in embarrassment.

"I'm just telling the truth, sweetheart." Mrs. Li smiles playfully at Connor before saying, "But, enough chatter. We all must be famished. Let us eat first."

"Ms. Lia, sit next to me!" Emily chirps from her seat.

I smile, happy to sit next to the adorable child. Connor

pulls out the chair on my right and everyone else takes their seat. Mr. Li hands the knife and fork to his wife who then proceeds to swiftly cut the turkey.

Once everyone has a mountain plate of food, Mr. Li holds out his cup of apple cider and offers a simple toast, "Happy Thanksgiving, everyone!"

I notice all the drinks on the table are non-alcoholic drinks. As if reading my thoughts, Connor leans towards me and whispers, "My family doesn't normally drink. Our line of work requires us to keep our minds sharp so we do our best to stay sober. Most of our family events contain only non-alcoholic beverages like cider or tea."

It pleases me to know this about the Li family. I can relax and don't have to worry about dealing with people pestering me to drink. I smile at Connor and then lift my apple cider cup along with everybody else and cheer "Happy Thanksgiving!"

The feast not only looks appetizing, but it also tastes exquisite. On a normal basis, I don't usually eat turkey skin. I'm more of a meat kind of girl, but this turkey skin is so crisp and juicy that I savor every bite of it. The turkey itself is tasty and the meat is tender without being too dry. The salad is so heavenly, I ate at least two rounds of it.

If I didn't need to save my stomach for other food, I'd probably go for a third plate. The corn bread is crunchy on the sides but it also melts in my mouth. It's taking all my will power to eat slowly and enjoy the food rather than stuffing everything in my mouth at once.

"How are you enjoying the food, dear?" Mrs. Li asks me with a bright smile.

The big spoon of baked potato I am chewing prevents me from answering right away. Not wanting to delay my response, I give a thumbs up with my left hand first before proceeding to wipe my mouth with a napkin. After I am sure I look like a proper human being again, I respond, "Everything is so delicious. Definitely one of the best meals I've ever had. Thank you, Mrs. Li."

"Don't be shy and feel free to eat till your heart's content." Mrs. Li smiles with her eyes closed and I swear I see angels floating around her.

I nod in thanks and continue to eat merrily as Mr. Li comments, "So, Lia, Connor tells us you're a very talented artist."

I direct my gaze to my friend who doesn't meet my eyes as he is seemingly too preoccupied drinking his clam chowder. Turning my attention back to Mr. Li, I say, "I'm not sure about the talented part, but I do draw and paint for a living."

"Nonsense," Mrs. Li chimes in. "Our son showed us your art pieces displayed for this year's city annual art gallery. Both pieces are so beautiful and stunning to look at."

"And we heard you had your artwork featured there two years in a row. That is very impressive," Mr. Li adds with a big grin before asking, "How different is studying art in college than being an artist out on your own?"

I pause eating my baked potato. It's a harmless question and I'm really touched Connor showed his parents my art. It makes me really giddy inside to know other people like my art. I swallow the lump of nervousness building up in my stomach. Flashbacks from the disastrous Wang family dinner causes me to shift in my seat.

The last time I directly mentioned I quit college in front of them, they lost it. I'm afraid of that very same reaction from Connor's family. The Lis are on a completely different financial status than most people, but from what I've seen, they are not obnoxious or snobby at all. They are all very nice and I can see where Connor gets his kind nature from.

I don't plan on lying or telling half-truths to his family, but it's been a while since people have been genuinely interested in talking about me and I start to feel anxious.

"Lia?"

Connor's gentle voice wakes me up from my daze and I snap to attention. Shaking my head, I say, "Oh, um I studied business in college, but didn't pursue art seriously until after I dropped out."

Every muscle in my body tenses for the impending awkwardness that will surely ensue, but to my surprise, Mr. Li rejoices, "Way to go, kiddo!" I look at Mr. Li in disbelief thinking I misheard him. He lets out a hearty laugh and notes, "Some people go to college because their occupation requires a college education and others go just to discover what they want to do. It's good that you knew what you wanted to do and went for it."

"I went to college to get my degree even though most of what I know came from working hands-on in the family business. But I am thankful for the people we met there and the connections we made," Karissa contributes as she directs a flirtatious gaze to her husband. Andrew winks at her and then she adds, "And you are really skilled at what you do, Lia. Your paintings are absolutely mesmerizing. One of our new tenants are in talks of renting our space to open up a new art gallery featuring a variety of different artwork and they are always on the hunt for more artists. I don't want to talk business during dinner, but I would love to give him your number if you are interested."

"Yes, that would be great. Thank you!"

Even though I got my hands full working on webtoons and teaching an art class, I always somehow squeeze in my own drawing and painting time too. It's my passion and I would love the opportunity to showcase my artwork to even more people.

"Connor, did you ever find a painting to hang on your dining room wall?" Grandma Li asks raising an eyebrow.

"Not yet. I didn't have time to find a suitable picture," Connor replies.

"How about you ask Lia to paint something for you?" Grandma Li turns to me with a mischievous look in her eyes, paired with another one of her sweet smiles.

"What an excellent idea!" Mrs. Li agrees clapping her hands together.

Connor darts a panicked look my way and says, "Only if Lia is interested of course."

I let out a laugh at Connor's consideration and the mere coincidence of that thought. "I noticed the empty space at your dining room and thought it would be a great idea to paint you something. I wanted it to be a surprise, but since we're on the topic, I hope you don't mind the spoiler."

Connor looks at me bewildered as if that was the last thing he expected me to say.

"And how many times were you at Connor's condo before noticing the empty patch of space?" Karissa inquires innocently as her brother glares in her direction.

I am saved from answering when Grandma Li says, "Oh, how wonderful of you, Lia. Connor, you should invite her to the Christmas party as a thank you for her kindness."

"Christmas party?" I ask confused.

"It's our family tradition to celebrate Christmas every year with a party on Christmas Day. It's a big party because most of our family and friends attend," Connor answers clueing me in.

"There's a bunch of food there too. If you liked today's feast, you will be blown away at the Christmas party," Andrew remarks raising his glass of cider.

"Yeah, Ms. Lia should go to the Christmas party!" Emily advocates as she bounces in her seat with so much enthusiasm.

"I heard you are best friends with Isabel. We're close friends with Jackson and his family so I'm sure he will invite her along too," Karissa mentions winking at me.

Mrs. Li smiles at me warmly, "We would love for you to attend, Lia dear!"

"Yes, you should come, Lia. The more the merrier!" Mr. Li affirms with an approving chin nod.

I abruptly get up from my chair and announce, "I need to use the bathroom."

There is an extremely long interval in the jolly atmosphere and guilt begins gnawing at me. My head is tilted down so I can't see their reactions and hopefully they won't notice me biting the inside of my mouth to quell the trembling of my lips.

"Of course, Lia dear." Mrs. Li is the first one who breaks

the awkwardness I caused in the air. "The bathroom is down the hallway to the left."

I nod in thanks and hurry out of there as fast as I can, but halt when I hear Emily's cheery voice. "Come back soon, Ms. Lia! We still have dessert to eat!"

Emily's radiant personality and eagerness to learn have always been such a delightful addition to the class and I am so grateful that her ray of sunshine is dissipating some of the fog I brought, whether it be intentional or not.

"Ok, I will. Thank you," I say with my utmost buoyant voice I can muster without sparing a glance back.

Finally finding the bathroom and closing the door, I crouch down on the floor and lean against the cold wood with my arms wrapping around my knees. Tears brim my eyes and I dab at them gently with my cardigan sleeve. I feel terrible for ruining the night. Everyone in the Li family were so welcoming and I'm the worst house guest ever. They showed me so much undeserved kindness and they made me—a complete stranger—feel right at home.

I don't want to disappoint them with my refusal, but there are so many reasons why I shouldn't attend. First of all, Re—R—

He and I usually spend Christmas Day together so I want to check in with his schedule beforehand. But then again, would we even have plans anymore? And if I do go to the party, I don't want to have another mental breakdown similar to what I am having now. It feels foreign to be around genuinely nice people who don't fake their smiles and lie about compliments.

I enjoy being in the company of Connor's family, but I'm afraid if I get so used to this positive energy, I won't be able to live without it. The people I met before have taught me to freeze my heart and always be on guard for an attack, but the Lis are penetrating my fortress with their warmth and love.

They are all so sweet and the type of people I would have wanted to meet earlier in my life, but now, after my parents and R—Re—R—Reed...I don't think I can open up my heart to any more people and risk going through another heartbreak.

After making sure my eyes no longer look teary and my face can form a natural enough smile, I exit the bathroom.

"Hey."

I see Connor waiting for me near the start of the hallway.

"Hey." I return his small smile with the upward tilt of my mouth and twist the ends of my cardigan before needing to spit out an apology. "I'm sorry about what happened, Connor. Your family is so wonderful, and I'm sorry I was so rude. I'm so sorry."

"No one thought you were rude. If anything, I'm sorry we put you on the spot like that. That was not our intention."

"No, don't be sorry! I just—I'm just—I...I'm just a wreck," I breathe out. "It's not you or any of your family's fault...it's just me. I'm sorry."

Connor puts his hands a few inches below my shoulders and his voice is soothing as he says, "Hey, it's ok. No one thought much of what happened. We're all good."

His eyes search mine and even though no words are exchanged, I see the recognition in his eyes. Connor understands why I freaked out earlier but doesn't press me for an actual explanation.

Instead, he gives me a sunny smile and tilts his head towards the dining room saying, "If you're ready, let's head back in. I think you'll love the dessert selection Jackson prepared for us a few hours earlier."

I smile and follow him as he leads the way back to the place I wish I could call my home, to the people I wish I could consider as my family.

"Perfect timing," Karissa observes when she spots Connor and me.

"Yeah. We were just about to cut the pie," Andrew says.

"Ms. Lia, you have to try Uncle Jackson's pumpkin pie! It's so good!" Emily beams with sparkles in her eyes.

Grandma Li waves us over with a big smile, "Come, sit."

Mr. Li hands me a plate of pumpkin pie Mrs. Li cut. "Enjoy, sweetheart."

I take the plate from him with two hands and thank him and Mrs. Li. They both give me a warm smile. We partake in the desserts as if the previous tension never happened. My eyes drift to Connor's and he meets my gaze. He gives me a reassuring smile which seems to reaffirm his words earlier.

His family really does not hold any lingering bad feelings against me or my brisk retreat earlier. Their ongoing kindness towards me thoroughly touches my heart, allowing me to fully enjoy devouring the rest of the meal comfortably.

By the time we finish eating, I am so full. Like one hundred and ten percent full. I probably shouldn't have stuffed that extra slice of pumpkin pie, apple pie, or crème brulee, but it was worth it. I'm about to get up from my seat to help with the cleanup, but Emily pulls my hand lightly to get my attention.

"Ms. Lia, we're going to watch *Shang-Chi and the Legend of the Ten Rings* after dinner. Stay a little longer and come watch with us!"

I meet the rest of Connor's family's eyes. I would feel awful for troubling the Li family any longer with my presence, but I don't have a good excuse to say no to Emily.

"Oh, did you watch the movie already?" Karissa asks before adding, "We can always pick out something else to watch."

Everyone else in the room smiles encouragingly, overwhelming me with so many happy emotions. I finally break and give in to my inner desire to stay.

"I haven't watched it yet. If you don't mind me staying longer, I would love to watch the movie with everyone."

"Of course we don't mind, dear! We'll watch it together as a family then," Mrs. Li declares with a big smile.

"I'll go set up the TV," Karissa offers.

"And I'll prepare the popcorn," Grandma Li announces following Karissa out of the dining room.

Emily takes my hand and guides me along as Mrs. Li calls out, "Boys, we'll meet you in the theater room when you're done."

Mr. Li, Connor, and Andrew who are all three already cleaning up nod in unison. Mrs. Li slips her arm in my free arm and says, "Let's go, Lia dear."

"Are you sure? I can help with the clean up as well."

"The boys can handle it and you're our guest. You just sit back and enjoy." Mrs. Li gives me a loving smile as the three of us walk together.

The Li mansion has their own freaking theater room. Judging from the size of their mansion, that was probably self-explanatory, but it still blows my mind. The room is enormous resembling an actual theater with a big TV screen in the center and an eight-seat sofa along with a few other individual chairs. Watching *Shang-Chi and the Legend of the*

Ten Rings is as marvelous as I expected. The whole cast did a fabulous job acting and I loved the movie, but Tony Leung is the real MVP for me.

I admit I already had a minor crush on him when he starred in *The Heaven Sword and Dragon Sabre* in the 1986 drama series, no doubt my favorite remake. No one can portray Cheung Mo-Kei's good-hearted nature and natural modesty as well as Tong Leung. He's such a heartthrob in that show and he totally reminded me of it in this film. But aside from the overall greatness of the movie, the large HD TV screen and sound effects amplified from the Li's theater room made the experience of watching the movie even better.

As I make my way back from the ladies room—finally actually needing to go—I take the time to stop and look at the Li family photos framed along the hallway. It's apparent in the photographs Connor and Karissa both had their good looks even in their childhood and teenage years.

And these pictures further prove how Mr. and Mrs. Li aged like fine wine. Their additional years of age somehow only seemed to enhance their already good looks. There are many happy pictures of the Li family and even some with Jackson and his family as well. Maybe because my family is no longer like this or ever was, it is really heartwarming and fascinating to see a family this tight knit.

"Our family loves taking pictures," Mrs. Li remarks coming up next to me.

"I can tell." Her lips form into a smile at my joke and I say, "Thank you so much for letting me join tonight's dinner especially under such short notice, Mrs. Li...and I want to apologize for my behavior earlier. I'm sorry."

Mrs. Li casually brushes off my apology with a wave of her hand. "There's nothing to apologize for. Besides my son and granddaughter, I know the rest of us didn't get to spend as much time with you, but we are all really fond of you. I'm not sure why such a humble, thoughtful, and kind girl like you is spending Thanksgiving alone, but you are free to come over any time, Lia dear."

Her warm words and smile move my heart and I can't help but smile appreciatively. "Thank you, Mrs. Li."

Connor's mother raises her hands to gesture to the whole house and says, "And as you know, due to our family background, Karissa and Connor did not grow up like normal children. I know it was hard for them to make real connections with other people their age. I can rest assured with Karissa since she is very sociable and holds her own in a conversation. My son on the other hand, he is naturally very friendly to other people but also very guarded too. Aside from Jackson, Connor doesn't easily let other people in his inner circle. But every time Emily mentions you or he talks about this new friend of his, he beams like a kid opening presents on Christmas morning. Besides cooking, I've never seen him that happy talking about someone." Mrs. Li places a hand on my shoulder. Her touch is soft but I can feel the love and touch of a warmhearted mother. "Thank you for being a part of his life."

I shake my head. "I'm lucky to have Connor as a friend. We only met this past year, but he has helped me in so many ways and I can't thank him enough. He's a really good friend to me and I hope I am as good of a friend as he makes me out to be."

"He has never brought a friend over to our Thanksgiving dinner before," Mrs. Li points out with a not-so-subtle wink. "You must be very special in my son's eyes."

I laugh nervously but don't know how to respond to her comment. Fortunately, Mrs. Li doesn't expect to hear a response from me. Instead, she pulls me in for a hug. Her action surprises me so much, my body goes taut without meaning to.

Not minding my odd reaction, Mrs. Li says, "It is getting late now, dear. You should go on and head home. We had a magnificent time and would love to get to know you more, dear. Come visit us soon, ok?"

I don't remember the last time I was hugged by my mother or at least hugged with her sincerity and love. Being embraced by Mrs. Li, I feel all the warmth and love from a mother, something I didn't know I missed. Tears are welling up my eyes again and my throat tightens from the emotions I'm feeling. Not wanting to leave her hanging, I hug her back tentatively.

"I will." My voice is slightly muffled by her clothes and me holding back my tears but I feel Mrs. Li nod and hold me closer in her arms.

On our drive back, Connor asks, "Did you have a good time, Lia? I hope my family wasn't too much. They were just really excited to meet you."

"I had a really good time and it was great meeting them too." I smile before glancing over at Connor and finally confess, "When you saw me earlier tonight, I was pretty miserable. We were supposed to celebrate our four-year anniversary, but...Reed's flight got delayed so he's stuck in New York until tomorrow."

At a red light, I can feel Connor's gaze on me. I don't meet his eyes because some of the bitterness of that thought returns.

I shrug those negative feelings away and carry on, "But

because of you and your family, tonight ended up being a really good memory for me. Thanksgiving has always been a day to celebrate family and because most of the people I know don't have the best relationship with their parents, not to mention my own family, I never really thought much about the meaning of this holiday. My last experience at a family gathering was when I met Reed's family which ended in me finally gaining ten percent of their respect by beating them at mahjong."

"Only ten percent?" Connor asks with his eyebrows raised but eyes still on the road.

"Yup. That ten percent probably isn't worth it considering how their dislike for me increased tenfold," I reply with a small laugh. "But the point is, aside from Isa, I never really got the sense of having a real family. And tonight, I felt that. I felt really comfortable and at ease with your family. So thank you for inviting me over, Connor. Tonight was really fun."

We arrive at my studio and Connor pulls over. He turns to me and says, "My family adores you and I think they won't stop nagging me about your next visit for a while. And I can't blame them because I am looking forward to it as well." Connor gives me a soft boy-smile that makes my traitor heart skip more beats as he continues, "Anyways, I promised I'd invite you over for dinner as friends so I plan to stay true to that. It was nice having you over for Thanksgiving, friend.

See you when I see you, Lia Bears."

"Can you stay another three minutes?"

"Hmm?"

I exit the car and turn around. "I'll be back. Don't go yet."

Connor nods and I close the car door hurrying to my studio. In a few minutes, I return with a bag that covers only eighty percent of the surprise. He is waiting outside the car and I hand him the bag.

"It's nothing special, but I wanted to thank you for all the things you've done for me. I hope you like it."

Connor takes the gift with a wide smile like I handed him a treasure chest full of gold instead of a mere painting. His joy is so apparent and I can't help but smile at him.

"Can I look at it now?" he asks excitedly.

I nod and he gingerly takes out the painting from the bag. We are standing underneath the street lamppost so there is enough light to clearly see my painting of the Ratatouille dish with a window frame showing the nighttime sky of the Eiffel Tower in Paris. A little shadow of a rat with a chef's hat can be seen at the side. I was inspired to paint this after listening to Connor's story of how he knew he wanted to be a chef.

After a minute, he looks up from the painting and then at me. The first thing he says after studying the painting is, "I'm going to hang this up on my wall tonight."

I laugh. "It's late. You can hang it up tomorrow or some-thing."

Connor shakes his head fervently. "This masterpiece needs to be on display tonight. Any later would be overdue."

I roll my eyes playfully and lightly punch his arm. He laughs in response and I'm not sure how it's possible but his eyes seem to sparkle in the dark night. Connor smiles at the painting and then back at me.

"I love it, Lia. I love it a lot. Thank you."

When he utters those words and gives me such a genuine happy boy smile, glee and nausea envelop me as I finally understand what Mrs. Li meant about Connor lighting up like a kid on Christmas morning.

Chapter 14

"Lia, I know there's nothing I could say or do to make up for missing our anniversary yesterday. But I am really sorry," Reed says as he brushes soft circles on my hands with both of his.

He texted and called a few times in the morning, but I didn't respond. I was planning on replying. It's just I didn't know what to say so I kept pushing it back. I was hoping to avoid confrontation for a few more days, but the universe wasn't feeling generous today. Reed took me by surprise when he showed up at my studio right after art class ended. His timing is impeccable this time because I'm one hundred percent alone and free right now. If only his timing was this perfect when I wanted it to be.

He pulls me in a hug and I hear the desperation in his voice as he continues on, "Lia, I know you must be mad, but please say something."

My arms don't go around him like they usually do. They

dangle limply at my side as he continues to hold me. Reed's embrace has always been my comfort place. They were where I wanted to be during my best and worst days, but the touch I used to desire and miss lacks its usual magic now. I want to be surprised and regretful things have totally done a 180 but I can't.

Everything has been leading up to this. The sadness, disappointment, and anger I didn't want to admit to myself that I kept bottled up from all the times Reed flaked on me finally tips over. When it is clear Reed does not plan to let go of me until I say something, I lightly tap his arm.

"Please let go of me."

My treacherous heart aches a little seeing his hurt expression as he takes a step back, but I stomp down hard on my sympathetic feelings. There's no chickening out of this now.

Swallowing the lump in my throat, I declare, "I think we should break up."

Reed's hurt expression somehow morphs into an even more pained expression as his mouth parts in shock and horror flashes in his eyes. He takes a step towards me but I step back putting a hand up to stop him. Trying to keep the tears building up at bay and my voice from cracking, I state my reasoning.

"I can't do this anymore, Reed. I know you didn't want to miss our anniversary, but you did. Every time you missed a date or important event, it was always because of work. I get that, but I can't keep waiting for you like this."

"I know I haven't been there for a lot of things, but I promise you I have a good reason. I wanted to keep it a secret until later but seeing that I have messed up bad enough for you to suggest breaking up, I can't keep it a secret any longer," Reed responds in an unexpected calm voice.

"What are you talking about?"

"I want to bring you somewhere."

Reading the apparent confusion on my face, Reed tries again in a softer voice, "Please give me one last chance. I promise this will explain everything."

Against my better judgement, I let emotions take over logic. I follow Reed to his car and we drive in silence with only the radio to lighten the awkward atmosphere. We drive for about fifteen minutes until he slides into a driveway of an unfamiliar house. Reed gets out of the car and I step out before he can open the door for me. Upon closer inspection, I realize that the house is a two-story house painted bright white with the windows painted charcoal black.

The house is nothing extravagant and the design is basic, but that's exactly what I like about it.

Reed rummages his coat pocket for keys to open the door and then signals me to come inside. Even more lost at what's going on here, I catch up to him and enter the house. The floors are wooden and there is a flight of stairs right in front of the door leading to the second floor above. The house looks clean but aside from a few tables and cabinets, it is practically barren. Reed walks into what I assume to be the living room towards our right and I go in with him.

There is a fireplace in the center of the living room accompanied by a bay window and a cozy area big enough to fit a couch along with a few other furniture. The window captures the neighborhood view perfectly and provides natural lighting which gives off a very homey vibe. Further down the living room, I see the kitchen. The kitchen area is small but has all the necessities of a sink, refrigerator, and cabinets.

This is only the first floor of the space but I have to admit, this house is quite lovely. This is the type of house I always pictured myself living in if I ever saved enough to purchase one. Realizing Reed brought me here for a reason and still has not provided me with an explanation this entire time, I spin around to face him.

"Why did you bring me here?"

"What do you think about this house?" Reed asks with a smile.

"It's nice. Now answer my question, Reed," I say impatiently.

"This house is ours."

My jaw drops. "What?"

Reed has a pleased smile on his face like he's glad for my shock. "Well, soon to be ours. We've officially been dating for four years now, Lia. I'm serious about you. I can picture you in my future and us living together. That's why I bought this house. I want us to live here together."

"This house and all the other expensive items you've purchased recently must have cost a fortune! Be honest with me. How did you manage to afford all that? Did you ask for a loan?" I ask with a stern voice.

"Long ago, my grandfather bought a few stocks under Alex's and my name. After turning twenty-one, I finally had full control of the account and could do whatever I wanted with the money accumulated in there. I decided it was time I use some of that money for good use. I only paid the security deposit for this house and will pay for the rest once we finalize the purchase," Reed replies in a carefree tone.

I heard everything he said but my mind is still reeling from information overload. Reed mentioned that his favorite relative from his family was his grandfather because he's the only one who looked out for him. He told me his grandfather left some money under his name but I didn't know it was that much to afford a whole house. This was not the explanation I was expecting. I'm not even sure how I should feel right now. To summarize this past year, my boyfriend ghosted me to plan the ultimate surprise of purchasing a whole house and other expensive gifts to make me happy?

In a way, that is a pretty romantic gesture but why am I not more excited about this?

"I know this is a lot to take in. You can take your time with all of this. I just wanted to show you this so you know I am one hundred percent into our relationship. Breaking up is the last thing I want, and I'm sorry my work drove a wedge between us. That's finally done and over with. Nothing will ever get in the way of us again. I swear it," Reed promises with a determined glimmer in his eyes.

He reaches out for my hands and when I don't move away, he gently puts them on his chest. "You have your own art studio and your career is continuing to reach greater heights. It might not seem like it, but everything I did was for you, Lia. I just want to be a man who deserves you. I want to fulfill your dreams and go travel the world with you like you always wanted. And when we get bored of traveling, we can come back home. To our home. The two of us, always and forever."

Reed gets down on one knee and takes a small box from his jacket pocket. He opens the box revealing a mini-white gold diamond ring. My hands automatically go to my mouth to cover a gasp. Seeing my surprised expression, Reed chuckles.

"I wanted to propose to you with a fancier proposal but due to the sudden change of plans, I hope you can overlook it and still consider making me the happiest man alive. I want you to be the first person I see every day when I wake up. I want to be first person you think of when you have good news to share and be the arms you go to when you have a bad day. I want to shower you with goodnight kisses every night until you laugh and tell me to stop. Will you give me the honor of being by your side and marry me?"

Tears stream down my face and I can't help but hiccup sob. If I'm being honest, I'm not sure why exactly I'm crying. Reed is telling me all the things I longed to hear, to have someone love me so much that they want to spend the rest of their life with me. Marriage is something I never thought about. I always wanted it, but after my parents' divorce, I guess I never saw it as a possibility for my future.

In spite of everything, I was always hopeful. I hoped to meet someone one day who could change my mind on marriage and convince me we could have a long-lasting loving relationship.

Reed wipes my tears away with his thumbs but I can't look him in his eyes. Upon meeting Reed, I thought I found the one. He is perfect in so many ways and I love him, but he never brought up marriage before. I didn't know he was thinking about it until now. I don't know how to feel or what to do. He tilts my chin upwards causing me to have to meet his eyes. He gives me an understanding smile like he expected this response from me.

"I know this is very sudden and I'm sorry for overwhelming you like this. You don't have to answer me yet. I can wait until you're ready. I just needed to assure you that you are everything to me. I never want to lose you," Reed says as he kisses my forehead.

Still dumbfounded from everything, I only manage to nod in response as I hiccup sob again. Reed smiles and wraps his arms around me as he murmurs into my hair, "I love you, Lydia Zhang."

Chapter 15

"So what is the big news you wanted to tell me?" Isa asks in a robotic tone as I hear the sound of her long fingernail scrolling through her phone.

"I'll tell you in a minute once we remove our masks," I reply in the same robot tone as I finish inputting the last dialogue of the webtoon chapter I'm working on.

Every once a week, Isa and I put on face masks and sit on the couch. That's how we spend time together while doing self-care. We usually watch dramas or do our own thing without looking at each other. The thing about us wearing face masks is we cannot look at the other person with it on. It sounds bizarre but the second we do, Isa and I burst out laughing. Like how yawning is contagious, our laughter is infectious.

Once one of us laughs, the other person will follow laughing right after. Normally that's a great thing. But when wearing a face mask, that's the worst thing that can happen.

Having to constantly fix the face mask from shifting is such a hassle every time so we agreed to never look at each other when we have them on. I close my laptop and put it away just in time for the timer to ding. My face feels wet and sticky so I know the mask has done its job of revitalizing my skin.

"Ok, so what's the big news?" Isa asks again as she faces me with her legs crossed on the sofa.

My best friend is wearing the matching bestie bathrobe I got us for Christmas two years ago and has her hair in a bun. Isa already takes good care of herself on a normal basis so her skin looks flawless, but the face mask makes her skin glow even more. I know it's Isa's job to keep her appearance in perfect condition, but sometimes I am in awe at her beauty up close. Beauty, brains, and a sweetheart? Oh, Jackson, you lucky boy.

Remembering I still have not shared the news with my best friend, I clear my throat and take a deep breath. "Reed proposed to me."

"Reed proposed?" Isa gasps. "Oh, my holy gosh! Tell me everything."

After I finish telling Isa the whole story without missing any details, I am about to run my fingers through my hair but pause remembering I have a few clips on to hold up my baby bangs from touching the mask. I resort to fidgeting with my fingers instead until I feel a gentle hand over them.

"How are you feeling, Lia?" Isa asks in a worried voice.

I sigh. "I know Reed did everything for me and swore all the missing dates will not happen again, but I can't completely let go of all the bunched-up anger and hurt I feel from what happened. If I'd known why he was so motivated on working and getting the new promotion, I would have tried harder to convince him that I am more than happy with what we have now. I trust Reed has good intentions and wants the best for me, but I'm not sure I am ready to jump the gun and marry him yet."

"Reed said he could wait for your answer and you can take some time to think about it. No need to rush and give him a reply just yet," Isa reassures me as she pats my arm for support. "But that's not the only thing on your mind is it?" My best friend has a knowing gleam in her eyes and a small, pained smile. "You're also thinking about Connor. I know you said he was just a friend, but did your perspective of him change even a little bit after spending Thanksgiving with him and his family?"

I grab the nearest pillow and wrap it around my arms like a kid hugging a teddy bear. "Isa, why do you know me so well?"

She laughs. "How could I not know you, girl? We're besties. We were going to marry and die together if we did not find anyone by the time we reach thirty-five. We are still going to die together but now we have our own respective partners–maybe even two for you–so let's settle on burying ourselves next to each other instead."

I want to stuff my face in this pillow but the nutrients from the face mask I put on earlier is still drying so I pout instead. "Can we fast forward to the burial part so I can jump in a hole and never come out until both Reed and Connor forget I ever existed?"

Isa puts an arm around me and I rest my head on her shoulder. She rubs my arm soothingly. "There, there. It's alright, Lia. At least you are basically now one of those female MCs where you no longer worry about financial problems but only boy problems." I sob more and Isa says, "Sorry, too soon?"

I continue to sob whine louder but I slip up when I start to giggle. Isa laughs with me and we both break out into a full-on cackle. My best friend knows exactly what to say to get me out of my funk.

After our laughing fit, Isa looks at me with a serious expression. "Lia, I know you are still dating Reed, but you have to be honest with yourself. How exactly do you feel about Connor? If Reed was not in the picture, would Connor have a shot?"

I bite my lip. "I like hanging out with Connor. We have a lot in common and I really like him as a person. He is sweet, funny, and an excellent chef. I think I would like to date him if I wasn't dating Reed. But at the same time, I only started noticing Connor after he's been there all the times when Reed wasn't. What if I am confusing my gratitude for Connor as a friend with romantic feelings?"

Isa nods in understanding and gives me a comforting hand squeeze.

I smile and say bitterly, "Reed and I have been together for four years and you guys were my rock during the hardest times of my life. I know I mentioned breaking up with Reed, but there will always be a part of me who loves him and can't let him go. I still do love Reed a lot but a weird uncertain feeling forms in my heart whenever I think of accepting his marriage proposal...ugh...I just want to take a break from everything."

Isa snaps her fingers twice and I know a brilliant idea formulated in her mind. "Let's do just that."

"What?"

"Jackson and Connor invited me to go to their family's beach house over at Flaira Lakes this weekend. It is only an hour drive from the city and it could be like our mini-road trip. We'll stay there for two days and one night. It's winter but barbecues are perfect all year round. Lia, you should come. It will be the perfect time to get some space from Reed so you could think about everything with a clear mind and spending more time with Connor, might help you sort out your feelings for him. And if it doesn't, just take this trip as two besties having fun together at a luxurious beach house."

Feeling rejuvenated at the mere thought of a weekend getaway, I agree to it before I can argue with myself and before Isa could start singing "Paradise" by T-Max to further persuade me.

"You know what, Isa? Count me in."

Time away from the city–away from Reed–is exactly what I need right now. I need to have a few days to think things through and let go of all my problems. Ever since Thanksgiving, Connor and I barely had the chance to talk. I think this trip will really help me distinguish how exactly I feel towards him.

"Great, I'll let the boys know!" Isa claps her hands enthusiastically.

I give my bestie a big hug, "Thank you, Isa."

"Anytime, girl. Now, let's start packing!"

Chapter 16

Reed: "Do you have plans this weekend? I still have work on Saturday, but I'm free Saturday afternoon and all day on Sunday. Do you want to come over to my place and watch a movie?"

Me: "I'm going to be out of town this weekend with Isa and some friends."

Reed: "Where are you guys going?"

Me: "Flaira Lakes."

Reed: "Sounds fun. Raincheck for next weekend? Let me know. I want to see you again. Love you."

Me: Heart emoji.

I review my text exchange with Reed yesterday and sigh. Sometimes when I don't know what to say, a simple emoji is all I need to text to communicate my message. But this time, the emoji is used to conceal my inner turmoil without worrying the other party. Until I have a definite response to Reed's question, I don't plan on seeing him face to face.

I want to give him an answer to set things straight between us and not drag on any more of the "non-existent" existent tension between us. I shove my phone back in the pocket of my light blue spaghetti strapped beach dress that I am thrilled to finally have the opportunity to wear.

When I look up, I notice Connor standing a few feet away from me. His white collared button up summer shirt matched with beige khakis and sandals look great on him. With his whole ensemble going on, he would fit right in as one of the F4 boys in *Boys Over Flowers*.

"Oh, hey." My voice comes out a little jumpy since I am startled by his sudden presence.

Connor shoots me an amused grin that I'm sure can make any girl fall head over heels. "Isa and Jackson are going to play another round of mahjong if you want to join."

"I think I'll sit this one out. I'm still stuffed from the

barbecue so I'm going to take a stroll down the beach," I answer and head outside.

Although this beach house shares the ocean with others nearby, they are spread wide enough to not have to battle over beach territory with fellow neighbors. There is something about the clarity and ambiance of Kahala Beach that can't be beat, but I have to admit, the Flaira Lakes Beach view comes a close second.

Air here is humid but the accompanying cooling ocean breeze makes me thank myself for grabbing my cardigan before going down the stairs that lead directly to the ocean. The booming sound of waves brushing against the shore is roaring and I can feel the raw power of the water current.

If it weren't for the lights outside the house, the ocean would look like a dark abyss that can swallow everything in its sight right up. That thought alone is usually enough to make my legs tremble but today, it doesn't sound as intimidating. As I walk bare feet on the sand, I hear shuffling behind me.

"Do you mind if I join you?" I twirl around to see Connor behind me with a small smile.

I wave him over and we walk in silence before he asks, "Is there something on your mind, Lia?"

Taken aback at the accuracy and suddenness of Connor's question, I stop moving.

Connor turns back to me with an apologetic smile, "I don't want to pry or anything, but during the whole day, you looked like you were having fun but I could tell you were troubled by something. I just wanted to make sure you're ok. I'm here if you need to talk or want someone to listen."

I resume walking at my slow pace and Connor strides along next to me. He is a lot taller than me so I have a feeling he is purposefully taking smaller steps to match my snail pace. During this entire getaway, I had lots of fun. The four of us sang K-pop karaoke with the windows down in Jackson's Jeep and I almost died from laughing too hard when his voice cracked at the high notes of "We Like 2 Party" by Big Bang. We played beach volleyball, made sandcastles, and even kayaked too. And on top of that, the outside barbecue was incredible.

I tasted Connor and Jackson's cooking separately before, but combining both of their culinary skills together was chef's kiss times infinity. The shrimp kabobs, meat cubes on a stick, curry fish balls, corn on the cob, grilled veggies, and watermelon pizza all tasted amazing. I never experienced an outdoor barbecue before, but after this, I can't imagine I went twenty plus years without one.

Today is definitely a day I will never forget. Not only was it awesome to have a whole beach house and a section of the ocean ourselves, but I also created a lot of fond memories with a group of friends. Growing up with little to no close friends, I presumed friends having fun at a beach was something only in movies or chaebol K-dramas. Despite feeling a surreal amount of joy with people I enjoy hanging out with, there was always something looming over me that made today not as fun as it would have been.

I finally speak. "We will be heading back home tomorrow. This might sound silly, but I don't think I'm ready to leave yet. I know I already got to spend a whole day here when most people don't even get to experience this once throughout their entire lives, but I can't help but feel this way."

"The beach house isn't going anywhere. We can always come back here whenever." Connor doesn't say more but I hear his unspoken words. "Things don't need to end here. Happy memories don't need to end."

As always, Connor really sees me. He knows I am missing the fun memories and happy feelings associated with our time here rather than the actual beach itself. I mean of course, I will totally miss the gigantic beach house and its lovely views and architecture, but I will miss the feeling of being at ease here more. Rather than keep quiet and continue to have it consume me from the inside, I tell Connor what's on my mind.

"Once we return home, I have to make decisions I am not ready to make. I want to keep running away and avoid my problems forever, but that is not an option. And it's just all too much."

"From the first time we met, I could tell you are someone who knows what they want and works hard to achieve it. I'm not sure what exactly you are going through right now, but I am sure you will figure it all out," Connor replies with a half-smile half-grin.

I hate how flawless Connor's response is. He doesn't know what's going on but gives me the encouragement and support I need. He even has the audacity to give me an adorable smile grin that I didn't know was even possible until now. I despise how the outside lighting from the house and the dark night sky makes his already widely known good-looking face look even more good-looking.

"Reed proposed," I blurt out.

I am standing a step behind Connor and this time, it is he who stops walking. His back is to me and he doesn't say anything. After a few seconds, he turns to me with a smile that doesn't quite reach his eyes.

"That's great news. Congratulations, Lia."

"I didn't answer him yet."

At that moment, Connor meets my eyes and I can see the spark of hope in his puppy brown eyes before he pulls his gaze away. That one second look at my neighbor friend's eyes tells me everything I need to know even if he doesn't say anything else.

Not wanting to lead him on, I continue talking. "Reed has been pouring all his attention and focus to his job so he can give me the comfortable lifestyle I wanted. He worked hard to make me happy so we could enjoy living in a house and traveling around the world together."

"Why do I get the feeling that that doesn't make you happy?"

The corner of my mouth twitches up at how fast he is to pick things up.

"I want to travel around the world, to see and experience new things. And once I get sick of traveling, I want to have a home to settle back down to. At least that's what I wanted before." I take a shaky breath and continue speaking, "My dad always loved to travel and my mom loved family vacations and to see my dad happy. Traveling was fun, I guess. But I think I enjoyed those times because my parents were happy and in turn, that made me happy."

"How about what makes you happy?" Connor asks me in a quiet voice and I can feel his gaze but my eyes are fixed on the ocean.

I think about his question before answering, "Living with Isa in our apartment makes me happy. Teaching art to people who love it as much as I do, drawing webtoons, and painting at my studio makes me happy. Being near people I love and doing what I love most makes me happy." Connor waits for me to say more and I do. "And maybe because I've experienced more things that as of now, I don't mind staying in one place and seeing where life takes me one step at a time. I don't want things to change yet. I want to continue living the way I'm living. I want to live in the moment and not have my entire life planned ahead of me."

My heart tightens as I voice aloud everything I feel. Even though I was pretty vague, I am certain Connor catches onto my meaning. A small part of me knew I had to turn down Reed's proposal, but the fear of things changing more between us made me want to delay the inevitable for however long I could. Reed seems to think what I wanted before is still the same thing I want now.

He hasn't considered my hopes and dreams could change or how I might not want those things anymore. Maybe it's because Reed is twenty-six and our four-year age gap affects how we see life. I want to continue things as is until I am ready for a new phase of my life while he is all ready to settle down and start planning ahead for the future.

Yet at the same time, our difference in age has never been an issue before.

We usually talk to each other and communicate our thoughts, but this time, I don't know why it is so hard to get through to him with my words alone. He is so sure my happiness depends on expensive gifts and traveling around the world. He is doing all the things he thinks will make me happy instead of really asking–really knowing–what makes me happy.

It makes me happy to go to diners and talk about CW shows. It makes me happy to dance barefoot on his apartment floor in front of his fireplace together. It makes me happy to be with him. Things were so perfect back then which makes me resent how our relationship is now.

Reed is never there whenever I want him to be. He doesn't seem to be present even when he is in front of me. And when I try to talk to him, my words go in and out of his ears. I have never felt so distant from him than I do now. I want things to go back to the way it used to be. I want to reverse time so we could go back to the way we used to be. But that's impossible.

Everything has changed and there's nothing I can do to change that.

Warm hands amidst the cool ocean breeze brush the tears off my face. Through my tear-filled eyes, I see Connor giving me a reassuring smile. Even in this moment, my friend is still giving me enough space to feel safe around him.

After wiping the last tear from my eyes, Connor holds my hands together in his. "Listen to your own advice. Take things one step at a time. It's ok to tell Reed how you really feel when you are ready. If a person's actions make you feel the opposite of their good intentions, you don't need to feel guilty about that. It's not your fault. You do not need to carry the weight of their feelings along with your own all on your shoulders." He lightly caresses my cheek with the back of his fingers and goes on, "You can be selfish sometimes too, Lia. You don't have to always put the other person's feelings above your own."

He lets go of my hand and is about to move away from me, but I take his hand to stop him.

"Connor, I—"

I stop mid-sentence because from the corner of my eye, I see a shadowy figure standing a few feet away from us. I'm not sure if my eyes are playing tricks on me but when I angle my head to get a better look, my blood turns ice cold. Connor turns to see what I'm staring at and his body visibly stiffens.

"R-Reed," I croak out.

My boyfriend watches us with the angriest expression I've ever seen. How long was he there? Did he overhear our whole conversation? So many questions pop in my mind, but I realize how bad this looks. Connor and I are pretty close and there's also the incriminating fact that I am holding his hand. I quickly let go of Connor's hand and take a step away from him. Reed shoots daggers in our direction before stomping away.

I run after him and touch his arm to stop him. "Reed, wait. It's not what it looks like. I can explain."

He jerks his arm away from me and puts his phone in between us. Reed shows me Isa's Instagram post captioned "Beach House Hangout w/my Bestie + My Boo + My Boo's Bestie: Arguably the Best Day Ever." The photo is a selfie of Jackson with his arm around Isa and you can see the back of Connor and me making sandcastles.

"Are you sure it's not what it looks like? I asked you if you had plans this weekend. You said you were with 'Isa and friends.' Why didn't you just say you were at a fancy beach house with Jackson and Connor?" Reed's upset voice rises with each sentence making me shiver.

"I'm sorry, I should have. But please don't misunderstand," I plead.

"What's there to misunderstand? I saw this post and texted Jackson for the address because I thought it would be a good idea to surprise you by coming here after work. And when I arrive, I see this!" Reed roars as he gestures between Connor and me.

I blink away the new tears forming in my eyes and use my best placating tone, "What you saw is out of context. Connor and I were just talking as friends. He just comforted me, that's all."

I hoped my explanation would calm Reed down, but he

looks even more perplexed.

Reed scoffs and says in a mocking voice, "It's not what it looks like? Why is my girlfriend confiding in a different guy about her problems and not with me, her boyfriend?"

As if factoring Connor in the formula to solve an equation, Reed looks at him and then back to me.

"Is he…?" Reed starts before pausing. I can see the twitch in his jaw and underlying hurt on Reed's face as he asks, "Is he the reason why you didn't immediately say yes to the proposal?"

I shake my head and try to say no, but tears get caught in my throat preventing me from saying anything.

Reed gives me a disgusted look. "All this time I was working my ass off for our future while you went and fell in love with some other guy?"

"That's not what happened. I'm not cheating on you, Reed. I would never cheat on you," I say begging him to listen to me.

"Fine, you didn't cheat on me. But do you have feelings for him? Do you have feelings for Connor because that is considered cheating too!"

"I—"

I glance over at Connor and his original "give me the sign and I will step in" expression turns into a curious one like he did not expect me to fumble with my answer. I clear my throat and try again, "It's not like that."

"What does that mean? You didn't say no so you do like him!" Reed accuses as he stares a hateful look my way.

"I didn't say that. Please don't be like this, Reed."

"Then what is it, Lia?"

"It's hard, ok?" I finally crumble altogether and my voice comes out sharp and broken at the same time.

"What's hard? You either like me or him. You can't like two people at the same time. Which is it, Lia?" Reed growls as he waves his hand like he's done with me.

"You've been so distant lately, working 24/7. You weren't there for me at all, Reed," I defend in a small voice.

Just saying the truth to him makes my throat clench. It's like having to confront someone about what they did to hurt you but when you are the least prepared.

"I didn't mean to. I already told you why I was working so hard," Reed tries more gentle this time before lashing out again, "And that in no way gives you a free pass to start dating someone else."

I gape at Reed in disbelief. "I can't believe you right now. I've noticed it a lot recently, but I kept on giving you the benefit of the doubt but the truth is you aren't listening to me. You haven't been listening to anything I've been saying at all."

I can't deal with Reed when he is this angry and not thinking straight. I begin to walk away not wanting to see his face anymore but he steps in front of me, "What do you mean? I am listening to you."

"No, you're not. I told you before I don't care about all the fancy gifts and how much money you make. All I wanted was to be with you. But you never listened to me. You kept missing dates and never spent any time with me," I answer trying to keep my composure as calm as possible.

"We still texted and called each other. And that time at the work party and the night you stayed over at my place," he counters.

"The art exhibition? Our anniversary day?" My voice cracks and I hate how much the pain of him not being there still lingers in my heart.

Reed falters before murmuring in a low voice, "I said I was sorry. I didn't want to miss out on any of them. It just happened that way."

I wipe my tears furiously away from my eyes and fire back, "That's the thing, Reed! Every time I wanted you there and you said you were going to be there, you didn't show up. You were never there. When we did spend time together, you weren't one hundred percent there either. You were present but I could tell your mind was still on work. And buying a house and planning our future without even considering that my feelings can change? You only thought about what you thought I wanted but never really what I wanted. And for some strange reason, even when you say it's all for me, it doesn't feel like it's all for me. No, everything you did was for yourself. Like you're trying to prove something!"

Reed goes still and this time, his expression tells me I hit the bull's eye. I caught him red-handed. I can't believe I never noticed this before, but now I can see clearly. There is something Reed hasn't been telling me. He has been feeding me lies or at least half truths up till now. I don't stop there and bulldoze right on.

"So don't tell me I'm the reason why you are doing all this because I told you before and always meant it. I don't need you to buy me things and fund my whole life to make me happy. You never listened to me no matter how many times I told you...and now, we have drifted far enough for me to have to let you go. And as for Connor, ever since I met him, he's been nothing but nice to me. So don't drag him in this mess because you are not willing to admit that you are the one at fault."

"Are you saying he's a better boyfriend than me?"

I can feel Reed's hot rage emitting from him despite the wind. It takes all my willpower not to roll my eyes at him. I thought I would know almost everything about my boyfriend after four years of dating, but I never knew he had this petty side to him.

"What I am saying is, I'm tired of you thinking you're doing everything for me when we both know that's not completely true," I correct him sternly.

Reed takes a step closer to me but I back away from him. I let him coax me time and time again with his touch, but not this time. I cannot turn a blind eye to his absence and actions any longer. I am about to walk away from him until I see Reed storm towards Connor–the poor bystander in this mess–with his hands curled into fists.

"It's all your fault!" Reed screams as he launches the first punch at Connor.

Connor luckily dodges the first strike, but Reed doesn't stop there. He continues to throw fist after fist at Connor.

"Reed, stop! Stop it!" I shout.

I want to step in between them but considering they are both physically bigger and stronger than me, I will only get mixed up in the brawl. Reed keeps attacking and Connor is put on constant defense as he tries to find an opportunity to pin him down.

"Stop, Reed!" I cry out again but to no avail.

Witnessing Reed and Connor this moment, a memory of my parents yelling at each other flashes in my mind. At least to my knowledge, my parents never got physical with each other. Their quarrel was loud and frightening, but it was never anything close to domestic abuse. For some reason, seeing Reed tussle with Connor, I see my parents' dispute as well. I shake my head trying to get a grip on myself.

"Reed, stop. Please...stop fighting..." I implore a little out of breath.

I try to breathe in through my nose even though air keeps entering and escaping through my mouth. My whole body feels weak and I crouch down unable to stand any longer. Putting my hands on the sand to steady myself helps me feel more grounded, but it still doesn't stop the pain of not having enough air. The ocean is right in front of me, yet all I can hear are my parents bickering and my inner pleas for them to stop.

It's like I'm a teenager all over again wishing my parents to stop fighting while never being able to do anything about it. No matter how much I wanted it to all work out, my parents never made up. They would keep up the appearance of a happy marriage but clash with each other behind closed doors.

"No, please stop fighting. Please stop." I think I whisper-mumble to myself.

I cover my ears with my hands like it will prevent me from hearing my parents' angry voices. More tears flow down my face and I can practically feel my rapid heart beating out of my chest. My vision blurs and just when I think I'm about to be swallowed up by darkness, a low voice calls to me.

I can't make out what they're saying but feel the safety and warmth of their hands on my shoulders. From this touch, the voices in my head dulls until the lull of ocean waves reaches my ears once again. My heartbeat slows down a bit and it becomes easier to breathe.

"Lia, you're ok. You're safe. Everything is ok." I hear a voice repeat like a mantra.

I hold onto that voice until I have full control of my body and my heartbeat is back to its normal pace. Finally able to flutter my eyes open, I see who the gentle calming voice belongs to.

"Are you okay, Lia?" Connor asks me in a soft voice.

Still not trusting my voice to say anything just yet, I nod. Connor helps me up but keeps holding my arms in case I need to lean on him. I want to stop time right now and have this moment be on a loop. The way his puppy brown eyes–the pair of eyes I find myself wanting to see every time things go wrong–look at me. The way I feel so secure in his strong arms. The way his number one priority is to be whatever I need him to be to help me be ok again.

It is in this moment I know what I need to do and say to make things right. It is at this moment right now, I finally know what I have been truly fearing all along.

Right when I am about to open my mouth to talk, Reed shoves Connor aside. He grabs my hand and blocks my view of Connor before snarling, "Stay away from my girlfriend, Connor. Let's go, Lia."

Reed marches away yanking me with him like Connor is the bad guy, but I stand my ground freeing my arm from his tight grasp.

"No."

He whirls around to face me, "What?"

"No to your proposal. It's over between us, Reed. It's not because of Connor but your own actions up until now. And you were wrong. It wasn't your work that drove a wedge between us. It was you." I point my finger at his chest. "You and your ambition for God knows what? I don't even care at this point. We're done so stay the hell away from me and my friends."

No scuffling sounds come from behind so I assume Reed has finally gotten the message. I feel bad for leaving Connor behind but I really need to get away from Reed right now. As I autopilot my way back to the house, the sight of Isa and Jackson standing near the beach stairway temporarily wakes me up from my flight mode. Judging from their expressions, they must have heard and seen everything or enough to understand the situation.

Jackson walks up to me first. "Lia, I gave Reed our address because I thought it would be a nice surprise. I didn't know you and him were going through something. I am so sorry."

"Don't be. It's not your fault, Jackson. Things just played out that way. I'm sorry you had to witness all that," I say as I try my best to keep my hiccup sob under control.

Isa puts a hand on my arm. "I'm sorry too, Lia. When I found out Reed was here, I tried letting you know but...it was too late."

I give them a small smile. "It's no one's fault, really. I'm glad things are sorted out now. Sorry for all the drama. I'm going to go back in and rest for a bit. I'll see you guys tomorrow."

After hiking back up the stairs and rinsing the sand off my hands and feet at the outdoor shower area, I dry off and hurry inside to my room aka one of the three guest bedrooms. I close the door and sit against the front of the bed with my arms around my knees. The tears I've been holding back finally bursts like a river dam. A minute in my crying session later, I feel a familiar arm around my shoulder.

I don't need to look up to know whose comforting arm is around me right now. Isa is silent as she gently pats my upper arm and I continue to bawl my eyeballs out, no longer caring how loud my cries are. I cling onto my best friend like she's my lifeboat in the vast sea and she cradles me closer with her warm embrace.

A sick feeling lies at the pit of my stomach. I know why these tears won't stop falling. Reed and I are over. Even though I was the one who initiated the breakup, it still hurt. The loss of Reed. The loss of those four years of us being together. Reed was someone I thought would be in my life forever. He was the one. I thought as long as we loved each other, we could get through anything.

How naive I was.

It didn't matter how much I loved him or how much he loved me as long as he let whatever was going on in his head dictate. I wanted to stay and help him through it yet he shut me out time after time. I love Reed, but he's too far gone. I didn't want to have to end things with him, although seeing that he kept blaming his actions on everything and everyone except himself, there was no other way.

That wasn't how I wanted it to end between us, but he left me no other choice. I had to end it.

I had to end us.

Chapter 17

It's officially been a week since the whole beach house fiasco. Reed has been calling, leaving voicemails, and sending me texts of apologies and asking if we can talk—all of which I have been ignoring. The logical course of action is to ultimately block his number if he keeps this up, but his most recent text makes me hesitate.

Reed: "Lia, can we please talk? I promise this is really the last time. I have something important to tell you, something I should have told you sooner."

I want to continue ghosting my ex-boyfriend, but part of me knows I cannot have complete closure until we have a final chat with our emotions levelheaded. And there's also the fact that I still need to return some of his belongings I kept throughout the years. But most importantly, the necklace he gave me. He did buy it as a gift, yet it doesn't feel right to keep it and throwing it away is such a waste of an expensive gift. I never knew the aftermath of breaking up requires so much cleanup work.

Reed arrives at our agreed destination earlier than me. I spot him already seated on the same Mel's Drive-In booth we shared years ago during our second date. How time flies. Instead of feeling butterflies and gazing lovingly at each other, we now sit directly across from each other deciding what would be the best course of action to ease the tension.

He breaks the silence first with a tentative smile. "Thank you for meeting me today, Lia. I'm really grateful for the opportunity to clear some things up."

I can tell he hasn't properly slept in days and it takes everything in me to steel my heart to not worry about his health and well-being. The waitress comes by, interrupting our awkward conversation or lack of thereof. "Oh, so good to see you two again! I was wondering where you guys went."

Reed gives his regular charming smile before handing her back the menu. "Hey, Carly, been busy lately, but we're back. We'll take the usual pancakes and waffles combo with two glasses of orange juice. Thank you."

I remember the first time Reed and I shared that order together. I could never choose between pancakes or waffles for breakfast, but if I ordered both, there would be no way I could finish everything. And if I brought home the leftovers, they would not taste as good heated back up the next day. To solve this dilemma, Reed suggested we order both and eat them together.

I felt bad if Reed was only accommodating me, but he re-assured me he liked the combo as well and he always wanted to share food together as a couple. Ever since then, pancakes and waffles became kind of our thing. It was something I always looked forward to whenever we managed to squeeze in a little us time and go to Mel's.

But now wasn't the time for me to get soft on sentimental feelings. It's been a week but if I don't be tough about this, I know there will be a chance that even if Reed doesn't give me a good explanation for his actions, I might want to take him back.

Before Carly leaves with our order, I abruptly call out, "Actually, make that only one order of waffles and one glass of orange juice."

She glances at Reed then to me before nodding and speed-ing away as subtly as possible. Reed purses his lips as if he's trying to think before he says anything else. Good choice.

Normally his shy contemplating expression would be cute, but I don't have time to beat around the bush. I agreed to meet so I could end whatever we have left between us so we could move on with our lives.

"Let's cut to the chase, Reed. I don't have a lot of time and need to hurry back to my studio. What did you want to talk about?" I ask with my best RBF.

Reed folds his hands together leaning forward, "I'm sorry. I'm sorry for not being there for you. For what I said at the beach house. For everything I did to hurt you. I am sorry for all of that and more. I miss you. I want us to give it another try. I was in over my head the first time, but now I learned from my mistakes. I'll give up my new position as editorial director and go back to lesser hours so it can be just like old times. I want you back, Lia."

"If you think we broke up because of your new promotion then you clearly have not learned anything from our time apart," I snap and fail not to let the frustration show in my voice. "I don't want you to give up your promotion or would I ever ask you to. Seeing you happy and succeed in your dream career is all I ever wanted. And if you're done repeating the same apologies over again, I'm going to take my leave."

I scoot out from the booth–without taking the box of Reed's belongings with me–and am about to get up before Reed grabs my wrist. "Wait, I have more to say. I'm sor–Please don't go yet."

I eye Reed's hand on me and he quickly lets go so I begrudgingly stay seated.

He doesn't say anything for a while and when he finally does talk, his voice comes out pained and hoarse. "You're right, Lia. I haven't been completely honest with you. The long hours, my eagerness to get the promotion, it was all because I wanted to give you everything you deserve but...I also wanted to prove something." Reed's jaw tenses and his eyes are glued on the table as he continues on, "I thought if I could get a higher position in my department, be able to buy expensive things, and drive a fancy sports car, my parents would finally stop comparing me to Alex. I thought if I proved I could be successful at my job, my parents would finally stop seeing me as second best and tell me they were proud of me too."

Hearing Reed's confession, my wavering heart breaks a thousand times over for him. His parents are awful to him and not even worth his precious time. I am sure Reed is aware of all of it, but that does not quell his desire to make them proud. Not one bit.

It seems the more our parents mistreat us, the more we long for their love and affection.

Or at least for us and our ingrained filial piety. I thought one day when Reed was ready to talk, I'd be there for him like he was for me. But I guess the conversation was put off for too long and everything spiraled out of control.

Reed clenches his fists so tight, all color drains out of his hands as he speaks, "All my life it's always been 'Alex is so great. You should follow Alex's excellent example. Why can't you be more like Alex?' My parents never listened to me but when Alex said the exact same thing I did, everyone praised him. And in school, whenever I got good grades, my parents seemed to expect that out of me like anything less than perfection would be deemed unacceptable. But whenever Alex got good grades, my parents complimented and rewarded him with delicious food. I hated how differently my parents treated my brother and me. I hate it so much and I wanted to prove my worth to them...at least once."

Despite everything Reed did, I cannot help but sympathize with him. I understand what it is like to crave for love and approval from our parents. Children are real people with real feelings who need a lot of love and care to grow. When we don't receive it, it only makes sense how that would affect our personalities and way of thinking as adults. But simply knowing about our situation doesn't immediately cause a change within ourselves.

We need to really accept what has happened and decide how to move on from it.

I used my awareness of all the toxicity going on in my life as fuel to work harder to become a better person and the opposite of my parents. It took me awhile to reach this state of mind, but it's still definitely a work-in-progress given how much of an emotional wreck I was in front of Connor and his family. As much as I want to stay angry at Reed, seeing things from his side of the story, I really know why he did what he did.

How can I continue to be mad at him when I also know what it's like to want your parents to be proud of you? To show that they care and love you?

Reed finally meets my eyes and goes on, "That was my end game. Become rich and successful in my own way to attest to my parents I don't need to be exactly like my brother to do well in life. And then along the way, I met you, Lia. You were the exact opposite of my traditional parents' ideals. A college dropout living in a small apartment with her best friend striving to make it big with an impossible dream. It felt nice to be with someone so different from what my parents approved of."

"So you only dated me to piss your parents off?" I ask trying not to sound like my entire life was a lie.

"God no." Reed immediately shoots down that idea as he fervently waves his hands in denial. "I confess that it was a bonus to tick my parents off, but I love you. How could I not fall for you with your kind heart giving me more chances than I deserve, the way you see the real me, and how your presence makes everything better. You are the light in my life. You make me happy and show me what it is like to be with someone who really cares. What we had was–is real. I never pretended with you and I genuinely love you with all my heart. You can still be mad and hate me because I deserve it, but just know I really do love you, Lia."

He slowly reaches for my hand and when I don't retract, Reed places his hand on mine. His hand is warm and I can feel a small tingling sensation of electricity I often feel whenever we touch. "You're my home, Lydia Zhang."

I don't know what to say. A bunch of mini-mes are running around and screaming with their red flags raised in my brain telling me to get out of here when I still can. Even if Reed is true to his word and does love me, dating me gave him an ego boost to his parents. The fact that I inadvertently removed some weight off of him and became the center of abomination in front of his parents doesn't make me feel too good.

Moreover, if we do get married, I'm not sure if Reed's parents will continue giving me the stink eye and have disapproval written all over their faces.

We might not need to see each other every day or that often, but if I ever get married to Reed, I would be evaluated by his family's standards and judged by them. They will have power over me since I married into the Wang family. Even if Reed sticks by my side and disagrees with them, it's hard for me to hold my head up high and pretend their words behind my back (and to my face) have no effect on me.

Because they do.

I care about Reed so I sort of want his family to approve of me too, despite being well-aware, they are not the best people I should associate my self-worth with. I am not sure I can endure living a life where I'm constantly under the lens of critical spectators I will never be able to impress. And besides that–in a way–I am no different from Reed.

I empathize and maybe even appreciate his complicated family situation because a nasty part of me feels relieved I am not the only one with Mommy and Daddy issues. It makes me feel less alone and abnormal when I hear it is not just me who does not get along with my parents. As much as I hate to think this way, it is maybe one of the main things Reed and I bond over.

We do not constantly trash talk our families, but it is the shared look of understanding and compassion whenever the topic of family pops up. Reed and I are always on each other's side making sure the other one knows we are there for them no matter what. Nevertheless, our dysfunctional relationship with our family is not the sole foundation of

Reed and my relationship.

I fell in love with Reed because of his way with words, the way he can make me smile and swoon with his charm, and his loyalty to the people close to him. Looking at Reed right now, I can tell the person I fell in love with is still sitting there in front of me and my heart yearns for him to stay with me forever.

When I continue my silence, Reed adds, "I know this is a lot. I didn't come here expecting us to pick up where we left off. I wanted to, but I know it's too soon for that. I'll give you as much space and time as you need, but I wanted to let you know I'm leaving again for a three-day work trip to New York tomorrow." My eyes automatically flicker to his and the earnest glimmer in his eyes makes me loathe this natural instinct of mine. "I'll be very busy and focused on work so I wanted to talk to you in person in case you texted me back or called and I wasn't able to answer you."

Reed holds my hands tighter but not tight enough to hurt as he says, "I haven't had a decent night of rest since our fight. I really want us to try and work things out. I know that mostly means me getting out of my own head and I will, for you. I want to attend the next art exhibition so I could share to everyone how great of an artist my girlfriend is, go to Mel's to order the same pancake waffle combo, and spend our fifth, sixth, and the rest of our anniversaries to come together. I want to grow old with you and be by your side every step of the way. I want to do all that and so much more. I am sorry my actions did not show how I truly felt, but I really do want that."

The honesty in his voice pulls at my heart strings and a choked cry of sorrowful delight comes out of me. With tears in his eyes, Reed smiles at me.

"You don't need to answer me right now, but can you give me some idea of where you stand? I'll be at the airport tomorrow morning at 9:30 a.m. and if I don't see you there, I will know I've screwed up too many times for you to forgive me and I should give up on us. But if I see you, I'll take it as a sign that it's not completely over between us."

For the past fifteen minutes, I do nothing but stare blankly at the white canvas in front of me. Usually my hands itch to dip my brush in paint and eagerly start painting, but for the first time, I'm utterly stumped. All the creative cells in my brain are gone and I don't know what to paint or draw. I lie to myself that I don't know the reason for my creative block, but the reminder of what's bugging me keeps echoing at the back of my mind.

Reed's words today really rattled me and my feelings are now even more tangled. Isa will be back home later in the day so I can ask her for help, but that is at least four hours from now. I am not sure if I can make it until then.

Finally giving up on forcing an idea out of me, I run a frustrated hand through my hair. Just then, a chime from the door rings and I see Connor walk in. It's been a while since I last saw him. Jackson drove Isa and me back to the city since Connor had to leave earlier to deal with some business matters at C&J's. Either him or Jackson could have gone, but I think Connor offered to go to give me some time alone and figure things out. I wanted to text or call him afterwards but I didn't know what to say and we kept missing each other during our morning runs.

That's probably for the best though.

I genuinely do not know how to act in front of him any-more and hurting him with my mixed signals is the last thing I want to do. But at the sight of Connor, my whole body relaxes and I let go of the breath I didn't know I was even holding. This longing feeling in my heart –which I have no clue when it manifested–is instantaneously quenched by his presence.

"Oh, hey, Connor." My voice is an octave higher than normal as I stand up from my chair to greet him as if I am back in middle school.

He greets me with a soft smile before answering, "Sorry for dropping by unannounced."

"No, thanks for stopping by." My reply still comes out a little too panicked and breathy. I realize Connor hasn't stepped more than two feet from the door. We are standing at least twelve feet apart and the strange long distance between us finally makes me get a grip on myself. I smile and tease, "You don't need to keep that much distance between us. We're still cool, right?"

Connor laughs and his broad shoulders visibly relax as he takes a few steps closer to me. "How are you, Lia?"

"I'm ok."

"You only say that you when you're not ok."

My preprogrammed response for the question I often heard as a child already slipped out of my mouth before I can think much of it, but the way Connor notices these tiny details about me moves my heart in a way I wish it didn't.

"Am I that obvious?"

"Only to those who know you," Connor answers with a kind smile.

"Thank you. For that day, I mean," I say quickly before I lose the courage to tell him everything I need to say to him. "I'm sorry Reed attacked you but thank you for not hurting him. If you didn't handle the situation as well as you did, I'm not sure what would have happened. Thank you, Connor."

He gives me another smile and responds, "I came here today to make sure you're really ok. I would have come by sooner but I wasn't sure if you wanted to see me and I've been tied up finalizing my leave from the youth center."

My face drops and I feel anxious all of a sudden. "What?"

"Today is my last day. The previous cooking instructor came back and will be taking back his position starting tomorrow. I'll finish removing all my stuff tomorrow morning so we probably won't be seeing each other as often," Connor informs me with a weak smile.

"Oh," is all I manage to say as my mind tries to comprehend how we will no longer be next-door-neighbors. A feeling of sadness washes over me from the news and I want to persuade him from leaving, but I keep my mouth shut since it wouldn't be right for me to tell him I don't want to see him less when my feelings are still all out of sorts for Reed.

Connor puts his hands in his pockets and says with a more convincing smile, "I'll miss teaching others how to cook, but I'm excited to get back to cooking full-time and working more with Jackson."

I nod and reply with my best enthusiastic voice, "Yeah, that's good news. Whatever makes you happy, Connor. I'm happy for you."

"But the thing I'll miss most is being a building away from

you and no longer seeing you during morning jogs."

I swallow hard and try to answer with a joke. "But we haven't even been bumping into each other as often anymore."

Connor smiles like he knows I'm trying to keep things light to prevent myself from getting too sentimental. "It always made me happy to see you. Whenever and however we kept running into each other. Every moment I got to spend with you became the highlight of my day. I'll miss you a lot, Lia. And if you ever decide to wander by C&J's, there will always be a seat waiting for you."

My heart aches from Connor's kind words. If this adorable cinnamon roll keeps this up, I might get a freaking cavity from all his sweetness. I give up on acting strong and throw my arms around Connor. I hug him tightly and whisper, "I'll miss you a lot, Connor. Thank you for being such a good neighbor friend to me."

He pats my upper back gently as he reassures me, "We might not work as near to each other as we used to, but if you ever want to talk or hang out, you have my number."

I pull away so I can wipe my tears I tried so hard not to spill from my face. Connor gives me a playful smile and adds, "And who knows? I might pop into your studio if Karissa or Andrew asks me to drop off or pick up Elly."

I laugh. "That's good to know."

Connor's wide grin turns into a more serious expression as he asks, "And if I have no reason to visit except just to see you, will that be ok?"

I freeze for a second and my heartbeat thumps faster. Connor backs away from me and goes on, "I know it has only been a week since you and Reed broke up. You must still be going through a lot and the last thing I want to do is make things harder for you. But that night, when Reed asked if you had feelings for me, you didn't confirm or deny it. I am more than content being just friends, but I want to know where we stand. Is there any possibility you might have some romantic feelings towards me?"

My brain goes to full panic mode. Why are both confrontations today? First it was Reed. Now it is Connor. I was ready for Reed, but not for Connor. My heart cannot take this much drama. Why is Isa always right? I have upgraded from financial troubles to love troubles.

I thought I made a decision, but Reed's explanation really threw me in for a loop. And seeing Connor now makes me even more confused. I have loved Reed for four years and I still do love him. To make matters even more complicated, there's something I feel towards Connor that keeps growing every time I see him and I can't pretend it is nothing anymore.

"I met with Reed today," I declare instead. His eyes widen

before settling back to a neutral expression. I continue on, "He told me what has been going on and we came to a mutual agreement."

Connor nods and smiles but I can see the spark in his eyes dimmer, "Are you guys back together?"

"I'm not sure. I'm still mad at him for what he did, but I do understand him. Reed is leaving on a work trip tomorrow and we agreed if I show up tomorrow to see him off, that means there might still be a chance for us," I answer with complete transparency.

"I see," Connor responds with an unreadable expression.

"I know I didn't answer your question and it's not like I don't want to or anything. It's just I really don't know. I'm sorry," I reply looking down at the floor in shame.

Connor has every right to be frustrated and angry with me at this point. He has been clear about his intentions while I say one thing and then say another. I have been a bad friend and person. I am sorry to Connor for hurting him with my indecision and hesitancy.

But being the nice guy he is, he puts a comforting hand on my upper bicep and tells me, "It's ok, Lia." I gaze up at him and he gives me a sincere smile. "I am happy you got to talk things out with him. I just wanted to know whether or not I should hold out hope in the future. If I could have the chance of pursuing you for real. But all I want is for you to be happy. Whether that means you being with Reed and us still being friends, that is all ok."

Connor begins to slowly walk backward with his eyes still locked on mine and pauses when he's near the door. "I hope to see you tomorrow morning, but if I don't..."

He doesn't finish his sentence but we both know what he is implying. I think Connor wants to say more, but he already conveyed everything he wants me to know. He trusts me enough to respect the reason for my choices. Like he's been being doing ever since I met him, he always considers my feelings first and my heart internally reaches out for him.

Connor gives me his infamous boyish smile I have grown to love and salutes, "I'll see you when I see you, Lia Bears."

Chapter 18

Even in the midst of numerous people in the airport, I can recognize that messenger bag anywhere. His brown messenger bag is made out of real leather so the skin does not peel off and still looks well-kept even after all these years. Being the last in line and waiting his turn for customs, Reed restlessly taps his foot eyeing his watch every other second as he scans the area. When he sees me walking towards him, he beams and spins me around in a big hug.

Last night, I talked it out with Isa and after our heart-to-heart, I made up my mind.

"Lia, I'm so glad you're here. Does this mean you'll give me another chance?" Reed asks and I can see the happy tears forming behind his glasses.

Pushing him gently back from me, I give him a pained smile. "I'm sorry, Reed. I came here to let you know I want to properly end things between us."

His joyful expression falters and his shoulders hunch in

defeat. "Are you still mad at me?"

"No, I'm not mad anymore."

"Then why? Is it Connor?"

Reed tightens the grip on his passport and I reach for his hand. At my touch, he loosens his hold and releases the remainder of all his suppressed hurt.

I smile at him and gently shake my head. "It's partially about Connor, but not entirely." I breathe in his scent of cedar wood one last time and then meet his eyes. "Reed, I gave you all of me and loved you with all my heart. You loved me, but you didn't love me enough to let me in." Reed opens his mouth to say something, but I push forward. "You didn't tell me what was going on all this time. You chose not to tell me the truth. You didn't trust me and I can't be in a relationship when trust is only given one-sided."

"I do trust you, Lia. That's why I told you everything at the diner."

I nod weakly. "It was already too late then. I'm sorry if I was not someone you trusted enough to confide in about your problems, but I gave you so many opportunities to tell me. Just to talk to me, Reed. And even if I didn't understand, we would have been communicating and working things out together as a team. That's all I ask for. You might have been alone in your family, but I thought you loved me enough to know I will always be on your side. That I will always love you and be there for you in every way I can."

He frowns unable to refute my words.

I speak with a softer tone, "But that's in the past now. I think it's for the best we break up. Even if I gave you another chance, too much has happened for us to go back to the way it used to be. I don't think I have the capacity to love you with all of me or ever be ready for us to try again. I'm sorry, Reed."

He brushes away a tear from his face and takes a moment to collect himself before giving me a meek smile, "Don't be sorry. It's my fault things ended up the way it did. If I had been a better boyfriend and listened to you, I wouldn't have lost you. If anyone should be sorry, it's me. I'm sorry, Lia."

I place my hand on his face and wipe away the rest of his tears.

"No more apologizing, Reed. I'm no longer sad or upset. Even though we are breaking up, that doesn't mean the four years we spent together was nothing to me. We shared plenty of good memories and you were there for me during the hardest times of my life. I only got to where I am today because of you and I will forever be thankful to you. I don't regret a single moment we were together. You were my first kiss, first boyfriend, and first love. It doesn't matter if we're no longer in each other's lives, you will always have a special place in my heart."

I step back from him and unclasp the necklace around my neck. I take Reed's hand with his palm up and return the expensive jewelry back to him. "I hope one day you will know you don't need to prove your worth to your parents. You are perfect the way you are and you should be proud of the person you've become."

He stares at me for a few seconds before pulling me in a hug and whispering into my hair, "I love you, Lydia Zhang. And I'm going to miss you like crazy."

"Me too, Reed. Me too."

He moves away from me and adjusts his bag on his shoulder. Reed smiles at me and then says, "Thank you for everything, Lia. I wish you all the best."

I smile back at him before tiptoeing to give him one last kiss on the cheek.

"Goodbye, Reed. Have a safe flight."

Finally arriving at my studio, I slide into my usual parking spot and get out of the vehicle. I don't care if other people watch me or think I'm crazy. I sprint to the youth center and stop only when I'm in front of the directory. The cooking classroom is located on the second floor and I jog up the flight of stairs even though there is an elevator nearby. The elevator would take eons to arrive and this can't wait.

I peek inside the classroom through the small window but no one is inside. Without catching a breath, I speed down to the parking lot. Coming to think of it, that probably should have been the first place I checked. But there's no time to dwell over it. Surveying the cars at the youth center parking lot, I finally find Connor's beige Lexus parked there.

He's still here.

I go to his car to look for him, but he is not there either. Where could he be? Maybe I missed him in the youth center? Or is this the wrong car? I spot a red envelope and a tangerine in the cup holder of the car and smile. Yup, that's definitely Connor's car unless someone else also drives the same car as him and so happens to be here at the youth center too.

Determined to talk to Connor one way another, I head back to my studio first. I originally wanted to talk face to face, but since push has come to shove, calling is better than nothing. I pull out my phone from my back pocket and my finger hovers over the dial button as I see a familiar figure standing in front of my studio porch.

His back is turned to me but I recognize that dark black hair, tall frame, and Pacific Ocean shoulders anywhere. My heart beats faster in excitement from seeing him and I whisper a silent prayer of thanks for letting me make it in time.

Connor simply stands there in front of my studio door without doing anything. I walk closer to him, yet he doesn't hear me. I'm about to call out to him but as if in unison, he sighs while turning around the same time. Our eyes meet and his face tells me he is obviously stunned to see me.

I grin at him, "You're a hard man to find."

He tilts his head confused at my statement but good naturedly chuckles anyways, "I finished packing everything in my car and was just about to leave. I didn't plan to say good-bye to you, but it felt weird not to stop by here one last time before I go."

I smile at Connor and he smiles back before hardening his expression. "Did you just come back from...the airport?"

"Yeah. I just came back," I answer without giving anything away. Connor nods and I see him shuffling his feet. Not wanting to torture him anymore, I ask, "Can you let your family know I plan to attend the Christmas party?"

He smiles but doesn't meet my eyes. "Great. My family would be over the moon to know. Should we also be expecting a plus-one or can Reed not make it?"

"Isa is already going to the party with Jackson so I don't think I'm bringing a plus-one. And as for Reed, I don't know. I didn't ask him."

Connor finally looks at me. He perks up and I swear if he had a tail, it would be wagging. I take a step forward and add,

"I came back from the airport after telling Reed it is over for good."

"Really?"

Connor's face is overcome with so much relief and joy. It is so adorable how he doesn't even try to hide it. Actually, I'm not sure if he could even hide his wide smile even if he tried. I bite my tongue to keep from melting at his reaction. He is too cute.

He clears his throat before correcting himself, "What I meant to say is I'm sorry it didn't work out between the two of you."

"Are you really sorry?"

"Not a single bit," Connor answers immediately and clamps a hand over his mouth. I burst out laughing and I think I see his ears turn a shade of red as he tries again, "That's not what I meant either."

I continue to laugh and he laughs right back. We smile at each other and he starts over with a shy smile, "What I wanted to say is, I hope you're not too sad over what happened. It must be tough getting out of a breakup so I hope you're really ok."

"The four years Reed and I dated will always mean something to me. But in the end, there was too much for us to work out and it was better to end things. I'm just happy all that is over and I can finally move on." Connor nods and

I continue, "Regarding my answer to your question yesterday." I pause to catch my breath and then say, "I know I just permanently broke up with my boyfriend and it probably is wrong for me to start anything new with someone else less than an hour after it happened, but I'm going to do it anyway."

Gazing into Connor's eyes, I straighten my posture and confess, "I eat really messy, am a semi-clean freak, and carry a lot of family baggage. I can't promise none of my issues will not affect our relationship because they will. It won't always be good between us, as you probably know. I might have another episode and be a wreck all over again. I might not be the best romantic partner, but if you're ok with that, I promise I will give you, me. You will have every piece of me through and through. My heart will be yours to keep."

Connor's mouth opens but nothing comes out. I worry he is thinking of how to kindly reject me–given all the times I inadvertently turned him down–so I keep talking, "I know everything I said might be too late. But I thought you had the right to know. I understand if you want to only remain fr—"

Right then, Connor stops me from finishing my sentence by gently pulling me to him. His strong arms are around me and we are so close I'm not sure if it is his or my heart beating out of our chests.

His voice is low as he asks, "Do you know how much self-control it takes for me to be around you?" I'm taken aback by his question and he continues on, "Even if I freely choose to be committed to an unrequited love with you, it does not change how much I want to look at you, talk to you, and kiss you in ways friends never would."

The rapid thumping of the heart is definitely mine this time. His straightforward honesty makes me blush with embarrassment and delight. My senses are going haywire from the intensity of his puppy brown eyes, his intoxicating scent of citrus and lavender, and our bodies pressed so close against each other.

I finally regain control of my body and land a soft punch to Connor's chest.

"What do you mean 'committed to an unrequited love?' You're young, incriminatingly good-looking, and have such a bright future ahead of you. There's plenty of other fish in the sea. Why settle on just me?"

He doesn't even pretend to be hurt by my thwack and solely caresses a strand of hair on my face.

"You're not just some fish in the sea, Lia. The first time I laid eyes on you, I immediately knew you were someone I wanted to get to know better. And your lovable demeanor, how you lose yourself talking about things you are passionate about, and those ridiculously adorable SpongeBob

SquarePants socks only drew me in more. As much as I shouldn't have, I completely fell for you that night at the art gallery when I saw the real you. You were so genuine and beautiful, I couldn't tear my eyes away from you even with all the other pretty things around us. All I wanted to see, all I could think about was you. But the minute you presented me with your painting, I knew it would never matter if you did not see me as more than a friend. You are the one for me."

I sob hiccup from the tears streaming down my face. I've cried a lot in my life, but I think this is the first time I'm crying happy tears. Connor's declaration of love makes me smile so much my cheeks hurt but I can't stop myself. I'm incredibly happy right now.

His eyes look slightly glassy as he tilts his mouth upwards and wipes my tears away. "I lived a happy life full of love and support. But when you came into my life, it's like everything fell into place. Everything I did would make me think of you and I couldn't stop anticipating our next coincidental meeting. Being with you makes me so happy and I'm not sure when people say this in a relationship, but I'd be lying if I didn't tell you tell this right now."

Connor stares deep into my eyes and confesses, "I love you, Lia."

If I was not holding onto him, I think I would have lost my balance and fell flat on my face. Connor standing this close in front of me and confessing that he loves me is too much for my little heart to handle. At this rate, I might short circuit from overheating before I can even return my feelings to him.

When Reed and I were dating, my heart still orbited around him and I only saw Connor as a friend. Yet I think with each minor interaction, I was slowly falling for him bit by bit. I fell in love with Connor as a friend. His warm personality and him as a person in general made me like him even more. I liked hanging out with him and started missing him when we didn't see each other after a long period of time.

I didn't know how else to describe it aside from us being really good friends.

But that night at the beach house, when it was Connor's face I saw and voice I heard drawing me back from the depths of my despair—as much as I wanted to deny it—my heart wanted Connor. And that terrified me because it didn't matter if Reed and I had four years of history together. The one year of friendship and close connection Connor and I shared meant more to me than all of that. He entered my life and became someone I couldn't live without.

It has always been Connor who kept his promises. It has always been Connor who prioritized me first above all else. It has always been Connor who loved me with all his heart.

I want to tell him my feelings are true and he is not just my second choice. Connor is the one I love, but his soft smile tells me he already knows without me voicing everything aloud. So instead of explaining myself, I shorten my sentence with those three magic words.

"I love you, Connor."

He smiles from ear-to-ear before his eyes glance from mine and then to my lips and then flicker back to my eyes. My heart somehow races even more and I want to give into my desire. Connor's gorgeous face tilts down closer to me as he moves his eyes to my lips again. It's like one of those drama moments where the guy is asking for permission to kiss the girl without asking for permission to kiss the girl. That has always been one of my favorite drama tropes and something I wished would happen to me.

I close my eyes angling my head upwards. Our lips touch and we kiss. It is exactly the way I pictured it to be but even better. Instead of feeling the awkward uncertainty of jumping trains from friendship to lovers, our kiss is heart-fluttering and passionate. He kisses me gently before tightening his grip on my waist and kissing me more. My fingers move on their own and learns the placement of every strand of his hair while I return his kiss. Everything feels so right that I start to wonder if I'm dreaming.

When we finally pull away from each other, the sensation

of Connor's forehead and breath against mine reassures me everything is real. No other words are spoken between us but with our eyes alone, we communicate. I have always been curious about what happens after the happy-ever-afters and perfect endings. But I think I finally understand my perfect happily ever after.

In this moment and every other moment after, it will be me and him.

Us together in this relationship. We both have equal chances of breaking the other's heart and having our hearts broken. We put our trust in each other to give our all to the other person. We promise to love each other with no restraints. That can be frightening and reckless, but with the right person, it becomes effortless and second nature. He loves me and I love him. Nothing is perfect in life, but this certainly feels close. I cannot be happier with the way things are now.

This year has been a wild rollercoaster with a lot of sad and painful moments, but I wouldn't change a single thing. It's all worth it. I'd go through the pain of reliving my darkest memories and losing the one I thought was the love of my life over again if it meant I could be living in this moment.

This moment with Connor looking at me with so much love in his eyes and lighting up as if it is already Christmas. Even if it hurt a trillion times over, everything I went through makes sense now.

It was to help me fully understand how to truly love the art of falling in love with you.

328

Afterword

Warning: Spoilers ahead. Please do not read this if you have not read the entire book or want to be surprised by the ending.

The Art of Falling in Love with You is such a long but perfect title I settled on sometime between 2020-2022. Even though it is such a mouthful, my gut told me it was the one. This novel is my first original work I ever finished and I can't be more excited.

The beach house fight scene in Chapter 16 was what inspired this whole story somewhere between 2019 to 2020. At the time, I didn't know the characters' names or any other details. On my notes/in my brain, the characters' names were Girl, Boy A, and Boy B.

Girl is dating Boy A who accused her of cheating on him with Boy B. (Yeah, I must have been craving drama or watching a lot of dramas during that time since I really vibed with this scenario.) Girl and Boy A argued and it got really intense. After their fight, Girl walks away from Boy A and it is revealed a little later how Boy B follows her and does basically everything that shows he is the perfect guy for her.

The basic gist of my idea and most of the dialogue were kept in the finished novel. But mainly, it was the concept of being in a relationship with someone who loves you in the wrong way, I really wanted to convey through this story. People can love you, but if the person who is receiving their love does not feel it or thinks that, it can really hurt the person instead.

I didn't want the Girl to come off as a two-timer cause she is definitely not one. She loved Boy A with all her heart, but because Boy A didn't love her right and never thought of communicating with her, she realized she couldn't hurt anymore and decided to end things with him. And since I live and breathe romance, it just so happened Boy B came along and stole her heart at the end.

After coming up with the idea, I deduced among all my other stories, this would be the fastest for me to write. Going with that idea, I focused all my attention and time I could to plan this sucker—I mean, lovely story—back in 2021 and finally finished in January 2022. Sorry to everyone disappointed with whom Lia chose, but the ending was decided since Day 1.

I want more representation for the swoonworthy Boy Bs/second male leads! They deserve their happy endings and I wanted to give it to them. Don't get me wrong, I do feel bad and am (mostly) sorry to Reed. It was difficult for me to think of a legit reason that would influence the once-perfect Boy A to do the not-so-perfect things he did while justifying his actions as well. But ultimately, I am satisfied with the idea I came up with and the ending I chose for everyone.

As the author, (to agree or disagree), I'm genuinely happy for Lia. She is someone I had a hard time understanding until a few rewrites, but hey, we did it. It was fun writing in her POV and a much better idea than writing in three alternating POVs between Lia, Reed, and Connor (also personally a lot easier for me too).

Lia is a character who has a lot of personal struggles, but she is a strong girl. Even though there were times I thought I was too mean to her, I knew she could take it. Similar to how Lia learned at the end of her story, sometimes people need to go through hardships to get to where they are now.

Despite this, that in no way justifies the tough journey. The pain was there—probably still is there—and it hurts. The suffering and the aftermath really suck therefore we can be happy and gloat how we managed to trudge through everything. Life is not easy so be proud of yourself for getting to where you are today.

Thank you for reading my debut novel and I hope you enjoyed reading it as much as I loved writing it (or somehow even more).

Much Love,
A. A. Jaeon

Acknowledgments

I would like to thank my parents for showing interest in this story idea while I was still fleshing it out and giving me the opportunity to bring it to life.

A huge thank you to my two best friends, Jove and Baylin. In the beginning, I thought there was no other way to get my book out except traditional publishing.

Thank you to Jove who brought up the idea of self-publishing and provided me with helpful tips to release my book. Ever since I had known you, you were/still are a walking dictionary with your vast amount of knowledge and ability to translate everything for me to understand.

And most of all, when I ran out of satisfying books, movies, animes, etc. to engross myself with, you gave me multiple stories and worlds to live in. The stories you told me will forever hold a special place in my heart. They inspired me to try making a story/stories of my own. I will always be grateful for the stories you shared with me and am eagerly anticipating your next story.

Thank you to Baylin Wing for all the times you lifted my spirits during my worst, listened to me complain about the difficulties of publishing a book, and reminded me to believe in my story when I lost faith in it. You always helped me in whatever way you could and constantly adjusted everything to fit my busy schedule. For all that and more, I am very touched and appreciative of you.

These past three years have arguably been the hardest times of my life and I can't stress enough how I never would have made it to where I am without you guys.

I want to express my gratitude to my proofreader, Jennifer Herrington. Thank you for catching so many of my typos, helping me with grammar, and noting down important items for me to look at. I will never forget how you kindly offered your help when I encountered a difficult situation and were the first person to ever read my completed manuscript. I really appreciate all you did for me, Jenn.

TAOFILWY's book cover would not have existed without Fran Hao Shuang. Thank you for replying to my request and drawing such a beautiful and one of a kind book cover!

The breathtaking interior illustrations, adorable logos/designs, and wonderful book cover(s) formatting are all done by Tanjibo. I am not gifted with Lia's drawing skills so I am really thankful to you for bringing my ideas to life and always seeming to understand my awful sketches. I can't thank you enough for your superb attention to detail and endless kindness for going the extra mile in doing everything over and over again until I am happy. Everything looks perfect and I can't ask for more. It was so great working with you. I cannot wait for our next collaboration! Thank you so much!

A big shout-out to the Kindlepreneur team and Mandi Lynn for being my guides to basically everything. As a complete newbie author who knew nothing, y'all were my bible. Words are not enough to express how much your blogs, tutorials, and videos saved my life. Thank you for being a helping hand to authors like me.

I want to also send all my love and thanks to my readers. Although I identify myself as a writer, the correct terminology would be an individual who uses words as a medium to convey their thoughts and ideas. Whenever I write stories, I usually have a story idea/vision in my head. Most of the time, I worry and get frustrated with myself whenever transferring what goes on in my brain to pen and paper (or typing it on my laptop) is not executed to my satisfaction.

With each story I write, I am continuously growing as a writer and (hopefully) becoming better at writing. Thank you for giving this story a chance. Even though I may not get the opportunity to connect with all of you, please know from the bottom of my heart, I am truly honored to have my story read by each and every one of you. This story along with my future works, I hope to make you fall in love with the limitless possibility of your imagination again and again.

Lastly, I want to thank the 2018 A. A. Jaeon. Because you finally knew what you wanted to do with your life, you took the steps to achieve it. It was not a stroll in the park so I am proud of you for standing your ground when things got hard, not giving into the pressure of abandoning your true dream, and making what seemed like the impossible then possible. You did great, buddy.

My first novel would never have been possible without these amazing people. Thank you to everyone.

A. A. Jaeon

A. A. Jaeon (can be referred to as A. A. or Jaeon) was born and raised in San Francisco, California. At a young age, A. A. often had an active and wild imagination. It wasn't until she grew older that she finally let her creativity guide her to the world of writing romance novels. *The Art of Falling in Love with You* is her debut novel. When she is not busy crafting her next work, A. A. enjoys listening to audiobooks, jamming out to music, and consuming anything romance. Please visit aajaeon.com for more information.

goodreads.com/author/show/30593977.A_A_Jaeon

instagram.com/a.a.jaeon/

youtube.com/@AAJaeon

Coming Soon

When Plum Blossoms Grow

Part 1

For more information, sign up for A. A. Jaeon's Newsletter

on her website:

www.aajaeon.com